The Wish

By

D.S. Affleck

Published by New Generation Publishing in 2013

Copyright © D. S. Affleck 2013

First Edition

www.newgeneration-publishing.com

 New Generation **Publishing**

In the beginning…

Acrid smoke billowed from the valley floor as a multitude of fires began to extinguish under grey skies and incessant drizzle. The remains of the town smouldered after the successful attack and nothing remained standing.

A figure, clad from head to foot in black armour, his face hidden by shadow, stood high above on a rocky outcrop watching with satisfaction as the prisoners were led away in chains. In his hand he held an orb which glowed fiercely, emitting an energy which seemed to envelop him. Behind him stood a younger figure, close to adulthood, observing everything and learning.

A frown crossed his face, as he thought about the attack. What should have been a relatively easy foray into enemy territory had nearly turned into a disaster and it had been his fault. He was distracted about something else entirely and his mind hadn't been on the attack. He hoped that his men hadn't seen his lack of enthusiasm as a sign of weakness. He'd have to watch out for some of his more ambitious lieutenants, this was just the sort of opportunity they craved.

He had been disturbed of late by peculiar dreams of the future. Dreams of a time he had no connection with, but somehow felt a part of. Dreams of a boy living in a strange land and a different time. He had connected with this boy and it had something to do with the object he held in his hand. He knew that soon he'd be making a bargain that could change his life forever.

The glass sphere he held seemed alive. Wisps of smoke swirled inside of it and sparks crackled from his fingers. He turned it over in his hand thoughtfully. It had given him great power, but for the first time in a long while all this pillaging and mayhem just wasn't as satisfying as it used to be.

He was brought out his reverie by a polite cough behind him. He turned to view one his captains, sent to retrieve their commander. Not wanting to lose face, he laughed maniacally and sent a bolt of lightning from his fingers into the valley floor below. It crashed with a sickening boom and rocks shot into the air in all directions.

This sort of behaviour was expected of him and his captain recoiled in terror. It would keep his enemies and his friends at bay for a while, but he didn't think he'd be able to keep up the pretence for too much longer. He knew he would have to be patient, but he was eager for events to unfold. He beckoned to the figure behind him to follow and they together, under the ethereal light of the orb, made their way back to camp.

Trouble at school

Jamie Lomax tried to pick himself up for the second time that day, but a heavy foot pinned him to the floor. Irritated at falling for the same trap twice, he tried hard to ignore the baying crowd a few feet away.

The day had started badly. Jamie was new to the school having recently moved from London. The school wasn't that bad really despite its name, Marsh Green, and the area they'd moved to was far better than the noise and pollution of Brixton in South London. The relative peace and calm of the countryside was a blessing and he didn't miss the constant scream of sirens or the dull throb of heavy traffic outside his bedroom.

Being new in an established year group is never easy and Jamie had been at Marsh Green for little under three weeks now. He was doing his best to get on with life without drawing attention to himself, but that had all changed after an encounter with Spencer Rogers early into his second week.

It hadn't taken Jamie long to realise Spencer Rogers was the self-appointed leader of the year group and from their very first meeting it was clear that he was a nasty piece of work. He wasn't your archetypal bully, because he was popular, charming, good looking and clever. Everyone wanted to be his friend. He used charm to fool everybody, the girls fancied him with his golden hair and piercing blue eyes, but above all he was clever, even devious. It was his quick wit and wily brain that drew everyone around him under his spell.

Spencer was the unofficial boss, or 'Don' of the playground. He had a gang that called themselves, rather unoriginally, the 'Jolly Rogers'. The name was ironic in the sense that nothing about them was jolly at all. But that was probably the point. They hung out at school, not doing an awful lot, affecting an air of importance. They tended to hang out near the school cafeteria, robbing smaller kids of their lunch money and playing it cool for the benefit of the girls.

Out of school, they did virtually the same thing, but hung out at the local skate park in dark hoodies, which is where they were now laughing nastily at Jamie. Not wildly exciting, but they thought they were cool and amazingly everybody wanted to be in on it. When Jamie had started, Spencer had invited him to be part of the gang. He'd been impressed by the idea of Jamie being from London. But being in a mob was not really Jamie's idea of a good time and he'd seen kids, friends of his, get into some serious trouble with the police for joining some gang or other. He had no interest in that, so he'd politely said no thanks.

Standing on the recreation ground now, possessions in the bin and an ominous crowd drawing in, Jamie thought back to the moment when he'd been invited to join the 'Jolly Rogers' on the playground and with hindsight was regretting his decision. Spencer's entourage had collectively shaken their heads in amazement and tutted with a sharp intake of breath. Spencer's expression changed from one of welcome to one of outrage. He wasn't used to people saying no to him; not that Jamie knew that, being a new boy.

Spencer had drawn close to him and whispered ominously that he should 'be careful and watch himself'. He had to save face after all! Jamie wasn't easily intimidated having grown up in London, so didn't think much of it. There had been the odd brush with one of Spencer's enforcers, but because Jamie was quiet and didn't cause problems on the playground, they had generally left him alone until now.

Jamie looked around desperately for an escape

route. Spencer was lazing on a swing eyeing Jamie like a cat just before it pounces. He was being played with and it was an uncomfortable situation. He'd walked home from school in London and never in his fourteen years encountered a situation as serious as this one was becoming! He knew he'd have to come back and retrieve his stuff later, so the trick now, before things got really serious, was to get past Spencer's bully boys.

These self-appointed bodyguards were huge twins called Francis and Charlie Crafter. They essentially did all of Spencer's dirty work because he was what you'd call a, 'hold your coat merchant.' Essentially, he'd hold their bomber jackets while they went and terrorised the rest of the playground on his behalf. Judging by the way that they had been let off the leash like a couple of pit-bull terriers and were now advancing on him, it appeared things were going to get nasty. He didn't like the idea of getting on the wrong side of these two behemoths; they looked like they could do some serious damage.

The trouble had started this morning on his way to Biology. He was late and lost as usual so wasn't watching where he was going. He was aware of a small crowd of people ahead on either side of the corridor, but was pre-occupied in trying to find the right classroom. As he went through the crowd someone stuck out a leg and he went crashing to the floor, his books scattering everywhere. Laughter erupted and he jumped up, embarrassed and angry in equal measure. He still held one book in his hand and he threw it at the nearest person, who ducked as the heavy textbook clattered against the wall.

Sounds of derision emanated from the assembled crowd and a chant of 'fight, fight,' began as Spencer, whose head had just been narrowly missed by the text book, shoved him in the chest hard and he stumbled back into the arms of someone very strong, who in turn pinned his arms back painfully. Jamie looked Spencer straight in the eye as he approached and watched as he motioned the other Crafter twin to come and finish the job. Charlie grinned nastily as his brother whispered in his ear.

"This might hurt a bit." Jamie tensed, readying himself for the blow, when a loud voice bellowed down the corridor.

"Just what is going on down there?" Instantly he was let go as the crowd dispersed in the opposite direction leaving a panting Jamie and a smirking Spencer to face the approaching teacher.

"Spencer, what is going on?" asked the teacher as he approached picking up books as he came.

"Nothing Mr Cook," came the innocent reply. "Just helping our new boy get to class on time."

"It didn't look that way to me. Was that the Crafter twins causing trouble again?"

"Don't think so sir!" Spencer stared at Jamie daring him to say otherwise.

"You boy," barked Mr Cook. "What's your name?"

"I'm Jamie Lomax sir."

"Ah the new boy. Is everything okay? Why are your books all over the floor?"

"I tripped sir," came the honest reply as the teacher gave him back his books. Jamie thanked him and said, "All is all right sir thank you. Nothing to report."

"Well, I'm not so sure. If those twins give you any trouble, or indeed our angelic Spencer here, you come and find me, you hear!"

Spencer smiled sweetly. "All perfectly innocent, I assure you Mr Cook."

"Well it had better be, now you two get to class, you're late already."

He went off in the opposite direction as Spencer and

Jamie trudged off to class. Jamie recognised where he was as they went around the corner and as soon as they were out of sight Spencer barred his way.

"You'll keep, loser. Watch your back." And with a laugh, he skipped through the door leaving a shaken Jamie to suffer the ignominy of being late for his first ever Biology class. He knocked on the door and entered. The Biology teacher was at the front of class and appeared irritated to have been disturbed again by yet another latecomer.

"Late and you're not the only one. Take a seat over there and see me after school for a detention." Jamie thought about protesting, but just sighed as he took his place at the front. He looked around the class as the teacher resumed the lesson and he recognised a few of the others who'd been a part of his public humiliation. He assumed by their looks of indignation that they'd be joining him, but no one looked at him. All eyes were lowered and he knew then that life was going to be difficult for him at Marsh Green.

It was on his way home after detention later that afternoon when he encountered the Jolly Rogers for the second time that day. He'd decided to take a short cut through the woods to the recreation ground, unaware that this was their stamping ground after school. He had his earphones firmly in place and was listening to some loud music, silently cursing his parents for bringing him to this god-forsaken place. He kicked a stone absent-mindedly. It was so frustrating that they'd moved him from a school where he was settled to start life all over again. They'd left London to make life easier for his mum and had moved in with his paternal Grandmother until they could find a home of their own.

But he didn't have any more time to think about this when he tripped over a branch held by the twins hiding in the undergrowth as he left the woods. They'd taken

9

advantage of him wearing his earphones and figured he couldn't hear them, so they'd lain in wait, having seen him enter the woods moments before. He stumbled and fell flat on his face, his rucksack slipping off his shoulders and his earphones popped out of his ears. He groaned, the wind taken out of him and groggily tried to stand up, but a heavy foot pushed him back to the floor pinning him there. He tried to wriggle away, but the fall had knocked the wind and the strength out of him. He lay still sizing up the situation as he watched a crowd of about six teenagers appear out of the bushes led by Charlie and of course Spencer.

"Told you this wasn't over didn't I?" crowed a triumphant Spencer walking over. He watched as Spencer picked up his rucksack and then seeing the earphones crunched them under his feet destroying them instantly. "Oh dear, sorry about that, I seem to have accidentally trodden on your earphones." There was a chuckle of admiration from some the others behind. "Shame, they looked quite good." Jamie groaned in frustration, they were a present from his grandmother. "You'll learn the hard way that crossing me is the worst decision you'll ever make. Pick him up fellas."

The Crafter boys lifted Jamie off the ground and half dragged half carried him over to the swings while a group of lads busily emptied the contents of his rucksack into the bin with great hilarity and back slapping. He ignored that and looked desperately for a way out of this situation, adrenaline pumping through his veins. He felt as though he was being tried in some sort of juvenile court as he stood there awaiting some sort of teenage judgement. He looked around, but there wasn't an adult in sight.

"Perhaps," declared the now moving Spencer, "you'll do the right thing and join us. It's always best to do what I say, as some of these idiots behind me will testify to." There was some nervous laughter behind him, but no one objected to the insult. "Now it's your turn." Spencer was swinging hard now and getting higher and higher. "I'll let the twins here have a go at persuading you that joining us will be a sensible move on your part. You might be sore for a few days though. Boys, do your worst."

The twins, fists clenched began to close in on Jamie, who had seconds left to think of something. Breath back and blood pumping, he knew he wouldn't win a fight against these two, so seizing the element of surprise he ran straight at the swinging Spencer, diving beneath him.

He felt his shirt rip as his momentum carried him safely underneath Spencer, who cried out in fury. Jamie scrambled to his feet and then ran as fast as he could away from the swings to the gate a hundred yards away. Once through this gate it was only another hundred yards to his grandmother's house and he hoped his surprise manoeuvre had given him enough of a head start to make it home before being caught again.

There were cries of surprise and anger behind him and he chanced a look back to see if anyone was in pursuit, which was nearly a mistake as he stumbled slightly. He was satisfied to see that Spencer had fallen off the swing and was rubbing his head, but it was clear that the crowd were hot on his heels. He sprinted for the gate. He couldn't remember if it swung inwards or outwards, so opted to hurdle it catching the top of it. He fell out onto the pavement heavily and rolled into the road. He was aware of a screech of brakes and an angry voice started yelling from the open car window, but he didn't have time to say sorry. He checked himself quickly. No broken bones thankfully. He jumped back onto the pavement, just as the gate swung inwards and a mob struggled to get through en masse.

A stone whistled past his head, but the motorist had been enough of a deterrent to halt the chase, but Jamie didn't take any chances and kept on running until with shaking hands he put the key into his grandmother's front door and literally fell into the front corridor relief flowing through him. He'd survived, but only just. He listened quietly for any more signs of pursuit, but apart from the sound of an approaching siren, which he assumed was down to the motorist, all was quiet. No one was home, so he trudged upstairs, grateful to have escaped intact.

The 'beast'

After a shower, Jamie felt much better. The hot water had a calming effect and washed away the horrific end to his week. Satisfied as he watched the dirty water swirl down the plug hole, he dried himself and popped his dirty laundry into a wicker basket. His shirt was ruined and he'd have to own up to that one, but he was sure he'd come up with some sort of suitable excuse as to how it ripped later.

As he padded into his room, he could hear the sounds of people downstairs busying away in the kitchen. It would mean his grandmother had returned and possibly his mother. He whistled at the top of the stairs and waited with a smile. There was a bark of delight and some scratching could be heard from behind a door. There was a laugh downstairs and the door was opened allowing the Lomax dog to bark excitedly as it tore up the stairs. Jamie braced himself as the dog got to the top of the stairs, skidded trying to change direction and with one more bark bulldozed into him.

This shaggy creature was Duster, Jamie's faithful hound who adored him unconditionally as only dogs can do. Duster was a beautiful liver and white Spaniel, full of life, and when not following Jamie, was forever chasing rabbits, squirrels and cats. Anything that moved really! They had a cuddle and then he rolled over onto his back so Jamie could tickle his tummy.

"Where's your toy, Duster? Go get it!" said Jamie.

Duster immediately bolted back downstairs and skidded into the kitchen whilst Jamie readied himself for Duster's favourite game. He reappeared with what can only be described as a green squeaky hedgehog. He growled good-naturedly as Jamie tried to take it from him. He managed to get hold of its nose and tried once again to prise it from Duster's mouth. A tug of war ensued for the next couple of minutes; Jamie had no chance of winning. Duster was just too strong.

After a couple of minutes they both went downstairs and entered the family kitchen. Busying herself at the Aga was Jamie's grandmother. Her shoulder length white hair was held behind her head in a ponytail and she was in her exercise clothes, a simple pink t-shirt and respectable black jogging pants that would embarrass his father; not like she cared. She was seventy, but in prime fitness. She'd obviously been out power walking with Duster, which explained her absence when he'd returned earlier.

She turned and gave him a big grin. "Hello dear, how was your day?"

"I've had better thanks Grandma, but at least it's the weekend," he replied.

Her face betrayed a look of worry. "Anything I can help you with?"

"Not yet, I should be able to cope. I'll let you know if I need your skills in ju-jitsu!"

She laughed and offered to do a spinning heel kick, but Jamie declined asking instead when dinner was ready. "Not long, your mum should be home soon, but your dad rang to say he would be late." Jamie walked over to the fridge and helped himself to a lemonade and sat down at the big oak kitchen table, relieved not to have been pressed further on the events of his day. As he sat sipping his drink he relaxed and thought about his family and the move to his grandmother's house.

Grandma owned a chocolate box house in the centre of the village, framed by a picket fence and neat privet hedges. It looked small from the front, but once inside and through the cheerful red front door, it was evident there was plenty of space. It had been the Lomax family home for many years and for the time being until they found their own home, Jamie, Duster and his parents were sharing it with Grandma.

The best thing about the house was its vast garden. It swept gently down to a river running at the end of the property, where she had full fishing rights and kept a dilapidated rowing boat. Jamie wasn't meant to use it, but his parents weren't generally around to tell him otherwise, so Grandma secretly allowed him to use it to swim from in the summer. Duster too was hugely fond of the boat, but spent more time out of it than in! He chased fish too!

Inside, the décor of the house was rather bohemian, awash with wonderful colour and adorned with wild and wacky pictures from all over the world. Grandma hadn't owned a television until they'd arrived, but Jamie's dad had recently installed an entertainment system in the living room, claiming that his mother really shouldn't be living in the dark ages. It was the only time he'd seen his grandma get cross and she'd disappeared to her study in a bit of a huff.

Dad bought her a huge bunch of flowers that very afternoon. She couldn't stay mad at him for long and once they'd made up, he also produced a digital radio that he showed her how to use. Her initial reluctance towards all things technological paled into insignificance when she realised she could record all her favourite radio shows. This, she thought, was awesome and was delighted to learn she'd never miss *The Archers*!

They'd moved out to the country to help Jamie's mum. She had been commuting to her teaching job at another school for a couple of years and found the driving exhausting. Dad was happy to catch the train into work so they'd made the big decision to relocate to the countryside. For various reasons, Jamie had decided not to go to the same school as his mum, preferring to avoid any stigma as a teacher's son.

Jamie was an only child and he'd always wanted a younger brother or sister to look after and grow up with. His parents had recently revealed that he'd had a twin. His sister had been still-born, but he had survived. He'd been a bit shocked by this and worried that he'd been the cause of his sister's demise. He'd done some research that had been largely inconclusive, but it did suggest that even in the womb, it was the survival of the fittest.

His parents were reluctant to talk about it, but it was obvious that they'd been heart-broken by the tragedy, yet delighted to have Jamie. His mum cried a lot when she told him. She didn't blame him, far from it, but he could tell that she'd been devastated.

Jamie's parents had always wanted another child, but their careers had taken off and this seemed to help take the pain away. His parents loved him very much, he knew that, but they were often too busy to spend quality time with him and for much of his life in London he'd been looked after by a nanny. He had grown used to it, but he did worry that they hadn't truly bonded with him. The revelation about his sister had stirred his innermost feelings of abandonment, but he still loved them whatever their faults.

Dad worked long hours in the city, so he often arrived home late, exhausted, haggard and desperate for a bit of peace. He often worked at weekends and, despite his best efforts, rarely spent enough time with his son. Jamie reluctantly understood, but looked forward to the holidays. This was when his dad would become Dad again. He lived for those precious moments and longed for the endless days on the beaches of Devon, where picnics and games of cricket would ensue until the tide came in.

Owing to his parents' busy lives, Jamie now spent most of his time with his grandmother, which was far better than a nanny. She was fun! Even if his parents were available, his grandma had often come to support events when they lived in London. His parents were definitely okay with this. They had to be really. Grandma was his paternal grandparent and the only grandparent he had! His dad always said that if they weren't around, he could think of no one better to look after him. He secretly thought his mum didn't really agree, because she always gave him one of her looks whenever he mentioned something interesting that Grandma had let him do.

His grandma was an unusual person with an unusual hobby! She was a witch and in his eyes this was very cool indeed. She was not a cackling, evil, broom riding, hooked nose, warty kind of witch, but a proper White Witch. It was not something that she kept secret. In fact, she was extremely proud of the fact. She was a part of the Wiccan coven, as it was called; it was a popular movement in the area and it was founded on pagan beliefs.

Jamie understood how it all worked because she had told him all about it. She explained that in order to live a full and successful life as a 'White Witch', you had to follow four simple rules. You had to live each day as if it were your last, for one day you will be right. Love yourself first and foremost. For when you truly love yourself, loving those around you will come as easily as breathing – and we all must breathe. Learn your life's lessons, each as it comes along, for that is the reason we are; and enjoy your life, because if you do not most likely someone else will enjoy it for you; then your time here will have been wasted. But the most important aspect of it all she had said in her most serious voice was to harm no man. It all seemed like sage advice to Jamie and made perfect sense.

Grandma was popular in her village and people did not hold the fact that she was a practising witch against her. Quite the opposite in fact and she was held in high esteem. She was seen as a wise lady, a kind person who helped others. People listened when she had something to say and her kitchen was always bustling with friends and visitors.

Jamie thought of her as a cool grandma; the envy of many of the kids in school. She had a big, booming infectious laugh and could make even the most serious teacher smile with a clever comment or aside. She was genuinely funny. High fashion was not high on her agenda, but she always looked smart and definitely wasn't old before her time when it came to matters of sartorial elegance.

Jamie took another sip of his lemonade and sighed loud enough to halt his grandma from her cooking. "Right that's it young man, I know just what you need." She took the bubbling pan off the stove and left it to cool on the side. "It's time to bring out the beast."

"Grandma, really, you don't need to. I'm okay, honestly I am." Despite his protestations, he had begun to smile. "I'm a bit old for rides in cars."

His grandmother was indignant. "Too old? Too old? Don't you believe it young man. Grab a jumper and that mutt of yours and let's go." Jamie jumped up, knowing arguing was futile and besides a ride in the beast would actually blow the cobwebs away.

The 'beast', as she affectionately called it, was her old E-type convertible Jaguar. It gleamed in its original British Racing Green paintwork, and worked as well now as it had the first time his grandfather had bought it and brought it home in the nineteen sixties.

It was a beautiful piece of machinery and the noise that the wonderful V8 engine made when she turned the ignition key made her laugh out loud every time. He wasn't sure whether it was the sound of the engine and the way that the car shook on its chassis as she revved the engine that made her laugh, or whether it was the memory of her deceased husband. Whatever the reason, his jovial grandma would smile even more behind the wheel of this behemoth of a forgotten age.

For years his grandma had zoomed up to London to pick him up to go for a jolly as she called them. The Jaguar was a convertible and inevitably the roof would be down. The only time it ever came up was when it rained. So on clear, rain-free days the roof would remain down and, whatever the temperature, the wind would whistle past Jamie's ears. Bracing was the word his grandma used.

He raced upstairs to grab a jumper as he heard the sound of the Jaguar being started. A blast of its powerful horn indicated that she was ready and with Duster close behind he closed the front door and hurried down the path. He opened the passenger door and pulled the seat forward so Duster could take his place on the doggy blanket on the floor. He woofed with excitement as he loved rides with Grandma. He popped the seat forward to allow his dog some space in the two-seater and settled into the comfortable leather seat, fastening his seatbelt as he did so. He looked over at his grandmother, who'd donned her leather driving gloves.

"Ready?" she asked.

"Always," was the expected reply.

She popped the old Jag into first with a satisfying clunk. She gave Jamie a gleeful thumbs up then revved the V8 engine unnecessarily, setting off a neighbour's car alarm, whooped loudly and roared away with a screech of tyres. She quickly slowed down to obey the village speed limit, but at the outskirts she floored the accelerator and the old car took off.

There was a general route she took which consisted of some twists and turns before joining a dual carriageway where she'd attempt top speed, before doubling back and entering the village from the other side. The ride as ever was exhilarating. Duster's ears were flapping behind him and his tongue was lolling happily. Jamie's hair flew around his head whilst his grandmother skilfully manoeuvred round bends, overtaking slower cars where it was safe.

The wind whistling past his ears helped to clear his head and he felt more positive as they slowed down on the approach to their village. As they burbled their way back home, he could see three figures walking towards them and, with a sinking feeling, he instinctively knew who they were. He was tempted to hide in the foot-well of the car, but decided against it. As they got nearer the three figures stopped to watch. The Jaguar was pretty distinctive and they knew who'd be driving. As they passed Spencer gave them a wave and the twins both glared at him with barely disguised venom.

He watched in the side mirror as they conversed animatedly for a moment before taking one look at the receding car and carrying on with wherever and whomever they were off to to torment next.

"Friends of yours dear?" asked his grandmother with a frown, as she watched the boys in her rear view mirror.

"Not really. Had a bit of a run in with a boy called Spencer and his two ogres have taken a dislike to me," Jamie replied.

"I know their parents if you want me to go round and have a quiet word," she offered.

"Thanks Grandma, but I have a feeling that would only make it worse. I'll have to sort this one out for myself. I think this is the sort of place where seeking adult help will only make matters worse."

"Well okay, but you let me know if it all gets too much." She looked worried.

"I'll be fine, Grandma, I'll just have to watch my back for a bit." Jamie continued to look in the mirror at the receding figures, but didn't feel that confident that would be the case at all.

Night-time liaisons

After the car ride, Jamie helped his grandma prepare supper. Before long, Jamie's mother returned exhausted from work and they'd all eaten together without speaking much. He spent his time thinking about his pressing agenda; how to retrieve his books without bumping into any of the Jolly Rogers. He still had a lot of homework to do.

As he helped clear away his things, it struck Jamie that the only way he was going to get them back was to sneak out in the middle of the night. He made his excuses and kissed both his mother and his grandma good-night before retiring up to his bedroom. He lay on his bed and flicked through the channels on his television but couldn't find anything to watch. He set his alarm clock for midnight and closed his eyes.

The sound of barking downstairs woke him up and he glanced at his clock. It read 10 p.m. His father had come home late tonight he reasoned and he listened carefully. Inevitably, he heard his dad start a play fight with Duster in the kitchen. He grinned as he pictured him on all fours batting Duster on the nose and wrestling with him.

Duster adored everybody, but after Jamie, Dad was the next best thing. Mum had persuaded him to have Duster, four years ago. Dad had driven all the way down to the West Country to pick him up. Despite an inauspicious start to family life (Dad had spent hours clearing up the dog mess from his car) Duster had become a firm favourite in the family.

He heard his dad's footsteps coming up the stairs with Duster following closely behind. He knocked on the door and poked his head around.

"You awake Jamie?" he asked.

"Yes Dad, I was just snoozing. Duster woke me up. Who won?"

"Duster as usual, look at my arm." He held up his left arm, which was covered in scratch marks. "He's too smart, your dog." Duster beat his tail against the doorframe upon hearing his name and nudged his way in hopping up onto Jamie's bed. They had a routine. He would give Duster a quick pat and cuddle his neck, then Duster would give him a couple of goodnight licks before retiring to the end of the bed, spinning round twice in a clockwise direction, and flopping with a sigh of canine contentment.

"How was your day?" Dad asked.

"Had better, but at least it's the weekend," Jamie replied.

"Me too, it's been a long one. I'm not long for bed myself. There's some Rugby on the television tomorrow if you fancy watching it with me?"

Jamie didn't like rugby very much, but a chance to sit and have a chat with his dad was a nice prospect. "Who's playing?"

"Some European fixture or other. I'll make us lunch if you like?"

"Soup and sandwiches?"

"Definitely!" laughed his dad in agreement. "Sleep well, see you in the morning. Good night hound." Duster wagged his tail as Dad shut the door quietly behind him.

Jamie gave Duster a pat. "Don't get too comfortable, we're off out soon." Duster settled quickly as Jamie turned off the light and he tried to doze off again. He lay in the dark, mulling over the day's events, trying to come up with some solution. He didn't want a physical encounter with the twins, they'd absolutely massacre him, but he wondered if he could get to Spencer before they got to him. He didn't think so,

Spencer was constantly surrounded. He could pretend friendship and join the gang, but he didn't like being accountable to anyone. It was a depressing scenario and he knew there had to be a confrontation at some point.

He turned over with a sigh and switched on his light. He'd been thinking for about an hour and it was just after eleven. He turned on the television again and found a programme that he liked and he settled down to wait for his parents to go to bed. Just before twelve, the doors to both his parents' and his grandma's rooms closed. Jamie waited patiently, giving them all another half an hour before sliding his legs out of bed. He was dressed in a flash, black jeans, t-shirt, a hoodie and a pair of battered trainers. Duster sat on the bed eyeing his master curiously. He knew something was up.

"Duster. Listen carefully. We are going to the park to get my books. It's not a walk, but I want you with me, okay?" The dog looked at him and cocked his head to show he was listening. "We have to be silent as we leave the house."

Jamie tiptoed downstairs avoiding the creaky third step from the bottom and stole silently into the kitchen. Jamie took Duster's lead from the hook by the back door, and unlocked it. It clicked loudly and Jamie froze, listening carefully. The house remained silent. Conscious that he wasn't breathing, he let out his breath and stepped outside. He locked the door and clipped the lead on Duster. He decided to use the gate down the garden rather that the front gate. It was a longer journey, but less likely to be seen by anyone on the roads. He didn't want to be questioned by any adults coming out of the pub, let alone a policeman doing his rounds. He didn't think being dressed from head to foot in black and out after midnight was something he could lie his way out of.

Duster pulled at his lead a little and a gentle tug

brought the dog back into line. "Careful boy," he whispered, "we need to really keep our wits about us tonight."

Progress was good and thankfully it was a clear night. Jamie had a torch in his pocket but he didn't want to use it, so he was pleased that cloud cover kept the moon out of sight, but gave him enough light to see. His eyes quickly became accustomed to the limited sight he had and before long they'd made to the recreation ground without any mishap. Jamie slipped through the entrance.

He walked to the bin where his books had been dumped and took the lid off. He reached in hoping there was nothing disgusting inside, but couldn't feel anything at all. It was empty! He reached inside his pocket and risked a quick blast of light from the torch. He held the torch inside the bin and switched it on. The bin had some general rubbish in there, but his books were definitely gone. Duster growled deep in his throat next to him.

"Looking for these?"

Jamie jumped, but had the foresight to swing the torch round. It illuminated Spencer. There was a pile of books next to him and he rested one foot on them, a hint of triumph on his face. Duster growled again and Spencer's expression changed. Duster appeared to be an unexpected development.

"Keep calm Duster." Jamie rested a hand on the dog's head, but he could feel that his usually placid dog was ready to attack if he gave the order. He didn't have a chance to think about this new side to his dog's character, but kept a tight hold of his lead just in case.

"Turn the light off you idiot," Spencer warned. Jamie immediately extinguished the light, but the moon came out at that moment illuminating them enough to see each other's faces. "I don't like dogs."

"I think it's pretty clear that he doesn't seem to like you." Bringing Duster had been a smart move, Spencer was definitely troubled by the dog. "I will let him off. I don't know what he'll do to you, but if the way he treats wild rabbits is anything to go by, I don't fancy your chances much."

Spencer took his foot off the books and backed away slowly, his earlier confidence gone. "All right, have your books, just don't let the dog go."

"That depends," countered Jamie sensing an opening, "I just need a few answers."

"Get lost!" came the angry reply.

"No problem, I'll just let Duster off his lead. Hold on a second." Jamie went to unclip Duster and he strained to get at Spencer, who cried out in alarm.

"Okay, okay. What do you want to know?"

"I thought it was pretty obvious. Why have I been singled out by you and your cronies?"

"I'd have thought that was obvious," replied Spencer, "no one says no to me."

Jamie was stunned. He really didn't think that Spencer was so narcissistic. "Do you expect me to believe that?"

"It's true. I have some hold over people and when you said no to me, I didn't want to lose face." Spencer was convinced by his own words and as if to highlight the point, he smoothed a lock of hair from his face.

"Are you that vain, that you think everyone hangs on your every word and action?"

"You've seen it. They do. It started at the end of primary school and it's continued into senior school. It's not my fault that everyone loves me."

Jamie laughed nastily. "I could let off my dog, he'd soon show you that not everyone loves you."

Spencer cried out again. "No, don't do that, please."

Jamie thought for a moment. "Give me one reason

why I shouldn't."

"Okay, I'll make sure that the twins leave you alone."

Jamie was instantly relieved, the thought of being beaten up by those two was really unpleasant. "Okay, deal, but what about you and me? Are we done?"

"I promise that there will not be any physical stuff, for now, but you'll still have to watch your back."

Again, Jamie was taken aback. Even with the threat of unleashing Duster, Spencer was still trying to gain some advantage. Jamie was tiring of the stand-off, he had no real intention of letting the dog loose to attack Spencer in front of him, but he had certainly been a useful bargaining tool. He made up his mind.

"Fine, that's a deal, but as you can see I am more than capable of looking after myself."

Spencer snorted, "A real big guy with your dog!"

"I could say the same about you and your heavy bodyguards. Why don't you and I have it out right here and now, get all this unpleasantness over and done with."

"I don't fight," was the reply.

"No, I suppose not. With Charlie and Francis about, why would you need to?" Jamie paused for a moment before continuing. "Right, it's clear you and I are never going to be friends, so just to let you know that I mean business I'm going to count to ten, and then I'm going to let my dog come after you. You'll have just enough of a head start to make it to the gate before Duster here catches up with you."

"You wouldn't dare." There was real fear in Spencer's eyes.

"You watch me. One."

Spencer paused momentarily.

"Two." With a yelp Spencer tore off, desperate to escape. Jamie slowly counted to ten, then let Duster off his lead. With a bark, he sped off in pursuit. Jamie casually picked up all of his books and put them into an empty plastic bag he'd brought with him. He listened for any signs of capture. There was another angry bark and a cry from Spencer, before he heard Duster trotting back with a piece of black cloth in his mouth. "Good dog." Jamie patted him on the head and examined the cloth. There was no blood and he quickly checked Duster's mouth. Blood free. He was pleased that Duster had done no damage, but he hoped he'd got a nip in before Spencer had escaped. "Let's go home."

They made it back to the house quickly and quietly, seeing no one else, and Jamie let them in the back door. Duster took a slurp from his water bowl then flopped contentedly into his bed. Jamie put his books on the table and gave Duster another pat. He smiled in satisfaction, then silently made his way up to his room and into his bed where he fell asleep almost instantly into a dreamless sleep.

A curious discovery

Jamie woke up the next day and groaned thinking he had school. He thought about sneaking back to sleep, but the house was quiet and it didn't have that hectic early morning feel to it. Usually the radio would be chattering away and his grandma would be clattering about in the kitchen getting breakfast ready. He turned over and glanced at his clock, which told him it was just after eight. He breathed deeply and relaxed. It was Saturday.

Jamie lay in bed for a while listening to the comforting sounds of the house. He could hear rain on the roof and absently wondered if Grandma and Duster were out for an early morning walk. There was no sound from his parent's room, so they must be having a well-deserved lie in. He swung his legs out of bed and stretched.

The kitchen was empty and Duster gone, so he was out on his walk. His books had been cleared from the kitchen table, which was now set for breakfast and a delicious smell of freshly baking bread emanated from the Aga. He thought about having a peek, but he knew that if the bread was rising, then this would be a disaster. He could wait. Yawning, he opened the door of the fridge and retrieved the orange juice. Pouring himself a glass, he took a long satisfying swig before placing it on the table and cleared a bit of space on the kitchen table so he could begin his homework.

He thought back to last night and smiled ruefully. He hoped it might cool things between him and Spencer, but he wouldn't know that until Monday morning he supposed. He worked through his homework, before clearing away his books with some satisfaction. He peered out of the window, where the rain had intensified, and thought how wet the walkers must be getting. The thud of footsteps above and the sound of the shower starting up meant his parents were up. His stomach rumbled. He was hungry.

A beeper went off next to the Aga and Jamie assumed it was to take out the bread. He found a pair of oven gloves and opened the door. A wave of steam poured out and once again the delicious aroma of his grandma's bread hit him full in the face making his stomach grumble in protest. He carefully slid the tray out of the oven, admiring the bread, and left it on the side to cool, when the door to the kitchen opened and his soaked grandma appeared, closing the door behind her. She was dressed from head to toe in a full length waxed jacket, wellington boots and a matching waxed hat. Raindrops slid down the jacket and began to leave a puddle on the floor.

"Oh, good," she said smiling at her grandson. "You got the bread out. How are you this morning? Good night's sleep?"

Jamie looked at his grandma carefully. She was remarkably astute and he wondered if she knew anything about his late night adventure. He didn't think so, but she glanced over to his books.

"Done your homework?" she enquired mischievously.

"All done Grandma. How was your walk?" Jamie asked in an attempt to deflect her.

"Wet. Duster is soaked through. He seemed quite tired this morning. I wonder why?"

"No idea. Do you need some towels?"

"Good idea, that dog of yours needs a rub down. Thought I'd walk him early as the rain is set to get heavier today. It's going to be an indoor kind of day."

Jamie padded into the laundry room to retrieve some dog towels, glad to have walked away from that potential conversation. He put two large ones on the floor and gave Grandma a thumbs up through the window to let her know it was all right to bring the sodden dog in. She brought him in and he sat on the dry towels, tongue lolling happily. Grandma took off her boots and carried them through to the utility room to dry off, whilst Jamie got on his knees and covered his dog in one enormous towel.

This was a great game for the dog and he nuzzled into Jamie, attacking the towel whilst his owner desperately tried to rub him down. Duster loved this drying game and made the process as difficult as possible! After a couple of minutes of vigorous rubbing down he appeared drier, but the dog wasn't finished yet. Grandma came back with another towel and formed a barricade protecting the rest of the kitchen. Duster stood up and shook himself, spraying Jamie and the new towel with the remains of the water from his coat. Grandma, safe behind the towel laughed and indicated that Jamie ought to go and have a shower now. Duster licked Jamie on the ear for good measure before disappearing out of the kitchen in search of his breakfast.

Wet and slightly muddied Jamie agreed and skipped up for a shower passing his mother on the stairs.

"Morning my love." She went to give him a kiss on the cheek, but stopped short. "Urgh, you're all wet!"

Jamie laughed and held out his arms for a cuddle. Mum skirted past him.

"I'll give you a cuddle once you've showered young man. Dad's out and there's plenty of hot water. See you for breakfast."

After a hot shower, Jamie dressed and came down for breakfast. Both his parents were there. He kissed his dad on the top of his head who held his hand up for a high five. He then went around the table and demanded a cuddle from his mother. Duster barked and tried to get between them both whilst this was going on. He always behaved like this where Jamie's mother was concerned. It was the same with Grandma. They couldn't work out whether Duster objected to public displays of affection or whether he was protecting the females of the house.

The rain beat down against the windows during breakfast and Dad seemed quite pleased with the weather prospects for the day. Both the ladies of the house usually had plenty of outdoor jobs for him to do, but owing to the pouring rain, he knew that he'd have a chance to laze around. Not wanting to encourage any indoor jobs he cleared the table after breakfast and did all the washing up before disappearing with a whoop to the lounge. Jamie heard the television turn on and the scream of a formula one car tearing around a track could be heard.

"Jamie. The qualifying for the grand prix is starting," Dad called.

Jamie was drying the dishes and he looked at his mother.

"Go on," she said. "I'll finish up here."

"Thanks Mum." He dropped the tea-towel on the side and jumped over the back of the sofa to join his dad.

As Saturday mornings go, it wasn't half bad. Jamie and his father watched the motor racing whilst his mum read her book in the kitchen. Grandma was picked up by a friend to go and play bridge, so for once in their busy lives there was a sense of stillness and relaxation. Jamie knew it wouldn't last, there were always things to do, but on this particular morning it was sheer indulgence for everyone concerned.

The qualifying session had been more exciting than usual and rain had affected their morning too, sending some of the usual front-runners off the track and lower down the grid than they would usually be. A relative newcomer in an unfancied car took pole position, which seemed to please Jamie's dad. A pause for a pot of tea and a game of rugby ensued on another channel.

Jamie enjoyed the time with his dad and popped in every so often to see how his mum was. She too seemed utterly happy with a lazy morning and was delighted when Jamie offered to make the lunch. As suggested by his dad, he heated up some tomato soup and made some ham sandwiches with the remainder of this morning's bread. He popped it all on the table and added some pickles and a large jug of water.

Once lunch was over, Dad disappeared into his office to catch up on some work and his mother begrudgingly started to mark a rather large pile of exercise books. Jamie looked out of the window, but the rain was still pouring down and there was no chance of a bike ride or anything outdoor related today. He was at a bit of a loose end and wondering what to do, when his grandma returned.

"Fancy a game of scrabble Jamie?" She asked as she hung up her coat in the hallway.

"Maybe later," offered Jamie. "Is there any chance I could go up in the attic and explore a bit?"

He'd done this many times as a smaller boy and had once found a hilarious dressing box up there. There was no way he was going to dress up but he recalled there were other things up there to discover. She agreed and helped him let the old rickety stairs down.

She told him to be careful and then grinning suddenly, reminded Jamie of the hilarious story which involved his dad falling through the ceiling when Jamie was five. He smiled, it was one of Grandma's favourite stories and she told it often, especially if any of Dad's friends were around! He and Mum had found him hanging halfway through the ceiling of the spare room, hooked onto a beam by his belt. He was a bit red in the face and decidedly fed up. Mum, barely able to suppress her giggles, had rescued him by cutting through the belt and he had fallen to the floor with a thump. Jamie had learned some new swear words that day. He even took a piece of the ceiling into 'show and tell' at school, although he didn't think his teacher had believed him.

They both laughed and, switching on the light, Grandma left him to explore, chuckling away to herself as she went back downstairs. What Jamie was looking for was his dad's old box of comic books. He still collected them now and Mum always thought it was a bit strange that a grown man read comic books. Dad's enthusiasm had rubbed off on him and he had inherited this obsession and would happily delve into the world of *Marvel* at any given opportunity. This is exactly what he planned to do now and he knew that somewhere in the attic lurked an old series of Spiderman adventures. Dad had always boasted that he had some rare early copies and he was desperate to hunt them out. He'd asked Dad where they were and he claimed that they were somewhere in the attic, but he couldn't remember quite where.

Before long, Jamie had forgotten about his real mission and spent a happy hour in the attic finding all sorts of weird and wonderful stuff. He found some marvellous vintage hats, which must have belonged to his grandfather. He paraded around in a fantastic trilby and hoped that his grandma might let him keep it. Despite his thorough and entertaining search there was no sign of Dad's infamous comic collection. Taking one last look around, he spied one corner that hadn't yet been explored. As he approached he could see some old boxes stuffed full. He hadn't been in this corner yet,

34

so feeling hopeful he examined them carefully.

As Jamie looked, he chanced upon one that looked suspiciously heavy and filled to the brim with what appeared to be paper. Dad's comics he thought. Bingo. But, in his haste to get to it, he prised it from the middle before taking the others off it from above. Disaster struck, as the top box fell. Arms flailing, he tried to catch it, but to no avail. The top came open and spilled its contents all over him. It made a lot of noise in the enclosed space and he listened hard, hoping Grandma hadn't heard and was coming up to see what had happened. He continued to listen, but he hadn't disturbed her. He began to rummage through the debris and was glad to see that nothing appeared to be broken.

Jamie thought he'd better put the contents of this box back before opening the potential comic box. But he soon completely forgot about the comics as he discovered all manner of strange and interesting things. He eyed with fascination feathers from magnificent birds, crystals of many shapes, sizes and colours and even a dried, shrivelled claw from what looked like a chicken. This made his skin crawl and he quickly popped it in the box with a shiver of disgust. He finished clearing everything up and was about to go downstairs to ask Grandma about these weird items, when he spotted a small wooden box.

The box was about the size of a Rubik's cube and made from a highly polished dark wood. It resembled a musical box because the lid was hinged and there was a metal catch on the front. It nestled in a pile of dust, but the box itself was completely clean. This was strange, as Jamie like everything else, was covered in dust. As he approached it, the box quivered slightly as if something was alive inside it. He jumped back, alarmed for a moment then plucked up the courage to pick it up. He was curious and turned it over in his hands. The box quivered again and Jamie nearly dropped it, but he held it firmly and with trembling fingers opened the lid.

Light poured out of it filling the attic with light and for a moment Jamie was dazzled. It wasn't a musical box that much was for sure. Whatever was in the box emitted an intense light, which glowed with such ferocity that it almost hummed with energy. He was unsure whether or not he should touch it, but his inquisitiveness got the better of him. He reached in and brought out a glass sphere about the size of a tennis ball. Intrigued, he took a closer look. The strange and ethereal light was emanating from its very core, and lit his face with a warm and pleasant glow. What a find he thought, as he reluctantly placed it back into its protective casing and shut the lid, blocking out the light and returning the attic to the light from the naked bulb above.

The bright light from the strange object had left images on his retinas and Jamie rubbed his eyes, trying to focus. He climbed down the rickety stairs carefully and then raced to the kitchen to find his grandma.

"Hello dear," she remarked cheerfully, sipping her herbal tea, "Fancy a chocolate hobnob?" Duster immediately woofed and thumped his tail on the kitchen floor. It was fairly obvious that he fancied a biscuit. "Not for you, you smelly hound," she laughed patting Duster on the head.

"No thanks Grandma." He looked around. "Where's Mum?"

"She's gone to the shops. Why?"

"Just wondered where she was, but it's you I really need. I hope you don't mind, but I think I found a box with some of your old witchy paraphernalia in it." Jamie was a bit worried that this might annoy her.

His grandma raised an eyebrow saying nothing, but motioned for him to continue. Jamie swallowed and continued. When she was quiet it often meant she was cross. He really didn't want to get on the bad side of his grandma, but he felt that she might understand and be the best person to explain what had just happened in the attic.

"I need to show you something. Look at this." Jamie carefully placed the wooden box on the table and looked up his grandma hopefully. "What is it?"

"Gosh," she whispered, recognising it, any irritation of him going through her stuff quickly dissipating. "I haven't seen that old thing for years. It was given to me when I joined my first coven down in the New Forest. I can't remember who gave it to me." She thought for a moment. "How strange. It's believed to have magical powers, but it was rumoured that only one person in every generation would ever be able to activate it." Jamie was beginning to get excited.

"How so Grandma?"

"Well, it has a strange name and even stranger origin if I recall. Hold on whilst I go and retrieve one of my books." She got up and disappeared for a moment then came back with an old leather bound book, weathered with age. She scratched her head for a moment and pushed her spectacles up her nose. She smiled as the name came back to her and she found the page she was looking for. She read out the entry.

"The Sacred Orb of Foden takes its name from an area in Scotland where it was reputed to have been found. No one knows for sure how old it is, or indeed where it originates from, but some very curious legends surround it.

"It was presumed in some circles of the faith to have been forged in the very depths of hell by the devil himself! It is believed that it holds great power, which in the wrong hands would spell mortal danger to all of humanity.

"Another states the opposite and that it was a present from a powerful wizard, possibly Merlin, to someone worthy and deserving. If they were such a person, then the orb would activate in a bright plume of light, letting that person know they were the chosen one.

"Like all of these legends, they purport to a quest of some sort. The first legend dealt with keeping a shadowy figure of some sort at bay, whilst having to fulfil some sort of bargain to keep hold of your soul, whilst the second promises a wish to the person who activates it, but only after helping five people.

"The orb has been lost for generations…"

"Grandma," said Jamie barely able to contain his excitement, "once activated, would it look anything like this?" Jamie opened the lid and removed the glowing orb. It seemed to shine even brighter in the cheerful kitchen. Duster sat bolt upright and stared at it, hypnotised. He whined quietly and slid under the table. Grandma gasped in astonishment, but didn't stay stupefied for long. Chuckling, she reached into her handbag and donned a pair of expensive sunglasses.

"Much better!" she exclaimed. "That is a touch bright isn't it? Well, well, well. Could you pass it to me dear?" As soon as the orb touched his grandma's hand, it ceased to glow and became an ordinary glass globe once more. "How extraordinary." She smiled, passing it back to Jamie. Again, it immediately came back to life and seemed to physically quiver in Jamie's hand.

"What does this mean Grandma?"

"I'm not sure dear, but if my book is anything to go by, you seem to be able to activate it and if the legend is correct you will be granted a wish if you help five people."

"I know you are a practising witch Grandma, but do you really believe in magic? This seems all a bit far-fetched don't you think?"

Jamie's Grandma took off her glasses and held Jamie's hand in her own. She looked very serious. "Listen, there is magic in this world, people just choose to ignore it. Miracles happen all the time and the most amazing things do happen to ordinary people."

"But that's not down to magic surely?"

"It definitely is, but it's not the 'pull a rabbit out of a hat' kind."

"What like those magicians on the television?"

"Sure, they are really very good at suspending belief. What they do isn't magic; it's all about illusion and detracting you from the secret of the trick they are performing."

"A bit like that guy who hangs from the double-decker bus with one arm whilst it's on the move."

"Correct, that's not magic, it's a carefully crafted trick to make you think it's magic. It's very smart I grant you, but not magic."

"So what is then?"

"Magic is the art of healing, of people being able to do unimaginable things that defy the limitations of the human body or mind. The father that lifts the wreckage off of his family with strength he never knew he had. That's magic of a sort. You just have to believe that you can do things."

"I'd like to be invisible or levitate!" Jamie laughed.

His grandma smiled, "It has been done. I've seen it."

"No way. Can you do it?"

"Now that would be telling wouldn't it? Put the orb in your hand again, I'm fascinated."

Jamie did as he was asked and again the glass sphere glowed brightly and fizzed with energy when he touched it.

"How interesting. Perhaps you should try to help

someone, see if the legend really is true."

"Who do I help, Grandma?"

"I guess you'll know when the time is right." She paused for a moment and a frown crossed her face. "Be careful though. You must tell me everything that happens, if this part of legend turns out to be true then we must assume that the other part might also be."

"What the bit about losing my soul?" Jamie looked worried.

"Indeed. Nothing to worry about I'm sure, but if anything strange should happen you must tell me immediately."

"Of course," laughed Jamie.

"Don't laugh, I'm being deadly serious. Promise me!"

Jamie was slightly taken aback by the urgency in his grandma's voice. "Okay, I promise."

"Good, but for now keep it a secret. We need to work out if it does anything at all, or whether it's just an illusion that you can activate rather than I."

Jamie agreed and unsure if he should be excited or scared, he placed the orb back in its box and took it up to his room.

The rest of Saturday passed uneventfully and he sat on his bed reading comics. His mind reeled with the possibilities. The discovery had left him feeling really excited about the potential reward, but in another sense a little nervous as to how he should proceed.

He still found it hard to believe that he would even be granted a wish; that was the sort of thing that only happened in fairy stories, surely? Other questions swirled in his head. Who would he help and why? How would the orb know that he'd helped someone? If it was all true and by some miracle he managed the task, what would he possibly wish for? Another three wishes? Would that be too greedy? He thought it probably would be. Besides, in all likelihood it was bound to be in a code of magic somewhere under the heading 'What not to do with a magic wish'! Despite all of this the other side of the legend kept springing into his mind. It all seemed completely unimaginable, wishes and losing his soul? He laughed at himself for beginning to believe.

He said goodnight to his parents and decided on an early night. The rain had stopped which meant he might get outside tomorrow. He was looking forward to some fresh air and he hoped it might clear his mind about what he should do, if anything at all.

He soon fell asleep and Duster, as ever, crept up to his room to join him, but as soon as he reached the bed to hop up, something made him stop. He looked at Jamie sleeping and whining turned tail and went back downstairs.

Something woke Jamie up. He had been dreaming and as the images drifted away, he was left with a real feeling of dread. He sat up and tried to recall what the dreams had been, but nothing came back to him except a feeling that someone had been watching him. Slightly spooked, he listened carefully, but the rest of the house was asleep. He shivered. His room was really cold; the heating must have gone off he thought as he got out of bed. He shivered again and turned on his bedside lamp and immediately wished he hadn't.

A thin veil of mist hung eerily a foot off the floor and swinging his feet from the bed disturbed it, sending the haze lazily in different directions. Jamie pinched himself. I must still be dreaming he thought as he looked around his room. The box containing the orb was still by his bed, so he opened it and held the orb in his hand. Like earlier, it glowed fiercely and the weight of it convinced him that he was indeed awake. It made him feel more confident and he decided to see if the rest of the house was in the same way.

He trod carefully to the door of his room, which was firmly shut, when a movement to his left startled him and he turned. His mirror, positioned over his desk had frozen over. He reached over to touch it when a mark appeared in it. Jamie took his finger away and watched stunned as the mark continued to grow and words began to form.

He couldn't move.

Slowly, but then more quickly a message appeared in the mirror. For a moment it made no sense and then horrifyingly it stated:

"Be seeing you soon!"

Jamie cried out in alarm, but was rooted to the spot. The orb glowed fiercely in his hand and then let out a glow so bright that he had to close his eyes. He waited, too afraid to look, when the room instantly warmed and his feeling of unease completely disappeared. He felt fine, no longer scared, and he opened his eyes.

The room had returned to normal. The mist had gone, the mirror was clear, but as he watched a solitary drop of moisture rolled slowly down the mirror leaving a streak. Jamie touched the mirror and jolted his hand back as haunting laughter emanated from somewhere. He shook his head in disbelief and again the orb glowed comfortingly, calming him.

Almost as if on autopilot, he staggered back to bad, still clutching the orb, got back under the covers shivering not from the cold but from a very real fear.

Bargains and threats

When Jamie woke, it was after ten according to his alarm clock, and despite the scare during the night, he felt fantastic. Totally refreshed, he jumped out of bed, placed the ever glowing orb on his desk, got dressed and made his way downstairs. The message on the mirror seemed a distant memory and he dismissed it as a figment of his over stimulated imagination. He didn't feel in the least bit worried and despite the warning from his grandma to report anything unusual, he'd decided not to share that with her.

Mum was beavering away in the kitchen, slamming doors, rattling pots and muttering about how little time she had and that no one ever helped. Jamie knew it was best to keep out of her way, but he popped in to say hi anyway and try to scrounge what might be left from breakfast.

"Morning Mum."

"Oh good morning sleepy head. You slept for over thirteen hours. How I'd love to be a teenager again."

He gave his mum a kiss on the cheek and smiled, not rising to the bait. It was obvious that she was in a Sunday mood. Dad was conspicuous by his absence and Grandma would have gone off to play her Sunday morning game of golf as the weather was fine. Mum professed to like cooking the roast dinner for the family, but it often put her in a strange mood. He was torn between sloping off quietly and offering to help. Even those invitations to 'help' were loosely veiled. Cooking with Mum usually ended up in an argument.

He poured himself a glass of milk and found a piece of cheese to munch on before deciding he ought to at least peel some potatoes. He finished his meagre breakfast and rolled up his sleeves. He filled the sink with cold water and poured in a healthy amount of King Edwards to soak.

Mum smiled gratefully and ruffled his hair. "Thanks Jamie, you're more help than your father." Jamie didn't answer and peeled the potatoes, popping them into a pan of fresh water, whilst he listened to his mum grumble about this and that. He skilfully said yes and no at the right times before he asked if she needed anything from the village shop as a way of escape.

"No thanks love I'm fine."

He popped on his coat and stuck his head into the living room where Dad was hiding. He offered to get him a paper and he agreed with a smile. He was about to leave when on a whim he decided to take the orb with him. He figured that if there was any truth to either legend, he ought to keep it with at all times just in case. He ran upstairs to get it leaving an agitated Duster spinning in circles by the front door desperate to go out.

"Hold on boy, I'll just be a second."

Jamie ran up to his room and picked up the orb that fizzled into life the moment he touched it and with a laugh put it in his pocket. He raced back down the stair and let Duster out the front door who flew down to the front gate barking loudly where he waited for Jamie to clip on his lead. With Duster trotting at his heels he strolled out into the village to the local newsagent. He spent his pocket money on a paper, some sweets and a magazine for himself. He popped a mint into his mouth, untied Duster from outside the shop and cheerfully began to amble home jiggling the loose change in his pocket, the worries of the past few days a distant memory.

Jamie had almost reached home, when he became aware of the sound of rubber on tarmac behind him. The orb vibrated strongly in his pocket as if in warning.

He turned, eyes widened in panic and took drastic and evasive action. He threw himself into the nearest hedge! Just in time as well, as Spencer came hurtling down the pavement just missing him, laughing maniacally. He whooped with amusement as Jamie disappeared into the spiky hawthorn hedge. He let go of Duster who gave chase barking frenziedly, his lead dragging behind him.

"Catch you later loser!" Spencer's voice called as he disappeared around the corner with Duster in hot pursuit. Jamie was furious and banged the ground in anger. The orb crackled deep in his coat and Jamie roared louder than he'd ever done before, sending birds nestling in all the surrounding trees up into the sky in a squawking cloud and shattering some glass somewhere in someone's garden. He felt a sudden shift in the air around him and he knew intuitively that something strange had happened.

Nothing moved as Jamie painfully disentangled himself from the hedge; all sound was gone. It was silent. He looked around and the world appeared to have frozen still. If he hadn't believed in magic before, he certainly did now. Cars in the road were stationary, birds above him were motionless in mid-air and in the distance he could see Duster in full flight with all four feet off the ground.

"Oh my God!"

"Almost," said a voice in his head, startling him. "Hold the orb tightly, it will guide you."

Jamie reached inside of his jacket and brought out the orb. It immediately shone like a beacon, sending a beam of light into the sky, splitting a cloud above him in two. The air around had begun to shimmer, as though it was disappearing and it took on a translucent quality. A hole in the air in front of him began to appear and he stepped towards it. He looked at it as if in understanding and then looked into it. His face, distorted slightly, stared back at him and then suddenly the world shifted.

Jamie held on tight to the orb as his entire world fell away. His feet were on terra firma, but all of reality seemed to shift around him. He closed his eyes as watching made him feel sick. He'd been on some serious roller coasters in the past, but this was extreme. The world shifted again and Jamie felt himself falling away from Marsh Green to somewhere else entirely.

Without warning the sensation stopped and the sudden return to normality made Jamie's knees buckle and he fell to the floor in a heap. Laughter brought him to his senses and he opened his eyes slowly. He sat up and looked around. He was in shock, as the reality of what had just happened became clear. It seemed incredible, but it appeared that he'd travelled in time and space to somewhere else. Amazing, but he suspected that he might be in danger. He studied his new surroundings carefully.

Jamie was in a tent of some sort. It was huge, with thick rugs over every conceivable floor space. The sides were draped with fine cloth and along one wall was a long table overflowing with food. The delicious aroma of fresh bread made his mouth water. In the centre of the cavernous space was a huge brazier that emanated a great heat. It sizzled and spattered, but the sparks that fell on the floor extinguished without setting fire to the rug on which it sat. He looked up and a small hole in the roof of this tent seemed to suck up all the smoke. What should have been an acrid atmosphere was anything but. The tent was warm and comfortable, but a sense of danger still pervaded his thoughts and his adrenaline was pumping in his veins.

Strange laughter erupted from the corner of the room. A dark figure got up from a pile of furs it'd been lying on and stretched luxuriously. Dressed from head to toe in black armour he was a fearsome sight. The armour shone like obsidian and on his head was a helmet with spikes protruding from its sides and sitting resplendent on the top, a plume of black feathers shone. A mask covered his face and the only feature of his face that could be seen was a pair of bright blue eyes. There were no other markings to suggest a rank or who this person was, but it was clear that he was a warrior and he exuded power.

The warrior silently padded into the centre of the room. He must have been over six feet tall with massive shoulders and a bulk about him that suggested a strong man. Despite his size, he moved with an agility and quickness of step that suggested great speed as well as brawn.

"Welcome young man." Despite the mask, Jamie could hear the warrior clearly. It was almost as if his voice filled the room.

Jamie looked at the figure towering above him and stammered, "Who, who are you?"

The man laughed without humour. "I'm not sure you'd believe me if I told you. Some call me Death, others the Keeper of Souls, but you may call me Lord if you must address me at all."

Jamie eyes widened with terror, the other part of the legend had some truth to it. He bowed his head trying to hide his fear.

"Look at me!" the figure ordered. He oozed with authority and stared at Jamie, making him tremble. His eyes bored into him and he knew that he was only to speak if he was spoken to. He'd never met an adult who'd had that effect on him before and he clutched the glowing orb ever more tightly.

"I wasn't expecting to see you so soon, most impressive for one so young. It took me years to be able to do what you just did."

"What did I do?" Jamie asked still trembling, but feeling a little bolder. He somehow felt that he had to appear to be brave if he was to get of here alive.

"You used your anger to stop time. Impressive indeed. Your aptitude surprises me, but as soon as you used the orb in such a way it meant that it was time."

"Time for what?"

"Time to come to me. I summoned you here." The warrior beckoned with arms to encompass the tent.

"Where am I?" Jamie asked tentatively.

"On your world, but in another time and possibly a parallel one to yours. You won't find me in any of your history books." He paused for a moment allowing his words to have an effect before continuing. "I rule here with an iron fist and all bow to me as supreme leader. You need know no more than that. You are here because I made it so, but also because you have activated the orb. My message got through it seems."

"That was you?"

"Yes, it was most interesting what I saw of your world. I rather liked it." Jamie suspected that this was an ominous statement, but didn't comment. "It was important for you to know more and your anger has sped up this process. Always remember that your emotions, particular those darker ones, make the orb you hold in your hand much more powerful. I can see that you want revenge on the other boy. I can almost taste it."

"It's true I want revenge, but I couldn't hurt him." Jamie paused, thinking, then decided to ask the question that was hanging over him. "Could the orb really make me powerful?"

The warrior laughed. "Of course, look what it's done for me. It feasts on your darkest desires. It loves revenge, hatred and control. If you allow it to overcome those emotions you can achieve anything you desire. It fed on me and now no one dares get in my way. I control an army of millions."

Jamie could feel his cheeks drain of colour. He was very frightened, but tried not to show it.

"But there are some truths you must know if you are to exploit the power in your hand. Show it to me."

Jamie was unsure whether he should, but did as he was asked. He opened his hand and the orb glowed fiercely.

"Ah," said the figure as he reached into his armour and brought out an exact replica, which glowed just as fiercely in the palm of his hand.

"You have one too?" Jamie asked.

"No, young man, they are one and the same. Watch." Both orbs rose into the air and then rushed towards each other, moulding into one orb which revolved in slow motion and glowed brightly. The single orb remained hovering between the two of them.

"Is the orb yours?"

"Yes it is."

"How does it work and is it magic?"

"It is a magical device created by a powerful magician in the dawn of time. It was created to help the human race achieve peace, by allowing one person in every generation in many parallel worlds the opportunity to be granted a wish. It was hoped it would be used for the good of humanity," scoffed the warrior.

"How did you get it then?" Jamie was surprised by his temerity and lowered his head in embarrassment.

The warrior growled, irritated by the flippant question. He was obviously unused to being spoken to without permission and in such a way. He took a step closer, but thought better of it and stepped back.

"I won it from the previous wielder. He now resides in one of those bottles behind me. I allow him out every so often, it amuses me to do so." Jamie looked and on a series of ornate shelves rested at least a hundred bottles which all swirled with a mysterious mist. He swallowed. "Ah yes they are the souls of those who didn't keep their end of the bargain."

"Bargain?"

"Oh yes, your lovely grandmother told you of the legend."

Without meaning to Jamie spluttered out angrily, "You leave my grandma out of this."

The warrior took one step towards Jamie and struck him hard across the face. Jamie fell to a heap on the floor, his cheek smarting from the pain. "How dare you talk to me in that way?"

Jamie got up slowly, anger raging inside him. He'd never felt this way before. Spencer had pushed him around and he wasn't going to allow anyone to intimidate him any more. Jamie's anger continued to grow and it wasn't an unpleasant sensation. He felt a power increasing within him and the orb hovering between them both began to glow even brighter. The anger teemed through his veins and he closed his eyes.

The warrior watched with great interest as the younger boy stretched out both his hands. Suddenly, the fire in the brazier exploded upwards and formed into a fiery ball that spun at incredible speed. Jamie's eyes flickered under his closed eyelids and the ball of fire moved between the two of them. He reached out the orb as well, but there was no response, which appeared to surprise him. He breathed deeply and folded his arms, waiting.

Jamie nodded once, and then started to gesticulate with his hands. The ball of fire was still spinning, but as he watched it began to get faster and faster, until it spun on its axis with such ferocity that it generated an eddy within the tent, which ruffled the expensive cloth adorning the walls. The warrior watched as the ball of fire spun its way higher into the tent. His eyes never left it, hoping to out manoeuvre it, if it came for him.

The ball seemed to be watching him before it came, rushing at him in a wall of searing heat. He had no time to react as it happened so quickly. The ball swirled around him trying to find a way in through the armour, a protective see through shutter slid down to protect his eyes. And then, suddenly, it was over and Jamie fell to the floor exhausted. The orb went back to hovering once more, its power for the moment spent.

The warrior clapped his hands together making the air ring. "Well, well, well. You are a terrifying prospect aren't you? It's a good thing that you've had no training, because without my enchanted armour you would have killed me."

Jamie was amazed and terrified of what he could do in equal measure. "Are you okay?"

"I am fine. A little hot in here, but otherwise fine. I look forward to guiding you if you agree to my bargain."

"Bargain?"

"You have seen what the orb is capable of. Your efforts to use it will have left you weak." It was true, Jamie was exhausted, but still managed to stand up straight. "The orb can be used as a powerful tool and no one will be able to stand in your way once you are its master. Maybe not even me. At the moment, you cannot harm me, but I can't say the same for your enemies back in your time."

"I couldn't do that to anyone. You just made me so angry."

"Well, that remains to be seen. You've seen the power it can unleash, but as you know there is another side to its origin."

"The wish?" Jamie asked.

51

"Correct. I've never needed a wish as I use it for my own means. I need no wish to make things happen for me."

"I could be like you?"

"Indeed, if you'll let me help you."

Jamie didn't like the thought of being all-powerful, but he nodded in understanding.

"If you agree, I will give you thirty days, one of your calendar months, to fulfil the legend of the orb. If you manage to help five people, one wish to you will be granted."

"And if I refuse this offer?"

"Refuse? Ha! Then you will never return to your world and stay with me forever."

Jamie was chilled to the bone. He was trapped. He contemplated staying for the briefest of moments and hoped the warrior would teach him the ways of the orb, so he could master it, defeat him and return to his world. He felt sure this wouldn't happen though and he'd become a slave. He made his decision.

"Okay, I'll do it, just to show you that I can."

"Fighting spirit. You are a worthy challenger my young friend."

"What if I don't help five people in thirty days?" asked a shaken Jamie, refusing to allow his fear to show.

"If you don't, then I will take your soul and you will become one of the undead, at my disposal and under my will." The warrior laughed nastily.

Jamie swallowed hard and said. "I'll do my best, but how will I know if I've helped someone? It would be no point in agreeing to do this if I don't know I've done it."

"A fair point. Use your eyes to help you."

"My eyes?" Jamie was dumbfounded.

"Your eyes will reveal all. You will understand

when it happens. If you manage to help someone, the orb will grant you a skill which will manifest itself to you, when you need it the most."

"Like what?"

"I cannot tell you, but it will cater to your own particular needs as the wielder. Now enough questions. Do we have a deal?"

Jamie hesitated, but knew he wanted to return home. He reckoned he'd need his grandma more than ever if he was to get through this unscathed. "Thirty days?"

"Thirty, starting from the very moment you return." The warrior stuck out his hand. Jamie hesitated before he reached for the offered hand and they shook sealing the agreement. Jamie could feel the warrior's immense power and knew that his hand would be crushed and every bone broken, if he decided to. The warrior held onto the hand and squeezed making Jamie wince.

"Good luck my young friend. Don't let me down, but if you do I have a bottle here waiting." Finally and much to Jamie's relief the warrior let go. "Now it is time to return you home. Hold out your hand."

Jamie did as instructed and watched as the warrior did the same. The warrior closed his eyes and appeared to concentrate. The orb spinning between them shuddered on its axis before it glittered with an intense white light and split in two. One orb raced to the warrior's outstretched hand, the other to Jamie's.

"Close your eyes and think of home," came the demand. Jamie obeyed and again he felt the unpleasant feeling of displacement as the world shifted once more. Again he kept his eyes closed until, with a jolt, he assumed he'd returned home. He kept his eyes closed and his senses told him that he was back; the air felt different, the smells familiar and he opened his eyes.

It was as he had left it. The same birds in the sky and Duster in mid-flight in the distance. For a moment he was unsure of what to do when a voice in his head surprised him.

"Don't delay. Time starts now!"

The light from the orb disappeared and the world started up once more. The birds continued their flight and Duster barking madly disappeared off into the distance. Jamie stood on the pavement in shock. Had he done the right thing? Should he have made that bargain? He felt as though he'd been coerced into making it against his will, as if he had no choice. He began to panic, as he just didn't know what to do. The orb glowed comfortingly, calming him. He began to think more clearly.

He knew that the situation was serious, but he also realised that he had to keep a clear head and that he had to employ the help of his grandmother. Without her, this quest that he'd somehow set in motion was going to be impossible.

He whistled for Duster, worried that his dog charging around the village in pursuit of a boy on his bike might get run over, so he whistled again.

Nothing.

He tried one more time and was rewarded with a happy bark. He was okay, but where was he? Jamie began to follow the trail blazed by his irate canine companion when he re-appeared being led on the lead by someone he recognised from school.

"Hello, is this your dog?" he asked.

"Yes, it is. Thanks for grabbing him."

"No problem. He was chasing Spencer like a mad thing, but he was too quick. He looked friendly enough, so he was happy to be led back here. I checked his collar and knew he belonged to you guys." He smiled. "I'm Tommy Jones. You're in a couple of my classes at school."

Jamie struggled to remember for a moment. His

brain was still a bit befuddled!

"Oh hi. Yeah, Tommy. I'm Jamie."

"Yeah, I know. I've been meaning to say hi, but you know."

Jamie smiled ruefully. "Yeah, I know. We've sat next to each other a couple of times. Right?"

"Right!" Tommy looked at Jamie curiously. Jamie had bits of hedge sticking out of his hair and his hands were scratched. "You been fighting with the hedge?"

Something felt right about this boy and Jamie decided to reveal a bit of his own predicament. "Yeah, Spencer ran me in there. I've been having a few issues with him since starting at Marsh Green."

"You're not the only one. Anything I can help with?"

"Nothing that a rocket to outer space wouldn't cure," retorted Jamie, picking thorns out of his fingers.

"Can't help with that one," laughed Tommy.

"Thanks for your help Tommy."

"Ah, it was nothing. Your grandma is great and when I saw he belonged to your family, I thought I'd return him. Any dog that chases Spencer is a friend of mine." He frowned a bit when he said that. "What's his name?"

"Duster," replied Jamie. "Hold on I'll introduce you properly. He took the lead from Tommy and asked him to crouch down. "Duster. Sit." Immediately the dog obeyed. "Paw, boy. Give Tommy your paw." Duster offered Tommy his paw and, laughing, Tommy shook it.

"Clever dog. Did you train him?"

"Dad showed me how. He grew up with dogs."

"Cool," said Tommy giving Duster another pat, who wagged his tail pleased to have a new friend.

"Look what are you up to today?" asked Jamie.

"Nothing, why?"

"Do you fancy coming over to mine after lunch? We could kick a ball about in the garden and play on the X-box?"

"Sure why not? I'll just pop home and check with Mum. I was going to the rec, but if Spencer's out and about I'll give it a miss. Besides, I've heard you're not a bad footballer and you can show me some more tricks with that cool dog of yours. If it's okay I'll see you in a couple of hours."

"See you in a bit hopefully." Jamie smiled and ambled home, having retrieved Dad's paper from the hedge. He knew he should have felt a sense of urgency, given the fact that someone had just threatened to take his soul, but somehow a kick about in the garden seemed the right thing to do. The orb in his pocket hummed confirming his decision not to worry. Perhaps Tommy would be the first person he'd help? Whatever the case, he hoped he and Tommy could be friends and after the few days he'd had, he could really do with one.

Number 1?

Jamie let himself in and delivered the paper to his dad.

"Thanks Jamie, fancy a bike ride?" his dad asked.

"No thanks Dad, someone's coming over to play some footy in the garden," Jamie replied.

Dad sat up and grinned. "Excellent, pleased to hear it. Let me know if you need a keeper!"

"There'd be a lot of goals then Dad!" goaded Jamie. Dad picked up a pillow and threw it at him. Jamie caught it and threw it back at his dad who dropped it. "See?"

Dad smiled and picked up the paper. Jamie poked his head into the kitchen where Mum was still cooking.

"Hi Mum, is it okay if someone comes over after lunch?"

"Of course dear, as long as you help with the dishwasher."

Jamie groaned.

Grandma returned for lunch and Jamie was desperate to talk to her about his encounter with the warrior, but was wary of involving his parents. He didn't think they'd believe him.

"I hear you've got a friend coming over this afternoon. Who is it?" she asked Jamie as they filled the dishwasher.

"Tommy Jones, Grandma."

"Ah Tommy Jones. A good boy, I know his parents well. I gather he's had a few problems at school recently. Spot of bullying. A bit like you I should imagine."

Jamie blushed a little, constantly amazed at how astute she was. "I had heard a bit about it, yes."

"Well, it sounds like he could do with a good friend. Hope the afternoon goes well." The door-bell went and

57

Duster started barking. Jamie looked at his grandma, a pile of plates still to load. She winked. "Go on, I'll finish off."

"Thanks Grandma." Jamie kissed her on the cheek. "Are you around later? There's stuff I need to talk to you about."

"I'm intrigued. Is everything okay?"

"Yes. I'll catch you later. I'd better get the door before Duster eats it!" He ran to the door holding the dog by the collar and opened it.

"Hi Tommy."

"Hi Jamie. Hello Duster."

Duster wagged his tail and immediately lay on his back for a tummy scratch. Tommy bent down to oblige then Jamie shut the door.

"Fancy kicking a ball about?"

"Sure."

The boys and Duster ran out into the garden and for the first time in weeks, Jamie felt relaxed. It felt good to have someone his own age around. They kicked a ball around for a while, but then the rain started to fall again. They retired up to Jamie's room to play a 'shoot 'em up' on the X-Box. Tommy began to chat more openly.

"You're pretty good at football. You should come to training next week. You could get in the team, we're already in the semi-finals of the cup. We could do with someone like you."

"Thanks."

As they chatted, Tommy asked why Spencer had it in for him. Jamie told him that he'd refused to join his gang. Tommy had nodded and said he'd seen that before. Then he revealed that he too was having trouble with Spencer and his cronies.

"They seem to have stopped at the moment though."

"That's because they've set their sights on me, but I

think I've sorted it."

Tommy paled a little. "I did wonder why they'd let me off the hook." He grimaced as a zombie on the screen drained the life of his on-screen character in spurts of blood. "Gross!" He put down his controller. "I feel a bit like that!"

Jamie paused the game. "What happened?"

Tommy began to explain. It was clear that Spencer didn't like Jamie, but he loathed Tommy. The fact that he was enjoying success in his studies as well as captaining the school football team seemed to be the main issues.

"Why should that bother Spencer, Tommy?" Jamie asked.

Tommy explained that up until fairly recently, he had been blissfully unaware of Spencer's increasing jealousy, but it all went horribly wrong when Tommy came top in his school exams and mopped up all the prizes at the end of the year.

"Spencer used to get them," he explained.

Tommy went on to explain that Spencer was livid. He took this as a personal insult and took out his disappointment on a bewildered Tommy, who didn't know what he'd done wrong! Until this point, he and Spencer had existed in each other's presence without a problem, but when he'd been named as captain of the football team this term things had got a lot worse.

They started up another game and Tommy seemed intent on destruction. As they blew things up Tommy revealed more. It was blatantly obvious that Spencer had it in for Tommy and because everyone was afraid of Spencer and his thugs, no one would hang out with him. He was effectively shunned and ostracised and there was nothing he could do about it.

The classroom wasn't a place of refuge either. Somehow, Spencer had been able to rig a recent

History test so it looked like Tommy had cheated. He hadn't of course, but it was very hard to prove his innocence to the teacher.

"That's so wrong."

"Tell me about it! I don't know what's worse, knowing Spencer had got the better of me, or the fact that the teachers now treat me differently. They give me that 'disappointed' look."

"Adults are good at that."

"Too right. It sucks." Tommy blew up an arms depot with a grimace of satisfaction. "Shame Spencer's not in there!"

"Too right," Jamie agreed. "Nice shot."

"Thanks."

"No probs."

Tommy looked at his watch. "Oops. Better go. Said to Mum I'd be back to finish my homework. You done yours?"

"Yeah, did it yesterday. Had nothing else to do."

"Swot," teased Tommy.

"I do my best to make myself unpopular," Jamie shot back with a grin.

Tommy stood up. "Thanks for this afternoon. It was good to chat about all that stuff."

Jamie got up too. "No worries. Look, I know I'm a new boy and all that, but I can handle myself all right. I'm happy to watch your back if you'll watch mine. Problem shared and all that."

"Why not? I don't think we'd win against the twins, but they might ease off knowing we're standing up to them together."

They shook hands. "Deal," they said at the same time.

"Jinx!" They laughed.

Jamie led Tommy to the door and said he'd see him tomorrow. He shut the door behind him and went in search of his grandma.

"Grandma?" he called. She was baking again.

"Yes dear. What's up?" she replied, brushing flour off her hands.

"I think you should sit down."

His grandma looked worried and did as he asked. "What's happened?"

"Are Mum and Dad around?"

"No, they've taken Duster for a walk and I think they were going to stop for a drink in the Cricketers on the way home," his grandma replied.

"Good. I'm not sure they'd believe what I'm about to tell you."

Jamie spent the next ten minutes replaying what had happened to him, starting with the mirror incident and then moving on to what happened after Spencer forced him into the hedge. His grandma listened and didn't seem at all fazed by anything Jamie told her.

"You actually stopped time?"

"Yes. Everything stopped. It was like pressing pause on live television. It was pretty cool."

"Gosh, I should think so. Then what happened?"

Jamie explained as well as he could the feeling of displacement and possible time travel. He paused for a moment checking the reaction of his grandma. He knew it had happened, but talking about it now made it seem so utterly implausible. She nodded for him to continue, her face set in concentration. She believed him. He told her about the meeting and left nothing out. He described in detail how the warrior looked and how he'd got angry when he mentioned her.

She smiled gently. "What did you do?"

"I got cross and then he hit me."

"He didn't!" Grandma was indignant.

"He did and then I did a really scary thing."

Jamie described how he'd conjured up the ball of

61

fire, which he'd intended to unleash on the warrior.

"Why didn't you?"

"I couldn't do it. Something inside me stopped me. I think I could have done. The warrior claimed I couldn't and that he'd teach me to use the darker side of my emotions."

"A bad idea definitely. You did well. So what happened next?"

He told her about the deal, which in his eyes was an agreement he had to make to get home in one piece. His grandma nodded again. He told her of the quest and the wish he would receive if he was successful.

"And if you fail in thirty days?" she asked trembling slightly.

"Then he said he would take my soul."

She breathed out loudly. "Oh my, oh my, oh my." She held her head in her hands for a moment. Jamie thought she was crying, but after a moment she looked up, steely determination on her face.

"Right," she said. "First up, why have you waited until now to tell me?"

Jamie hesitated for a moment, but then replied. "I felt okay. The orb reassured me somehow and then Tommy appeared and hanging out for a bit seemed right."

This seemed to satisfy her. "Where is the orb now?"

"Upstairs."

"Go and get it would you?"

Jamie raced upstairs to his room and retrieved the orb, which instantly glowed the moment he picked it up. A rush of pleasure swept through him and he grinned uncontrollably. He felt no compunction to rush when he was holding it and for a moment he stood there admiring its glow, lost in its beauty.

Grandma called from downstairs. "Come on Jamie, your parents could be home at any time."

"Okay, just coming." Jamie tore his eyes away from the orb and made his way back to the kitchen. He placed it carefully on the table.

"Right, so my book was correct. This amazing little thing is very magical indeed. Everything you've told me confirms that. What worries me though is the emergence of this warrior. That's the bit that makes me nervous. You were right to get out of there, but it does leave us in a perilous position."

"Us?"

"Of course silly. I'll guide you all the way, you'll not be able to do it on your own. I may not be able to perform magic of my own, but I can certainly help. Underneath all this grey hair is a sharp brain."

Jamie was relieved and reached over to squeeze her hand. "Thanks Grandma. Despite it all I feel very calm, but I'm glad you can help."

"Let's not get complacent. We still need to get a shift on if you are to help these five people. Whatever you do, try to discuss it with me first and under no circumstances are you to try to contact this warrior. Agreed?"

"Agreed."

"Right, let's start thinking. Who can you help?"

They paused, thinking and then Jamie suggested trying to cure famine in Africa or helping the Prime Minister win the next election.

"A bit grandiose I think my dear, but noble sentiments. I think it needs to be a bit closer to home."

Jamie slammed his hand on the table making her jump. "I've got it. I think I've decided who to try and help first."

His grandma smiled, coming to the same conclusion herself. "That wouldn't be poor old Tommy Jones would it?" He nodded in agreement.

"A good choice. That poor child has been dealt a

poor hand by that Spencer boy."

"How do you know about that?" asked Jamie, amazed at his gran's sharpness.

"Word gets around. There isn't much I don't know."

"Trouble is how do I help him?"

"Only you can work that out Jamie. The power, so to speak, is in your capable hands. You'll know what to do when the time is right, but I wouldn't wait too long," she urged.

Jamie picked up the orb and turned the glowing sphere in his hands. It sparkled with energy. "I have a feeling it'll come sooner than we both expect."

Twenty-nine days to go

On Monday morning, a very nervous Jamie popped the orb into the pocket of his school blazer. The thought of carrying something so precious and important made him both excited and anxious at the same time. It was a strange feeling! He didn't want it damaged and he certainly didn't want to lose it. His parents had already gone to work and he popped his head into the kitchen to say goodbye to his grandma.

"See you later," he called.

A voice cried out from the pantry. "Hold on. I've got something for you."

Jamie walked into the kitchen and sat down at the table, waiting. His grandma reappeared a moment later with a small figure, rather like a pendant on a silver chain.

"What is it?"

"It's called a Netsuke. It's Japanese and they were worn to keep out the evil eye and ward off evil spirits."

Jamie shrugged and picked it up, but immediately dropped it back on the table again as if stung. He winced in pain and looked beseechingly at his grandma. He shook from head to foot and she watched in horror as his eyes glazed over.

"Help me," he managed to splutter out before another voice entirely spoke through Jamie. She clung on to his hands and watched helplessly as Jamie spoke, but it was a different, distinctly cold voice that emanated in the cosy kitchen. It was the voice of the warrior.

"That will not protect him from me, foolish woman."

"You're not welcome here. Leave Jamie be."

"Ha, the feeble old lady speaks. Well, let's see if he

can get through the day without losing his temper and letting me in."

"He will, he's stronger than you realise."

"No one has defeated me in a hundred years."

"Perhaps you've met your match this time whoever you are."

"You'll find out soon enough who I am." Laughter erupted from Jamie, unnerving his grandma. "Be seeing you soon too old lady."

He emphasised the word 'you' which sent shivers down her spine. She watched as Jamie collapsed onto the kitchen table. "Jamie," she cried out. "Jamie? Are you all right? Jamie?"

Jamie groaned and sat up. "I think so. Wow, that was weird! I hope he doesn't do that at school today. Not sure I'd be able to explain it," he tried to joke.

His grandma was worried. "He is powerful, too powerful. How did it feel?"

"I was aware of him in my head and I tried to push him aside, but he was too strong. He just took over. I was still there, but watching. It sounds mad."

"Not mad at all Jamie." She paused for a moment thinking. "Okay, good luck charms won't work. Keep the orb with you at all times and don't whatever you do lose your temper. I think that might be catastrophic. That's what he's waiting for."

"I'll try."

"Good. Now you must try to start helping someone, anyone and soon. The longer you leave it, the worse it could be for us all."

Jamie gulped and said, "I don't know if this is the right thing to do, but I'm going to speak to the orb!" He retrieved it from his pocket and held it glowing in his hand. "Okay," he instructed it feeling a bit silly, "today we are going to help Tommy Jones. Spencer Rogers will no longer control Tommy."

He thought it clearly and directed the thought at the orb in his hand. As if in answer the orb vibrated strongly and the strangest thing happened. He felt the orb direct power into him. It flowed into his veins and every part of his body tingled from the tips of his toes to the cuticles on his head. He felt his hair rise up ever so slightly as if he'd rubbed it on a balloon. He looked at his fingers and stretched them out experimentally. Tiny sparks fizzed from his fingers. He jumped, amazed by the sensation and looked at his grandma.

She smiled and nodded sagely. "Time to go," she said.

Jamie hurried into school. The strange possession had alarmed him and he really hoped that wouldn't happen again. His senses were on high alert and he kept a very wary eye out for any trouble. Relieved, he made it to school just as they were shutting the pedestrian gates and hurried in.

As Jamie walked into the main hall, Spencer was already there. The twins were on either side and it was obvious they were up to something. They ceased whispering to one another, looked up and grinned nastily at him giving an ominous 'thumbs up'. He smiled back, as humouring them was surely better than having a bad day at their expense. The effect this had on them was instantaneous. Energy flowed out of him and caressed the entire room with a feeling of peace and serenity. He could just make it out as the room shimmered imperceptibly for a fleeting moment and then was gone. The orb ceased to vibrate in his pocket. He smiled again at the twins, certain this was the right thing to do. They sat bolt upright as if they'd been shocked.

Bewildered for a second or two, they scratched their shaven heads and looked at Spencer in an odd way, almost as if they didn't know or recognise him. They looked as if they'd just been woken from a hypnotist's spell. Spencer, aloof and full of self-importance as ever, hadn't noticed. The twins looked at him again and physically moved away from him a fraction.

How interesting, thought Jamie. He looked around the room to see if his actions had affected anyone else. They had. As he scanned the year group, others had begun to move away from Spencer, isolating him in the middle of the floor. The rest of the year group came in and as each person entered, they paused momentarily as if lost, before smiling in a satisfied and peaceful manner and sliding contentedly into a vacant position away from Spencer on the floor of the hall.

The majority of Spencer's gang, the Jolly Rogers, sat down without even saying hello to him and it was only when Miranda, the school sweet-heart, skipped in and sat well away from him that he began to suspect that something was different. As if awoken from his self-satisfied reverie, he looked around with a puzzled expression etched on his face and glared at Jamie as if it was all his fault!

Tommy was last person in and he looked around nervously. He paused before walking in and Jamie cringed as he tripped over a stray bag and fell flat on his face. He rushed over to help him as he sat up embarrassed and dusted himself down. Spencer sniggered loudly, pointing at Tommy and looked around the room for encouragement. No one followed his lead and he shut up quickly, cowed by the silence. A few people went over to check that Tommy was all right and many of the girls stared at Spencer, cross that he should laugh at someone else's misfortune. This was an interesting development thought Jamie.

He assessed the assembled crowd again. The change in everyone was quite profound. Instead of being ignored with all eyes lowered, Tommy's classmates looked him in the eye and smiled or nodded in acknowledgement. Even a couple of people Jamie had seen around school, but who had ignored him thus far, came and sat down and introduced themselves to him as Toby and Calum. It seemed people were prepared to accept him as well as reacquainting themselves with Tommy. Things were looking up.

Jamie looked over at Tommy and shrugged his shoulders, who in turn shrugged back, confused but not altogether upset at the perceptible change in their year group. Tommy turned to see Miranda staring at him and he blushed as she gave him her sweetest smile and shyly giggled with her friends next to her. Even the twins, who usually reserved their most sarcastic greeting for Tommy, greeted him with a friendly salute. Spencer looked completely horrified and turned to them to issue orders.

Jamie watched with interest and a certain sense of satisfaction as Spencer looked in surprise at the space vacated by the twins. He frowned and coughed beckoning them over, but one fierce look from Francis stopped him in his tracks. The bell rang and they lined up in their two forms as their teachers came into the hall.

Spencer's and Tommy's form teacher, Mr Andreck, appeared from the staff room and led the form into their classroom. As they went, Tommy sidled up and whispered.

"What's going on?"

"Search me," Jamie fibbed, patting the orb in his pocket. "But the twins don't look too happy with Spencer." Francis and Charlie were glowering at Spencer who appeared to have shrunk into his school uniform. He looked like the prey of two very hungry, very angry bears just out of hibernation.

The rest of the morning didn't pan out well for

Spencer. During a Maths test, he attempted to get Tommy into trouble with the same trick he'd staged in a recent History test. They sat on the same table and he'd slipped the revision notes for that week sneakily under Tommy's chair. He usually got someone else to do that, but for some reason everyone seemed to be pointedly ignoring him. The test ended and his hand shot up.

"Sir. I'm not usually a sneak as you know, but Tommy has cheated. Look under his chair."

The class fell silent as their teacher stood up. He took a very dim view of cheating. He was strict, but extremely fair and it took a lot to get him annoyed. His glasses slid to the end of his beaked nose, a sure sign that he was taking the accusation seriously.

"Tommy. Please bring me that piece of paper." Tommy looked crestfallen. The orb burned fiercely in his pocket and again Jamie felt a surge of power flow through him. The room shimmered once more as Tommy did as he was asked, carefully handing the offending sheet to his teacher.

He took one look at it and frowned. "Sit down please Master Jones." Spencer was looking rather pleased with himself. Mr Andreck looked at the sheet carefully again and said quietly, "See me after the lesson please Spencer." Spencer's face fell and the classes' eyes widened in astonishment. Was Spencer in trouble? This would be the first time ever!

After the lesson was over, the class trooped out to break discussing in excited tones what might happen to Spencer. It seemed implausible that he was in trouble, but it seemed that way. This was all quickly put to one side as a lively game of football began, with Francis and Charlie as captains. Charlie who blew a raspberry at his brother picked Tommy quickly. Tommy was the best footballer and everyone knew it, but instead of being last to be picked, he was one of the first. Jamie smiled as he waited to be chosen. How quickly things change, he thought.

It was the best game of football in a long time. There was no underlying menace about it and the twins drew everyone in with their good humour and banter. Gone was the threat of having your legs broken by one of them and they led the game with huge smiles. Their enthusiasm rubbed off on everyone and soon a crowd had gathered to watch.

Break time ended and as they bundled back into class laughing and fooling around, it was obvious that in their absence things had not gone well for Spencer. He had red puffy eyes and it looked like he'd been crying. Mr Andreck looked thunderous.

As they all went to their next lessons, the twins sidled over to Spencer to find out what had happened. Jamie watched carefully. He was concerned that Spencer might ruin the good feeling of the morning and he began to feel his anger bubble to the surface. He breathed deeply and touched the orb in his pocket, which calmed him. He continued to watch as the twins listened intently to Spencer. They nodded as he spoke, but then something Spencer said angered them and Charlie pushed Spencer back against the lockers. Francis pointed his finger at Spencer shaking his head as he did so and together they left a confused Spencer standing at the lockers.

They found out from the twins that Spencer had admitted to the whole thing. He'd been sent to the headmistress, a fiery lady in her own right, to explain his actions. It was rumoured that a headmistress' detention was the punishment, which was generally unheard of in their school. They didn't see him that lunchtime and his absence had a remarkable effect on the year group. Spencer's gang disbanded instantly.

Boys and girls who only hung out with each other because of Spencer's influence were reacquainting themselves with old friends and making new ones. Spencer's hold over them appeared to be waning. It was amazing, like waking up out of a bad dream. Jamie couldn't believe it was really happening.

Spencer appeared in lessons, but for the rest of the time he was noticeable by his absence, as if he was avoiding everyone. As the day ended, Jamie and Tommy were getting ready to walk home, when Spencer appeared and barged passed them.

"Oi," cried Tommy.

"Leave him," urged Jamie. "Something's about to happen. Watch."

Spencer had seen the twins on the other side of the playground and he was striding over; someone said something to him. Jamie and Tommy could see Spencer mouthing off, clearly annoyed, but instead of cowering this person was having a go back. Spencer obviously couldn't believe it and marched over to Charlie and Francis. He must have forgotten about the earlier incident at the lockers, as it was clear that he tried ordering them around. He was obviously telling them to get involved when something curious happened instead. Jamie felt the orb vibrating in his pocket and he directed this energy at the twins, urging them to deal with the situation as only they could.

They nodded and looked over at Jamie. For a moment he felt awful. This is what Spencer would have done, but he put aside his doubts. He knew this was the only way to stop Spencer's bullying. Tommy watched, as did many of others. Something incredible was about to happen. A lot of people had been on the receiving end of something Spencer had initiated and his comeuppance fuelled the mob's desire for revenge.

Jamie nodded at the twins and they understood what

to do. Grabbing Spencer, they picked him up and carried him over towards the school bins. He bucked in their arms wildly and cried out, but no one helped, instead the crowd, growing larger by the second, followed. Tommy caught the eye of the twins and they beckoned him over. He saw the plan and opened one of the school's industrial bins where the discarded food from the canteen was dumped and stepped back without saying a word.

The gathering crowd watched in an eerie silence. Incidents like this had happened before, but they had been loud affairs that attracted the teachers and never amounted to anything but widespread detentions. This was different. No one chanted or bayed for blood, instead hundreds of pairs of eyes watched in reverent silence. The twins, without betraying any emotion, began to swing Spencer's body as he cried out for them to stop. They carried on regardless and when they'd got the momentum right they let go and he sailed through the air and into the bin with a distinguishable squelch. They too stepped back and then turned to go, leaving Spencer in the dustbin.

The crowd as one turned to leave. Jamie was amazed and slightly perturbed as this happened and it was like watching a flock of birds in the late summer sky. He waited to see if Spencer would reappear and after five minutes or so one of Spencer's legs appeared over the rim of the dustbin and then another as a bedraggled Spencer slid out of the bin and collapsed on the floor. His school uniform was soiled and bits of vegetable matter clung to his hair. He held one of his shoes in his hand and his once clean white shirt was stained with tomato juice.

Jamie walked over to him. "Are you okay?" he asked.

"What do you think?"

"Learnt anything today?"

"Only that you had something to do with this."

Jamie smiled. "What if I did?"

"It means that between you and me, things aren't over."

"Fine by me, but it looks like people have seen you for what you really are. A nasty bully."

"Oh and that makes you feel special does it?" Spencer growled standing up and facing Jamie.

"Not really, but how about a temporary truce between you and I?"

"You must be joking!"

"Fine, but what about Tommy and all the others?"

"Tommy?"

"Yeah, Tommy. Leave him alone."

"Sure. He wasn't worth the effort anyway."

"So you'll leave him alone then?" Jamie persisted.

"Yes, I'll leave him alone. Promise. Hope to die, stick a needle in my eye."

"That could be arranged you know. Things have changed, Spencer."

"So I see," spat Spencer plucking a piece of carrot out of one of his pockets. "You're the new leader now is that it?"

"No it's not. I just want to go to school without fear of being bullied or beaten up."

"Does that happen to me now?" Spencer asked.

"Not by me it won't."

Spencer shrugged. "You done?"

"Sure. Don't forget about Tommy now."

"I won't. Haven't forgotten about you either. Be seeing ya." Spencer walked off without a backward glance as Jamie reached into his pocket to touch the orb. It pulsated strongly at his touch and he wondered if he'd done enough to have helped his first person.

He thought about it all the way home and just before

he got to his front gate Tommy appeared out of breath and grinning.

"Jamie, hold up," he panted.

"What's up?"

"You'll never guess what just happened?" Jamie could guess, but he kept quiet. "Spencer just apologised and promised to leave me alone."

"No way."

"Way!"

"That's epic news Tommy."

"Sure is. Can't tell you how that makes me feel."

"Pretty good I reckon."

They both laughed. "Hey, wasn't it weird how everyone turned on Spencer today?"

"Sure was."

"What happened?"

"Not sure. It was as if everyone suddenly saw Spencer for who he was once he'd tried to get you in trouble and got caught."

"Yeah, and that thing with the twins was…" Tommy was lost for words for a moment.

"Weird?" Jamie suggested.

"Yeah, what with everyone watching. No one said anything and then everyone left together."

"Yeah it was a bit strange," Jamie agreed.

"What happened to you?"

"Oh nothing," Jamie lied. "Just collected a book I'd forgotten."

"Oh okay. Cool. Do you think Spencer will leave you alone as well Jamie?"

"Let's hope so. See you tomorrow."

"Laters." Tommy turned to go, but changed his mind. "Jamie. Come to footy practice in the morning. It's before school. Fancy it?"

Jamie thought for a moment about the quest, but decided that he had to lead a normal life despite the threat of losing his soul hanging over him. It was too surreal! "Yeah. I'd love to. What time?"

"I'll knock on your door at seven. Practice starts at seven thirty. Okay?"

"Cool. See you tomorrow."

Jamie closed the gate behind him. He was about put his key in the front door, when it opened revealing his grandma staring at him impatiently.

"Well? How did it go?"

Jamie laughed. "Can I come in?"

"Sorry dear. I've made tea. Come into the kitchen." Jamie followed her and sat at the kitchen table where tea and some freshly baked cookies sat waiting. Duster barked outside the back door and Grandma let him in and he jumped up putting his front paws on Jamie's lap.

"Hello boy," he said ruffling his dog's head. "Catch any rabbits?"

Grandma coughed getting his attention. "Did anything happen today?"

Jamie placed the glowing orb on the table, and relayed the events of the day. Grandma frowned when he described the dustbin incident, and gasped when he described the emotionless crowd reaction. He told her about his last conversation with Tommy and she jumped up.

"That must be the first person then, surely."

"How will I know?"

"What was it the warrior said?" She paused recalling Jamie's conversation with her the other day. "Oh yes. You'll see it in your eyes. She popped on her glasses and peered intently into Jamie's eyes.

"You don't think you'll actually see it do you?" Jamie asked getting up to look in the mirror.

"It was a bit cryptic, but you might. If something happens, tell me instantly okay."

"Okay. Can I have my tea now?"

"Of course you can. What was stopping you?"

That night Jamie sat at his desk readying himself to begin his homework thinking about the weird day he'd had. He reached into his blazer pocket to retrieve the orb and put it on his desk. The moment he touched it the most incredible thing happened. A fierce bolt of light flew from its tip and hit Jamie between the eyes, knocking his head back. His whole body twitched and jerked alarmingly as the orb's intense power surged into him. Duster watched the whole thing unfold with his head to one side and barked quietly.

Jamie sat pinned by the light for a minute, unable to move but filled with a power that was unimaginable and ancient. He caught glimpses of heroic deeds and people from the past as he allowed the power into his system. It felt enlightening and he groaned out loud when it stopped all too soon. Barely a minute had passed.

"Wow, that was intense!" Jamie reached down to touch Duster, who yelped as sparks emanated from Jamie's fingertips. "Sorry Duster. I wonder what that means eh boy? I suppose it means I helped one person." He looked for the orb for confirmation, but nothing happened. "Better tell Grandma hadn't we?"

As he got up to leave he caught a glimpse of himself in the mirror and did a double take. "What the…?"

Jamie looked hard at his reflection in the mirror. There was something different about him. He looked again and there it was, his eyes!

"You'll see it in your eyes," he mouthed. He looked again to check he wasn't dreaming. None of what was happening really made any sense at all, but he was beginning to embrace all this magical stuff. His eyes had changed colour. Not by much, but enough for him to notice. His dark brown eyes were now lighter. Hardly possible, but there was the evidence, right in front of him. His eyes were now a lighter shade of brown. He raced downstairs and into his grandma's study.

Without pausing for breath he told her what had just happened, but left out the last bit for the moment to see if she would notice.

"I feel fantastic." He grinned.

"How so?"

"I feel more confident, stronger. The stuff I managed to do today was amazing. I know it was the orb that guided me, but without my input, nothing would have been resolved and Spencer would still be out there causing mayhem."

"Anything else?"

"Yeah. I got the feeling that it gave me something that I now need to pass on to someone else."

"A message?"

"No, not a message, more like an emotion or something of that sort. It's hard to explain."

"Well done. You're doing so well. I'm finding it hard to concentrate on anything! So, are we any closer to knowing when you've helped someone? Was it the experience you've explained?"

"That's part of it. Look into my eyes Grandma."

She peered into Jamie's eyes and her own eyes widened as the words of the warrior made sense. "Oh my goodness. Your eyes! They've changed colour. Incredible. That's what he meant."

"Mad isn't it?"

"Yes. Let's hope your parents don't notice. Gosh, if they change any more we'll have to get you some coloured contact lenses. Goodness gracious me. Amazing."

Training

Jamie tossed and turned in his sleep the following night. He couldn't get comfortable and although he didn't dream, he kept waking with a feeling that time was passing him by. He looked at his alarm clock hoping it was morning. It read three fifteen and he groaned. Still another three hours to go. He scratched his head sleepily and thought about reading his book when the temperature changed dramatically in his room.

He reached for the orb on his bedside table and held it in his hand. It gleamed comfortingly and illuminated his face in the dark of his room. He wasn't scared and knew that he was about to receive a message of some sort from the warrior. The temperature dipped quickly and he wrapped his duvet around his shoulders. He looked for Duster, but the dog had gone downstairs. The door closed quietly and mist began to seep under it filling the floor of his room and tickling the furthest corners with its silent fingers.

Jamie watched fascinated as the room swam out of focus for an instant, before settling and becoming eerily silent. Jamie listened hard for a movement when a voice very close to his bed startled him.

"Good morning."

Jamie tried not to sound alarmed. "Hello?"

The mist cleared and sitting at his desk was the warrior watching him with those piercing blue eyes of his. Despite the fact that this alien figure was sitting in his desk chair, he looked quite at home!

"Not sleeping well?" he asked chuckling to himself.

"No, not the best."

"Oh dear, I am so very sorry."

"What are you doing in my room?"

"I came to pay you a visit and to congratulate you on the completion of the first part of your quest. Quite impressive."

"Thank you, I think."

"Yes, you should thank me, although I was most disappointed that you did not lay waste to that troublesome boy. I'll take him if you wish, he would be a most useful addition to my army."

Jamie knew he had to be careful. "Um, a nice suggestion, but I can handle Spencer."

"Can you now?" The warrior chuckled again. "I think he will continue to trouble you on your mission. He may even hinder your progress. Are you sure you don't want me to deal with him?"

Jamie was tempted for a moment, but quickly dismissed the thought of sending Spencer to the warrior. "No, it's okay. I can deal with whatever Spencer can throw at me."

"Hm, we'll see." The warrior looked around Jamie's room.

"What are you doing here?"

"I was going to ask you the same question. You summoned me."

"I did not," stammered Jamie.

"Well perhaps the orb decided to throw us together again for its amusement. The link between us is growing stronger. Can you not feel it?" Jamie wanted to admit that yes, he did feel stronger and yes, he was tempted to ask for help from this powerful man, but he was wary of him and stayed silent.

"No answer eh? Well, nevertheless your quest will prove more difficult now you have started. I thought maybe you needed my help?"

"No thank you." Jamie tried to be polite remembering the last time he spoke out of turn to the warrior.

"It's good to be polite," the warrior said. "I could still stop you right now and take you back with me."

The orb glowed strongly in Jamie's hand and the warrior laughed. "Ah, it seems our little friend thinks otherwise. No matter." He looked around the room again and paused at a poster of a fighter plane on Jamie's wall. "What is that?" he asked.

"That's a fighter plane, a Typhoon jet. It's used for defence."

"Defence! Pah! It would be useless against me. Does it fly?"

"Yes."

"Does someone fly it?"

"Yes."

"It looks most amusing. I'd like a few of those, it would rid me of a few pests that strike the furthest regions of my empire. I must get my people on it. A plane you say?"

"Yes."

"Most interesting. I must visit you more often."

Jamie stayed quiet not wishing to encourage the warrior any further. He knew that his presence could be dangerous for everyone in the house and he hoped that this meeting would end quickly.

"How are your eyes?" Jamie was taken aback by the sudden change of topic.

"Different," he replied.

The warrior sat up. "Indeed, keep a close watch on those, they'll tell you everything you need to know. Any idea of what to do next?"

"I think so."

"Care to share it with me?"

"I don't think so, as I'm not entirely sure yet."

The warrior thought about that and nodded appreciatively. "Sensible. Don't give too much away." He stood up and yawned. "I tire of this and wish to

81

return. Fancy coming with me?" The eyes glared at Jamie with a hint of amusement and Jamie shook his head. "Shame, but you'll come and see me soon. I'm sure of it. Fare thee well."

The room shimmered again, leaving Jamie on his own. He breathed a sigh of intense relief as the mist dissipated under the door of his room. The air warmed and feeling very tired he lay back down and fell asleep.

He awoke with a start. The alarm clock hadn't gone off and it read six forty-five.

"I'm late," Jamie exclaimed. "Blast!" He jumped out of bed and charged around his room getting everything he needed for school and changed into his football kit. He raced downstairs just as the doorbell went and he opened the door.

Tommy stood waiting.

"Morning mate."

"Morning. Just coming. Hold on." Jamie dumped his stuff by Tommy's feet and raced into the kitchen to pick up something to eat. Mum and Dad were eating breakfast.

"Morning everyone. Can't stop. Off to footy practice."

"Morning love," said his mum.

"Play well," said his dad.

"Oversleep?" asked his Gran. "All okay?"

"Yes fine. Are there any more bananas?"

"In the fridge."

Jamie wrenched open the fridge and picking up a couple of pieces of fruit he said a hurried goodbye and joined Tommy outside.

"Ready?"

"Think so."

"Let's go."

Jamie was feeling a bit nervous. In his haste to leave the house, he'd forgotten the orb. He was sorely tempted to go back and get it in case another opportunity presented itself. He had twenty-eight days left, surely that was enough time? He shook off his unease and asked about the football coach to take his mind off his bad planning. He wondered idly whether the visit during the night was a ploy by the warrior to slow him down but he shrugged off the notion as paranoia.

As they walked, Tommy reported that their sports coach was an amiable Scotsman called Mr Fitzgarret. He explained that he allowed the children to call him 'Fitz' as he always claimed his name was too much of a mouthful to use all of the time! He was an excitable man and he was particularly enthusiastic about the teams' potential this season. He worked them hard in practice and was brutally honest in his opinion of each and every child's skills.

They arrived at school, dumped their kit in the changing rooms and ran out to join the others on the training pitch. There were some familiar faces and Jamie groaned when he saw Spencer glaring at him, but he quickly felt better when he saw the twins who came over to say hello. Tommy introduced Jamie to Fitz, who nodded and asked him what position he preferred.

"I like to play in defence sir," Jamie stated.

"Sir? Call me Fitz laddie," smiled the coach. "You're gonna have to work hard if you want to play in defence for me."

"Okay sir. Fitz I mean. I'll give it my best shot."

"Good lad. Now go and join the others and we'll make a start."

It was a full on training session that Jamie really enjoyed. He kept worrying about Spencer, but after the initial glaring contest, Spencer ignored him and got on with the training session like everyone else. The session ended with some five-a-side games. Jamie played well, defended sensibly and even scored a couple of goals. All without the help of the orb. He was a good enough player not to need any magical intervention. Fitz was impressed.

"You're fast and read the game well enough, but you need to be more aggressive. If you want to play for me, you'll need to tackle more like Nobby Stiles!"

"Nobby who Fitz?" Jamie didn't have a clue and looked over at Tommy, who shrugged.

"Nobble Stiles wee lad. Ask your father."

"Okay I will."

"Listen Jamie. We have a game tomorrow afternoon after school against another local team. It's a big cup game and I could do with someone like you in the team. Ask your parents okay?"

Jamie was thrilled. "Yeah, okay. Thanks Fitz."

"Nae worries. I'll leave Tommy to introduce you to everyone." Fitz left and Tommy bounced over slapping him on the back.

"You in the team Jamie?" he asked.

"Yeah I think so." Jamie was a bit surprised at the speed of his inclusion.

Tommy laughed. "Fitz does that. Goes with a hunch. Good work. You know most of this lot, but come and meet the rest." As they were changing Jamie was introduced to the rest of the team. The twins, now content to play fight with one another rather than bother anyone else, gave him a curt well done. Jamie was still worried that they might hold a grudge after he'd fooled them the week before, but they seemed to have forgotten all about it. Spencer on the other hand barged into him on the way into the changing rooms.

"Lucky!" he growled quietly.

Jamie ignored him and was interested to observe that everyone had accepted the new way of things as if it was normal. Spencer was just a part of the team. Part of the year group, but without the destructive influence of before. Tommy on the other hand was a changed person. Full of life, he chatted to everyone and insisted on formal introductions.

"No point being in the team if you don't know everyone's names Jamie."

Jamie was certain that he'd forget. There was Zac, who would be playing in defence with Jamie and the twins. Tommy played in midfield and he was introduced to Alex, Daniel and Guy. Alex and Daniel were full of mischief and looked like best mates, but Guy was especially pleased.

"Thanks Jamie," he said as he shook Jamie's hand. Jamie looked a bit lost, so he carried on. "For getting me out of defence."

"Oh sorry Guy. Didn't mean to take your spot."

"Don't worry, I hated being in defence. Might mean I can score a few more goals."

Jamie laughed at that and Tommy swiftly introduced him to Geoff, their goalkeeper, who Tommy proudly announced as the next England keeper. Geoff shook Jamie's hand and quietly said.

"He does exaggerate!"

"He's the only player in the team who plays for the county, plus he's got trials for a big club coming up soon."

Geoff waved him away. "We'll see. Good to have you in the team. You were all right out there. Looked as though you could handle yourself."

"Thanks Geoff. Nice to know I'll be playing with the twins."

"Yeah, they are good to have on your side. Wait to you see them squash someone on the field!"

Jamie said hello to Eddie whom he'd met before. Eddie, Tommy explained, was the team's super substitute. Their secret weapon. He was the fastest kid in the year group and the school's top athlete. The head of games didn't like him playing football in case he got injured, so the arrangement with Fitz was that he would be used sparingly. This was a shame as he was the team's top scorer.

"Just imagine what he could do if he was on for the whole game." Tommy was obviously an admirer. "As for goal scorers, you've met Toby before and Spencer you know."

Toby gave Jamie a cheerful wave and Spencer just stared with his usual hostility.

"You've forgotten the person he's going to replace!" Spencer growled pointing at Jamie.

"Now, now Spencer. I hadn't forgotten actually. Jamie, come and meet Calum."

Jamie had heard about Calum. He was liked by everyone and was one of the good guys! He was nicknamed the gentle giant and Jamie could see why. He sat hunched over in the corner and when Tommy said his name he sat up and smiled at both of them. Jamie instantly felt guilty. Had he taken Calum's place as Spencer had suggested? They'd know later when the team sheet went up, but judging by the resigned look on his face before he smiled, he thought so.

He stood up to say hello. At well over six feet tall, he towered over the both of them. He held out one massive hand, which Jamie shook, and he smiled.

"You played well out there."

"Thanks Calum. Look, I'm sorry if…"

Calum cut him off. "Mate, if you're picked instead of me, then that's okay. My size makes me a bit clumsy. Fitz is always having a go at me. I'm happy to be on the subs bench." He brightened a bit. "Perhaps I'll be a secret weapon like Eddie."

Spencer was listening to the exchange and coughed loudly into his hands. The twins stopped what they

86

were doing and glared at him.

"What?" he said pretending to be innocent.

They got up and Calum intercepted them. "It's okay fellas. Leave him be."

"Yeah, leave me alone," crowed Spencer. Grumbling the twins continued to get changed as Calum shook Jamie's hand again.

"No hard feeling, all right?"

"All right!" They grinned at each other and Jamie knew they'd be okay, which came as some relief. Tommy continued to chatter away and the rest of the day whizzed past in a bit of a haze. The team sheet appeared and Calum was indeed on the substitute's bench. Despite what he said earlier Jamie still felt bad and Spencer caught him looking at the board and growled.

"You'd better play well tomorrow."

Jamie sighed. "Any chance of bothering someone else Spencer?"

"No one else will have anything to do with me." Which was true. Since yesterday's incident, the year group had settled into an existence without him. There was less of a menace lurking about in the corridors.

"Whose fault is that?" Jamie asked.

"I wonder?" Spencer said staring at Jamie with a cryptic look on his face. Jamie tried not to panic. He couldn't know surely? Had the warrior paid him a visit? "Time will tell. Watch yourself loser."

Everyone else seemed rid of Spencer's antics, but it was obvious he'd have to watch his back. He watched Spencer disappear and then followed him out of the building towards home. It was a strange journey home in that Jamie didn't remember any of it. His mind was totally preoccupied with other things. He paused, surprised as he turned the key in the lock. He shook his head, unsure of how he'd got home, before hurrying upstairs to check that the orb was still where he'd left it.

Before the discovery of the orb, he was just like any other teenager. He lived in the moment, tried to get his work done and played as much football as he could. He had had his worries that went with the territory: spots, girls, fashion and family. All teenagers did. His worries were just ever so slightly different now. Hanging over his every decision and aspect of his life was this quest. He would have laughed if it weren't so serious. There wasn't any teenager anywhere who had the prospect of losing their soul preying on their mind! The constant niggle from Spencer and his unease of taking Calum's place on the team paled into insignificance really. He was pleased that he'd made the team on his own merit, but he wasn't going to leave the orb at home again. He held it in his hands and it helped him relax.

He sighed and looked at his calendar. He stood up and crossed out day two. He had no idea who he would help next. He began to panic, but again the orb radiated a sense of peace and he knew instinctively that patience was the key. He would know when the time was right. He sighed again and got out his homework. Even boys with magical quests had to keep up with their schoolwork! All was quiet downstairs, so it was a good opportunity to get it done before his family returned.

An hour or so later the front door slammed and Jamie heard his dad's voice. He was home early!

"Jamie? Are you there son?" he called.

Jamie got up, his homework complete and poked his head over the bannisters. "Hiya Dad. You're home early."

"I know, it's fab. My final meeting was cancelled, so I snuck off early. How was your day? Did the trial go well?"

Jamie came down the stairs. "The best, Dad. I got in

the team. There's a cup match tomorrow. Will you be able to watch?"

Dad looked troubled. "Ah, no sorry chap. Tomorrow I have meetings till seven. If I have another day like today, I'll sneak in. Are you playing at home?"

Jamie tried to hide his disappointment. He loved having his dad watching. "Yes Dad. Kick-off is at four thirty."

"I'll do my best." Both Jamie and his dad knew this wouldn't happen, but he came and gave his dad a hug anyway.

"What's that for?" his dad laughed.

"It's just good to see you. Do you want a cup of tea?"

"Do you know what? No. Let's pop up to the pub for a pint."

Jamie grinned. "Cool. I'll get my jacket."

Over a lemonade and a packet of crisps Jamie asked his dad who Nobby Stiles was.

"Good heavens, who's been talking to you?"

"Our coach said I needed to be more like him!" Jamie explained.

"He's given you a back handed compliment my son." He smiled and got out his smartphone from his pocket. "Let's have a look at what the Internet has to say about him." Dad typed in the name and instantly Nobby's achievements scrolled down the screen. As it turned out Nobby Stiles was an England international who had played for Manchester United in the 1960s. He was a part of England's triumphant World Cup winning team of 1966. They scrolled through the article and at the bottom of the page was a grainy picture of Nobby holding the World Cup aloft in one hand and his false teeth in the other!

This made Jamie laugh out loud. "Does this mean I need false teeth then Dad?"

"No, you definitely need to keep those, although he wasn't scared of getting stuck in! He was a fairly uncompromising sort of player."

"What does that mean Dad?"

"It means he'd get stuck in and wasn't afraid of throwing himself around a bit. Was probably why he lost his teeth!" Dad took a sip of his beer. "Typical. Your coach would choose a United player, wouldn't he? What's wrong with QPR?" This was a common and light-hearted argument between them.

"'Cause they're rubbish?" Jamie smirked.

"Cheek!" retorted his dad chucking a peanut at his son, who ducked as it bounced off a picture on the wall.

They continued to banter away for a bit, when the door opened and his mum and grandma appeared.

"We thought this is where you two would be," they laughed joining them at the table. Dad was in a great mood and offered to buy everyone supper. Mum agreed and as she and Dad stood at the bar ordering the food and catching up with each other, Jamie took the opportunity to tell Grandma about his day and the night-time visitor. She paled slightly as he quickly relayed the conversation they'd had.

"Did he take anything?" she asked.

"Take anything?" Jamie was confused.

"Yes, take anything? Think Jamie. This is serious."

"No I don't think so, but he was really interested about a picture on my wall."

"Of what?" she asked.

"It was of a fighter plane I think."

"Are you sure?"

Jamie was taken aback by the seriousness of her tone. "Yes, I'm sure."

"Look, I'm trying hard to find some way of protecting you from these 'visits'. Please do me a favour and not engage him in conversations like that."

"Okay, but why?"

"I just have a feeling that this whole quest thing isn't as straightforward as it seems. Promise me?"

"I promise, Grandma."

"Good," she said brightening up. "Let's eat."

This worrying conversation did little in the way of calming Jamie's already fragile state of mind. His mum sat down and pecked him on the cheek.

"Hello love. Your grandma was looking pretty serious there. All okay?"

"Yeah, we were trying to think of a way of stopping Duster from burying his bones in the garden." Jamie was amazed by his ability to lie quite so seamlessly, but this seemed to satisfy his mother. "I hear you've had a good day." Jamie forgot about this minor indiscretion with his mum and tried to change the subject as the smell of food wafted deliciously from the pub's kitchens.

The semi-final

The football match was against another state school from the next town. It promised to be a feisty affair and Tommy was doing his best to encourage up the team. There was a quiet determination about the squad, but Jamie was very nervous as he tied his shoelaces for the umpteenth time in the changing rooms. He avoided eye contact and felt a little sick.

Fitz was in the final throes of his team talk. Everyone knew the game plan. Total football. Pass the opposition into submission and use the wingers to attack from out wide. Simple stuff, but really effective if practised correctly. Jamie wasn't really listening; he was desperate to get some fresh air. With one final instruction Fitz got everyone into a huddle in the middle of the changing room and with a final word of encouragement it was finally time.

The team clattered out onto the pitch, the sound of their metal studs echoing loudly. They took up their positions, eyeing the opposition warily. The two captains shook hands and the referee threw a coin into the air to see who would kick off. The referee reached for his whistle and blew once, loudly, to indicate the game should begin. Immediately a cacophony of noise emanated from the sidelines, as parents and friends cheered them on.

Not much happened at the start and it was a scrappy match. No team seemed able to take control or string a series of meaningful passages of play together. Some fairly serious challenges were going in and the referee was trying his hardest to maintain some semblance of control without tempers boiling over.

"Remember the game plan, the game plan!" Fitz ordered at the top of his voice. "Tommy, rally the troops. Get them to listen to you!"

Fitz was right. The implications of winning this match had made them anxious and all their carefully trained plans weren't working. Tommy started charging around the pitch, calming everyone down, encouraging them to remember their roles and to tune out the noise from the large crowd who'd come out to support.

This seemed to work. A ball thrown out to Jamie from his goal-keeper made its way to Guy in midfield. He beat one player and passed it to Tommy. Tommy immediately looked up and fired a pass beyond the midfield to the on-running Alex, who shaped up to go inside, but at the last moment dropped his shoulder and went around the defender with a burst of pace.

For a moment it looked as if he'd been too enthusiastic as the ball looked to be going out, but he managed to whip in across from the corner. As quick as a flash, Tobias darted away from his defender and flicked the ball on with his head at the front post, a tactic that is almost impossible to defend against. Spencer arrived beyond the goal-keeper to volley the ball into the top corner.

1–0.

Spencer was ecstatic and commenced with an elaborate celebration. Charging to the corner flag, he flipped head over heels and landed acrobatically on his feet. This was followed by an Elvis hip wriggle, using the corner flag as a microphone and a finger pointing to the sky. The crowd went wild, but Spencer was given a swift and stern talking to by the referee about showing off. The headmistress, Miss Bareham, who had come out to watch didn't seem pleased either, as she glowered at him through her horn-rimmed glasses.

Marsh Green quickly went 2–0 up with another Spencer Rogers goal. He was about to start his show-boating again, when he spotted Miss Bareham staring at him sternly, arms folded across her chest. He quickly changed his mind and instead high-fived everyone around him making the most of being the centre of attention again. He cheekily tried it with Miss Bareham, who raised one eyebrow and with a hint of a smile, declined and ordered him to get on with it!

Half time soon arrived with the score unchanged and Fitz was encouraged by their performance. He warned against complacency and urged them not to be over confident. More of the same was required. He also informed them that Eddie and Calum would be coming on soon to inject a bit of new life into the game.

The opposition came out in the second half looking very determined. The half-time team talk from their coach had obviously had an effect. They wanted to get back into the game and created some decent chances. It was developing into a stalemate, with no team gaining the upper hand, so Fitz made his switch, bringing Eddie on and taking Alex off. The result was immediate.

The opposition were so momentarily bamboozled by Eddie's searing pace that they froze, unsure of what to do. Eddie, being an opportunist, gleefully said 'thank you very much,' weaved in and out of three bemused players, reluctant to put a foot in for fear of bringing him down, played a sublime one-two with Tommy, which put him clean through on goal. With just the keeper to beat, he looked up and gracefully slotted the ball into the far right corner, sending him the wrong way and scoring the third goal.

Eddie was mobbed by his teammates. Jamie was ecstatic and joined in the celebrations. At three nil, they were surely in the final now. Eddie was being held by four of them and was being cradled like a baby. They let him down and he crawled into a ball sucking his thumb and pretended to cry! Jamie and the others were laughing out loud at this pre-arranged goal celebration but the referee was not amused. Eddie was warned for over-zealous celebrations.

The opposition coach was almost incandescent with rage. He bellowed at his team to sort themselves out. The next time Eddie got the ball one of the opposition exacted revenge and a small boy with red hair, eager to please his coach, flattened him. Jamie froze, anxious for Eddie who lay on the ground, but more for the small boy, as the twins, curiously quiet until now, growled with menace and raced aggressively to Eddie's aid.

They surrounded the red haired boy who'd made the tackle towering over him. "Do that again," started Charlie, "and we'll knock you're block off," continued Francis, finishing his brother's sentence as they closed in menacingly, fists clenched. The referee blew his whistle to try and calm things down and Eddie sprang up from the floor.

"It's okay boys, calm down."

"You sure Eddie?" they questioned.

"I'm sure," he replied, "now go on, and let me deal with this." The twins took a step back, unwilling to go too far just in case. He stuck out his hand to the small red haired boy who was keeping one fearful eye on the twins and he took it gratefully.

"Sorry," he muttered. The twins took a step closer. "Sorry," he said again, louder this time and Eddie accepted the apology wincing slightly as he began to walk away.

The game settled into what was looking like a comfortable victory for Marsh Green, but the last ten minutes were approaching. This is what Fitz termed the 'zone of unpredictability' in the team talk before the match. He explained that legs often were tired and that their focus could slip.

Jamie was new to the team and was doing his utmost to remain focused, but despite his best efforts his thoughts were definitely elsewhere. He'd caught sight of one of the girls in the year watching and his teenage hormones were definitely kicking in. The girl in question was Jane-Claire, or JC as she preferred to be called. She was in Jamie's form and he secretly had a bit of a crush on her. He'd watched her from a safe distance with her friends. She appeared quirky, loved a laugh with her friends and Jamie thought she was gorgeous. He'd noticed her the moment he joined the school, but was pretty certain she hadn't noticed him. Until now.

She waved from the sidelines and Jamie did a double take. Was she waving at him? He quickly looked around but there was no one else around. She said something to a friend and together they giggled and she waved again. Feeling supremely confident, he received a ball back from Tommy in midfield. Instead of setting up another attack sensibly, which nine times out of ten he would do, Jamie decided to go off on a run in an effort to impress this girl on the side-lines.

But disaster struck! He pushed the ball too far in front of him and lost possession. The ball was quickly passed through to the opposition's centre-forward, who gleefully received it and set off unopposed toward Marsh Green's goal. Jamie looked on, horrified, hopelessly out of position and tried desperately to get back. Geoff came off his goal line to try to rectify the mistake. The centre-forward pushed the ball past Geoff, who dived at his feet, missed the ball completely, which brought him down in the penalty area. The home crowd groaned as the referee blew his whistle for a penalty. Jamie held his head in despair as the opposition celebrated, surrounding their player. Something was horribly wrong and Jamie's teammates were crowding around Geoff who was writhing on the floor in absolute agony.

Fitz raced onto the pitch, quickly followed by the school nurse. The situation looked grim. Geoff was clutching his arm, obviously in pain. It seemed that as he had reached for the ball, the centre-forward had accidentally stepped on his wrist. The school nurse, concern etched on her face, declared that he wasn't fit to continue and ought to go to hospital for an X-ray. She thought it was probably broken. Jamie held his head in his hands. He couldn't believe what he'd just done! Tommy came up and gave him a light punch on the shoulder.

"Not your fault mate. Could have happened to anyone," he remarked. This didn't make him feel any better and for a moment, he was tempted to go and get the orb from the changing room to sort out this mess for him. There was no time.

"Calum," Mr Fitzgarret ordered, "on you come chap. I've got some spare gloves. You can go in goal." Calum looked terrified, and with shaking hands put on the gloves. He gave Fitz a pitying look, then with wobbly legs unsteadily made his way into the goal. What a baptism of fire! His first task was to attempt to save the penalty!

The crowd held their breath. Quietly confident, the centre-forward placed the ball on the penalty spot. Calum looked enormous in goal, but despite his size he looked very vulnerable. His knees were visibly knocking together.

Jamie crossed his fingers as the whistle blew. The centre-forward stepped forward eyeballing Calum who avoided his gaze. He paused, uncertain for a moment before taking a step forward and blasted the ball goal-ward. It looked a certain goal, but at the last moment Calum threw himself to his right and managed to somehow tip the ball over the crossbar and safely out for a corner. The centre-forward was devastated and collapsed to his knees holding his head in his hands. The home support cheered wildly and a hugely relieved Jamie was the first to reach Calum and congratulate him. He didn't have much time as quickly the opposition got over their disappointment and readied to take the corner.

The whistle blew harshly once again and the ball sailed into the six-yard box. It was just the right height for Calum who, feeling more confident now, rose to catch the ball, but mis-timed his jump. The ball sailed past him, and fell at the feet of the same boy who'd just seconds before missed his penalty. He couldn't believe his luck as he gleefully tapped the ball home to make it three goals to one. Calum looked mortified. He'd gone from hero to zero in a matter of moments.

Sensing a comeback, the opposition quickly picked the ball out of the net and raced back to the centre-circle, so the game could restart. Spencer tried to waste time, but the referee just tapped his watch and told him to get on with it. He passed the ball to Tobias, who was quickly closed down by three players. He panicked and lost possession as another attack was mounted against them. Jamie's team were in complete disarray and nothing Tommy could say or do calmed them down.

Suddenly, a shot by the little midfielder who'd floored Eddie earlier zipped from twenty yards towards their goal along the ground. Seemingly innocuous, Calum reached down to retrieve it, but the ball went through his legs and trickled into the goal to make it three goals to two. The crowd groaned as Calum disconsolately picked the ball out of his net. The opposition, anxious to get the game going again, quickly snatched it off him. There was only three minutes to go and they could sense a major upset. Marsh Green's players looked at each other anxiously.

Fitz was desperately firing instructions at his team

as the final minutes played out, but nothing he said seemed to make any difference. It was nerve-wracking stuff and, for the home crowd, hard to watch. Another shot came in, which Calum caught this time much to the relief of his teammates. Instead of holding onto it and wasting time, he threw it out to Zac, who wasn't expecting it and was closed down by the opposition, losing the ball. Fitz cried out in frustration.

The opposition launched one last, desperate attack. The ball was crossed into the box and headed out again by Charlie, but only to the feet of the opposition captain who half volleyed it towards goal. Jamie could see that Calum was hopelessly out of position and he jumped up to the cross bar, in an effort to head it away. The crowd held their breath as the ball sailed towards the top corner, but Jamie had timed his jump to perfection and headed the ball over the bar.

There was no time for a corner and the referee blew his whistle for the end of the game. Jamie was mobbed by his teammates. He'd saved the game, but he felt awful about Geoff. Calum was no keeper that was for sure.

Marsh Green had won the game and reached the final, but judging by the atmosphere in the changing room, you'd never have known it. The victory had come at a great cost to the team, as news filtered in that Geoff had broken his arm and was effectively out for the season. Jamie was distraught, blaming himself and although they tried to be positive, a final without their premier keeper had them all worried.

They'd won and played some good football at times, but Fitz was irritated that they'd made so many mistakes and lost concentration so dramatically at the end. He had some pretty harsh words to say to everyone, but when he got to Calum, his mood amazingly softened.

"This boy," he began, putting a reassuring hand on his shoulder, "is a shining example to you all. He took on a responsibility that many of you would have run away from. The fact that he did it is testament to his courage. With all of our help, he is going to make a fine keeper and I need everyone's support in doing so." He looked around the room, daring anyone to say otherwise. "Good, then we're agreed. See you all for training tomorrow."

As Fitz left the room, Jamie sat thinking. He wasn't so sure, but he was determined to make up for his mistake. He'd personally help Calum with the extra training and he thought a little extra help from the orb might just swing the balance in Calum's favour. He was startled for a moment, because quite by accident he'd stumbled upon the second person in need of his help.

A helping hand?

Jamie sat at the kitchen table feeling morose. His parents listened with a sympathetic ear as he shared the tale of the football match. They'd allowed him to finish without interruption, then tried to reassure him that it was not his fault and that accidents happen. He sighed dramatically and told them that it didn't really help, he still felt bad. His dad smiled and said that sometimes things were just meant to be. His mum laughed and warned Jamie that his dad was about to embark on one of his 'romantic theories' as she liked to call them. Dad had pretended to look hurt.

"Have you heard of fate Jamie?" his dad had asked. Jamie shook his head and waited quietly. "Fate is a peculiar phenomenon. No matter how the circumstances might have changed, the same outcome would have occurred. For example, the opposition may have created that very chance without your initial mistake, resulting in the same save and the same injury."

Mum nodded. "For once I agree with your dad Jamie. Geoff's accident was always going to happen during the game, whether you had made the mistake or not. Some things are just meant to be."

Jamie felt better. "Thanks Mum, thanks Dad that does make some sense in a strange sort of way. Could I ring Geoff after supper?"

"Sure," replied his mum.

After supper and feeling a lot better, he gave Geoff a ring. He was pleased to hear from Jamie and certainly wasn't blaming anyone. He was disappointed that he couldn't play football, but he was a positive person and joked that he'd broken the wrong arm, as he was left handed and had broken the right one. This meant he still had to do his schoolwork! Jamie felt relieved when he put the phone down, but still considered using the orb to speed up Geoff's healing process.

Mum and Dad had gone to watch television and he wanted a bit of reassurance so he popped in to have a chat with his grandma. Picking up a tea-towel he offered to dry up the pans.

"Grandma?"

"Yes dear?"

"Do you think I should use the orb to heal Geoff's wrist?" he asked.

His Grandma thought for a moment before answering. "This may sound a bit odd, but I would say no. What your dad said earlier made some sense. Perhaps now you've got a real opportunity to help someone else."

"Like Calum you mean?"

"Like Calum. Definitely. Put it this way, he saved a penalty, so he can do it."

"Fitz certainly thinks he can and I've offered to help with some extra training."

"Well there you are. What you've got to do is think of a way of helping him out. Any ideas?"

Jamie scratched his head and laughed at an idea that popped into his head. "Not really. Perhaps I can just zap him somehow."

"What, you mean stick out your finger and zap some confidence into him?"

"I know, I know it sounds a bit out there!" Jamie shook his head.

"Might work you know," conceded his grandma.

Jamie laughed again. "I'm not sure, but you think I should help him?"

"I think so."

"Okay." Jamie finished with the pans. "Thanks Grandma, I'll see you later."

Jamie wandered upstairs thinking hard. It was evident that Calum had some talent as a goal-keeper. It was definitely worth a try, but how would he achieve it? He sat down at his desk and gazed at the orb. He wondered if he'd be able to release any of its power again, or whether it would give him some kind of sign. He concentrated hard and pictured Calum in his mind hoping that might help and tried something different. Instead of holding the orb he stretched out his fingers but didn't touch it. He watched curiously as the orb quivered on the desk and began to glow. He closed his eyes again and refocused his energy picturing Calum saving the penalty.

He felt a power begin to bubble to the surface within him and he opened his eyes. He could see faint sparks of electricity crackle from his fingertips. There was a faint smell of sulphur in the room as he stretched his fingertips towards the glowing orb on his desk. It began to vibrate and all the items surrounding it began to move away as if pushed aside by an invisible force, clearing a path from itself to Jamie's outstretched hands.

The effect was spectacular, as the same intense light as before streamed out of its tip and hit Jamie between the eyes. This time he was ready and welcomed the power in. Images of past times swept before him, indistinct images of faces, people aided by the orb in ages long ago. Each image vanished almost as soon as it had appeared and the visions sped up making Jamie gasp. Without warning, they came to an abrupt halt.

It was if a switch had been turned on and power surged through Jamie's body, charging him like a battery. He felt electrified and every hair on his body was standing on end. He felt incredibly powerful and was tempted to see what he could really do, when the most remarkable thing happened. He began to rise off

103

the chair slowly at first and then his whole body was suspended above the floor, no part of him touching anything in the room. He relaxed allowing it to happen, until he was floating in a dream-like state above his desk. He wasn't sure that having this new found skill would help, but he felt calm and clear-headed.

He focused his thoughts once more on Calum and an idea began to formulate in his mind. It was all about the hands? The hands! Giving Calum a helping hand. Jamie was sure that the solution was there when it suddenly became clear. It was the gloves. They were the key. He knew what to do. Triumphantly, he opened his eyes and cried out in surprise. He was still floating. If only I could do this in exams, he thought, I'd pass everything without any bother. Everything was so clear. He enjoyed the feeling for a little while longer, but heard footsteps on the stairs. Grandma would be all right with it, but he wasn't sure how he'd explain it to his parents.

He enjoyed the sensation for a moment longer, not wishing it to end and tried to levitate across the room. Worried for a moment about floating out of the open window, he concentrated on his bed on the other side of the room. Duster nosed his way through the door and watched wide-eyed as his master moved in mid-air. He began to bark, breaking Jamie's concentration and he fell laughing to the safety of the bed below with a thump.

The orb continued to glow in his hands, but without the intensity of before. He knew for certain what he had to do and jumped off the bed, placing the orb back safely on the desk. With Duster chasing after him, he raced down to tell Grandma his plan and what had just happened.

He didn't think he'd be able to sleep that night, but recalling how relaxed he had felt when he was levitating helped to clear his mind and he was soon sleeping fitfully. His dreams were vivid that night. He dreamt of knights' quests and feats of kindness that should have exhausted him but he woke up feeling refreshed and fantastic. For the first time since this strange series of events had begun, he hadn't felt that someone was watching him in his dreams. He jumped out of bed and crossed out day four on his calendar. Twenty-six days left.

Over breakfast, Jamie and Grandma discussed how to set the plan in motion. Jamie thought he had it all figured out, but he needed an opportunity and that might not materialise until training later in the day. Unfortunately, an uneventful and dreary day followed, which drove Jamie mad with impatience. He spent a long morning watching the clock and barely engaging in the lessons and finally lunchtime arrived. He decided he'd had enough of clock watching; at least he could eat.

He found an empty table in the dining room to eat his lunch and to go over his plan, when a friendly female voice brought him out of his reverie. It was JC.

"It's Jamie isn't it?" she asked. A couple of her friends were behind her giggling, but she shooed them away. "Is it okay if I sit down?"

Jamie couldn't believe his luck. Here was part of the reason why everything had gone wrong yesterday. Jamie felt himself blush a little.

"Sure," he managed to stammer. "Have a seat." He pushed out a seat for her and she sat down.

"I really enjoyed yesterday's game," she began.

Jamie didn't know if she was toying with him. "Really?"

"Yes really. I don't watch football that much, but it was exciting at the end," she replied watching him carefully.

"I didn't," replied Jamie, "I feel guilty about Geoff."

"It's not your fault. It could have happened to anyone."

"That's what my dad said."

He's right." She paused for a moment and then added coyly. "Besides, you were just showing off!"

Jamie felt his cheeks redden and stammered, "I…I…don't know what you mean."

"Yes, you do," she remarked, a coy look on her face. "It's quite flattering really."

Jamie was really uncomfortable now! "Um, well, um. Not my finest moment."

"I realise that," she replied, "but I was impressed at how you saved the game at the end. I'll take that as your moment if you like." She touched his hand lightly with hers and she reacted with a little yelp.

"Wow. You gave me an electric shock!"

"Sorry about that." Jamie thought quickly. "It's my new shoes. I keep getting shocks myself." It might have something to do with a magical orb in my pocket, he thought, but you'd never believe me.

"It's okay. It was quite nice." She touched him again. "No shock this time. Be seeing you soon hopefully." She grinned, took a bite out of his apple and skipped off, leaving him wondering what had just happened.

School didn't seem to drag quite so much after that, but when it did end, it was time for football practice. Whilst they were changing, Jamie saw an opportunity to execute his plan. He was changing next to Calum who was preoccupied. He glowered at his gloves in disgust, turning them over and over in his hands.

"Go on Calum, pop them on they won't hurt you," Jamie cheerfully chided.

"That's what you think," murmured Calum grumpily ramming his hands into the offending items.

106

Jamie reached into the pocket of his blazer and asked Calum to hold onto the orb for a moment.

"What is it? It looks valuable?" He looked at it curiously and added with more than a hint of sarcasm, "I'll probably drop it!"

"Don't be daft. You made some great saves the other day," Jamie encouraged holding it out in front of him.

"And some bloomin' awful ones!" he quickly reminded Jamie.

"True," Jamie conceded, "but with the final coming up, we've got to be positive."

"Positive? You sound like my mum," he laughed. Jamie was pleased he'd lightened the atmosphere a little, as he popped the orb into Calum's hands. Quickly, before Calum could say anything, he projected his thoughts to the orb.

The air shimmered as Jamie felt the peculiar power he was able to create flow from him to the orb. The sphere began to glow, faintly at first and then more brightly as Jamie's plan almost came to a grinding halt. He wasn't quite sure of what he should do and he certainly hadn't practised! He panicked momentarily and then calmed. He breathed deeply and then feeling a bit daft started moving his hands in a circular motion. He hoped this would encourage the energy to swirl around Calum's hand before flowing into the gloves themselves. He waved his hands a bit quicker and was amazed to see something beginning to happen.

"Blimey Jamie. This is a bit of all right. How do you make it glow like that?"

"It has a gravity generator and if you rotate it correctly, it spins so fast that it generates light," lied Jamie easily. He couldn't believe how quickly, how effortlessly, the tale just popped out, without his even having to think about it. A distant voice inside his head congratulated him and reminded him he'd lied quite a bit recently. He shook the unwelcome thoughts to one side.

"Cool. Where did you get it?"

"I got it from my grandma. Chuck it back here and I'll pop it back in my pocket." Calum was still staring at it in amazement, as were a few others. Jamie was aware of the gathering interest and was eager to dismiss any unnecessary attention quickly. Calum reluctantly handed it back to Jamie, who pocketed it.

Calum sprang up from his seat and announced loudly with a double clap of his hands that it was time for practise. His enthusiasm, although surprising to most of the room, seemed to encourage them all and they clattered out to the playing field laughing and joking. Jamie patted the pocket of his blazer in thanks, unaware that Spencer was staring at the jacket with suspicion.

The training session began and at first Jamie suspected nothing had happened. Calum let in goal after goal! He wasn't entirely sure what he should do, when a shot was fired at Calum, who without really thinking, reached out one massive hand and caught it. He nearly dropped it he was so surprised, but the same thing happened the next time and when he dived at full stretch to flick the ball around the post Jamie allowed himself a satisfied grin.

Calum looked a different player and as his confidence grew he appeared to actually grow in size! He still made the odd mistake, but unlike before, he didn't allow it to get to him. With Jamie's guidance, he learned how to come off of his goal line, discovered where to stand for corners and how to time his jumps, grabbing the ball literally from the heads of attackers and he even worked out how to punch the ball. His goal kicks quickly became legendary, easily reaching the half-way line and beyond. His dramatic turnaround enthralled everyone and Fitz was understandably impressed as he approached Jamie and Calum at the end of the session.

"With just a couple of days to go until the final, you might just be up to scratch Calum," he remarked.

Calum was chuffed. "Thanks Fitz. I feel different today."

"You look different today. Keep up the good work."

"I will do. Thanks."

"Give him some extra shots just to make sure eh Jamie?"

Jamie grinned. "Will do Fitz."

The others went in, as Tommy joined them for a final save and shooting session. Calum's save rate had increased dramatically and Jamie was very satisfied that things were appearing to happen for Calum. With any luck and with a bit more practice, they might just have a good enough keeper for the final. Tommy passed him a ball that he blasted towards goal. Calum reacted and tipped it over the bar.

Jamie nodded. "So far so good," he thought.

Playing the waiting game

The next couple of days passed even more slowly if that was possible. It seemed that way to Jamie. He crossed off the days on the calendar and gulped. Twenty-four days left! A week had passed and by his reckoning he'd only helped one person! He was trying to help Calum, but when would he know whether it had been a success or not? Only time would tell he surmised, but time was ultimately against him.

He'd had no more visits from the warrior thankfully, but there was no new insight into his quest nor had he levitated again, no matter how hard he'd tried. He was beginning to get frustrated with his lack of action and he ploughed himself into training to take his mind off his increasing sense of unease.

One interesting development was that Spencer was avoiding him completely and that JC was taking more of an interest. This was great and she had even walked home with him yesterday. They chatted easily and it turned out that she had a dog too and they decided to get them together. He wasn't sure if this was a date or not, but he was looking forward to spending more time getting to know her.

In training, the change in Calum's skills was dramatic. Jamie spent every moment he could running through extra drills with him. Calum had become totally focused and his new found confidence was rubbing off on everyone at training. Geoff had even remarked to Jamie that his place in the district side would be in jeopardy if the selectors ever found out about him!

Although this change was intense, Jamie did have one worry that plagued him. Was it the gloves or Calum which had brought this incredible turn-around in his fortunes? He mentioned this to his grandma as they sat down for supper.

"I'm worried," Jamie began.

"What about dear?" replied his grandma wiping her hands of flour and sitting down.

"About the so called help I've given Calum with his goalkeeping."

Grandma looked confused. "I don't understand! That's great isn't it?"

"Yes, but what bothers me is that it could be the gloves and not Calum."

"Ah, I did wonder if you'd had a bit of a 'hand' in that," she cackled to herself, pleased with the joke. She paused for a moment thinking. "I think you should just allow this situation to work itself out."

"I'm worried that it's taking too long."

"I agree, but perhaps you have to be more patient?"

Jamie considered this option and then said, "It's definitely helped with Calum's confidence and he's become a great keeper, but nothing has happened like last time."

"Perhaps you have to wait until after the final?"

"S'pose so, but I'm still nervous."

Grandma smiled broadly, got up from the table and stood next to Jamie. "What's the problem? You've helped a friend; the gloves were just the catalyst, you'll see. Stand up and give your old grandma a cuddle."

"What for Grandma?" said Jamie standing up.

"You're completely missing the point here. The orb chose you for a reason. That reason is pretty clear to me. You have a kind nature and believe in right and wrong. You want to help people. Look what you've done already and Calum now believes in himself. You were the person who saw something in him and he followed it through."

Jamie sighed melodramatically and his grandma

111

continued.

"Look, this may sound a little far-fetched, but there's a little magic in everything we do and what happens to us in our lives. For whatever reason, you and the orb are intertwined and I really believe it wouldn't have just picked anyone. Go with the flow and see what happens, or if you're really worried, switch the gloves."

"Switch the gloves?"

"Why not? You'll have your answer won't you?"

Change the gloves, why not indeed? He was contemplating this option as his parents bustled into the kitchen for supper.

"Looking forward to tomorrow Jamie?"

"Bit nervous Dad."

"You'll be fine. Sound like you've got a good team. I hear that you've got a replacement keeper."

"How did you hear about that?" Jamie asked.

"Met his dad on the train," Dad answered. "He can't believe the transformation in his boy. Talked all the way to London about it."

"That's so cool," said Jamie.

"Yeah, he definitely thought so." A cheeky look appeared on his face. "Shall we wind your mother up about the opposition?"

The final was against The Deacon, a local private school and the current local champions. They were a strong unit and Jamie knew them well, as it was the school where his mum taught!

"Who will you cheer for Mum?" Dad asked trying to look innocent.

"Oh, ha, ha. Very funny. You're such a comedian aren't you? Of course I'll be cheering for Jamie, but I will be there officially as a Deacon teacher. I am their head of year after all."

"But when you cheer Jamie's winning goal, will you

receive your marching orders from The Deacon?"

Mum bristled and glared at her husband. "This is the twenty-first century you silly man. They couldn't do that."

"Of course not Mum," reassured Jamie as his dad laughed behind an enormous piece of pizza. "You'll just have to remain diplomatic at all times and cheer for both sides."

"I've got it!" exclaimed his father. "You should wear your Deacon school scarf, but underneath you'll have to wear Marsh Green colours."

"Not a bad idea for you," she agreed. "I'll add a splash of green to my ensemble. No one will ever know."

"Thanks Mum."

She winked at him. "I'll be cheering you on, don't you worry. I may just have to be a bit more subtle about it."

To switch or not to switch?

The next day at breakfast, a nervous Jamie picked at his cereal. He'd decided on a course of action and really hoped that it was the right thing to do. The letterbox clanged, taking his mind off the problem and Duster raced to the door barking furiously. Dad appeared at the doorway dragging the dog through the doorway, paper firmly clamped in his jaw.

"Jamie! For heaven's sake, can't you train your dog to leave the paper alone?" Jamie smiled as Duster growled playfully deep in his throat and tried to wrestle the paper from Dad. "Duster. Drop it!" he ordered. Duster immediately dropped the paper and went and sat next to Jamie to receive his pat. He obliged and sneakily fed him a scrap from the table.

"How do you do that?" his dad asked, making a meal of opening the slightly soggy newspaper. "Pass the toast would you?"

Jamie passed the toast and continued with his breakfast as Dad spread out the paper and began to read it. It was the local edition and he watched as his dad's eyes widened.

"Blimey Jamie. You ought to read this. Where's your mum?" He passed the paper to Jamie and jumped up to find Mum. Jamie began to read the front page. It said:

'The Chiltern Press Cup always throws up a few surprises, *reports Dom Affleck*, and this season is no different. The competition, now in its twenty-fifth year, was set up to encourage local schools, both state and private, to play alongside and against one another for this prestigious trophy.

In what is being hailed as one of the potential games of the season, Marsh Green Senior School are taking on the relative might of the reigning champions, The Deacon, in today's county Colts final at Wycombe Wanderer's stadium.

What makes this final so interesting is the fact that for the first time in years, a state school has reached the final. In a competition dominated by the private sector for so long, Marsh Green will have it all to do if they are to win the cup for the first time in their history.

Mr Geoffrey Thomas, Head of Games at The Deacon, was in confident mood yesterday. He didn't rate the chances of the opposition when he said, "Marsh Green are like a third division team on a good cup run. They don't have the resources available to us and have had an easy set of fixtures." He went on to add with a laugh, "We've definitely had the more difficult run in and are not beset by injuries. I believe they also have an untested goal-keeper in their team! I know who my money would be on if I was a betting man." No one from Marsh Green was available for comment.

The game kicks off at 2 p.m. today. Tickets are available at the ground's box office and all proceeds go to the winning team's chosen charity.'

Jamie didn't really know what to think about the article, as he read it a second time. Mum came into the room, followed by Grandma. They peered over his shoulder to see what the fuss was all about.

"Well I never," remarked Grandma.

"Oh, give me strength. That man is a menace." Mum was obviously referring to the Mr Thomas in the article. "Who gave him permission to speak to the press?" She stormed off.

"Whoops!" remarked Dad as he came back in to resume his breakfast. "Wouldn't want to be in his shoes today."

Jamie trudged to school with the paper in his bag. An increasingly agitated Fitz had scheduled a light early morning training session. He was a like a cat on hot bricks, he couldn't keep still and talked tactics to anyone who cared to listen! However it was a vastly different Fitz who joined the rest of the team this morning. Talk amongst the squad inevitably was of the article and they were unsure of how Fitz was going to react. Suddenly, everyone could hear him. He stomped up the corridor and barged loudly into the changing rooms, banging the door, brandishing an edition of his own. The first person he clapped his eyes on was Calum.

"Have you read this utter drivel boy?" he barked. No one dared move. The old Calum would have crumbled, but taking a deep breath he stood up and told his stressed master that they'd all read it, but had taken no notice of it. What he failed to tell him though was that they were all secretly pleased they'd even made the paper.

"But it's complete nonsense," continued the red-faced master, calming a fraction, "this bit about us not standing a chance. I've a good mind to go up to that posh school and give their Head of Sport a piece of my mind. My God, we'll make him eat humble pie."

Calum agreed that it was nonsense and in an effort to calm their coach, offered to help collect the cones and balls for the session, leading him out of the changing room and out of harm's way. Everyone breathed a sigh of relief and gave it a moment before following them out. Jamie remained pretending to look for something.

He reached into his own bag and retrieved a pair of gloves identical to the ones Calum had 'conveniently' left behind. It's now or never, he thought. His fingers fizzed for a moment as he swiftly popped Calum's gloves in his bag, substituting them for his replacement pair. He hoped it would work as he mulled over once again whether this was the right thing to do. The orb buzzed again in his pocket and feeling a bit better, he ran out to join the others.

The training session was supposed to be a light-hearted affair, as the match was that afternoon but Fitz's mood was wearing off on them. They began to feel really nervous. Incredibly, it was Calum who made light of the situation. Jamie had given him the gloves as soon as he'd joined the others and watched carefully as he put them on. He looked at them strangely for a moment, but then shrugged, banged his hands together and bounced off to get in goal.

The session ended and Fitz stomped off still in a bad mood. Everyone looked a little deflated and Calum looked at them all and started laughing.

"Come on, cheer up, let's have a penalty competition!" he declared. "We might need it!"

No one argued or hurried to change, wanting to avoid Fitz, so they took their positions outside of the penalty box. Eddie stepped up first. Calum stood in the middle of the goal and made himself look huge, arms and legs outstretched. An enormous gap lay between his legs, inviting Eddie to aim the penalty in that direction.

He took a couple of steps forward and placed the ball gracefully into the far right corner of the net. Calum barely moved. He looked stunned and was gazing at his gloves uncertainly.

Jamie's heart nearly stopped.

Francis pushed past his brother and declared that it was his go. Calum smiled more confidently as Francis was not known for scoring goals. He didn't bother with a run up and simply swung his left boot at the ball. Calum dived in the right direction and decided to leave it, but the ball had some serious swerve on it and as it brushed his fingertips, it ricocheted off the post, hit

Calum on the back and ballooned into the goal. Francis was beside himself and set off on a protracted show of celebration.

Calum was crestfallen and dejectedly picked the ball out of the net. Jamie decided to take the next penalty, snatching the ball from a startled Spencer who was eager to rub Calum's nose in it further. Spencer objected, but Jamie took no notice. Calum must save this he thought.

He placed the ball and looked at Calum. His shoulders were slumped and he was showing signs of his old self, all that newfound self-confidence beginning to flow out like a leaking tap. How do I take this without drawing attention to myself by missing it on purpose? The air in front of the ball shimmered slightly as Jamie felt a blast of energy course from him. It was decided. He'd blast it straight at Calum. He knew, with absolute certainty, that his big friend would second-guess him.

Jamie took a deep breath, took two steps back and looked Calum in the eye. Read my mind Calum he instructed, and for a fleeting second their eyes met. Calum nodded, as he stepped forward. The rest of the team watched with interest as he blasted it goal-ward. Calum smiled as he reached up with both hands and plucked the ball out of the air. With a cry of triumph he booted the ball high into the air and celebrated as if he'd won the cup.

"Anyone could have saved that Calum," piped up Spencer. "You hit it straight at him. Stop celebrating and see if you can save this."

Tommy interjected. "Come on Spencer. Leave him. There's no point."

"Yes there is. We have to trust our keeper. If he saves this, I'll be satisfied." Spencer stared at Tommy, daring him to say otherwise. There was an uneasy silence as the rest of the team looked on. They all knew that Spencer rarely missed. Calum made the decision for them.

"Bring it on Spencer!" he goaded.

Spencer grinned in triumph and placed the ball on the spot. Calum concentrated hard. Jamie felt curiously relaxed. It was now or never. If he had helped Calum, now was the time to show it. He watched on as intrigued by the outcome as much as the others.

"Ready?" Spencer asked.

Calum didn't have time to answer as Spencer stroked the ball with unerring accuracy towards the bottom right hand corner of the goal. Jamie kept his mind blank. If Calum were ready, he'd have to show it now. The ball flew through the air. It looked a like a certain goal, when suddenly Calum reacted. He flung himself to his left and with an outstretched hand punched the ball against the post, which rebounded out of the goal towards a very surprised Spencer. He didn't give a second thought and hit it back towards the goal, as would happen in a match. Calum reacted again and sprang back to the centre of the goal in time to flick the ball over the bar and out of play. There was a hushed reaction for a moment. All eyes were on Spencer. Calum stood in goal, watching him carefully.

"Well done I suppose," Spencer said quietly.

A cheer went up and the others mobbed Calum. Jamie watched Spencer as he shook his head. He thought he could just make out a hint of a smile on Spencer's face as he returned to the changing rooms. Maybe there was some hope for him after all?

After lunch, they had travelled together on the school mini-bus with Fitz driving. The atmosphere had been one of wild excitement and the dulcet tones of a bus full of teenagers had been heard all the way to the ground.

The game was to be played at their local football stadium. It was not Wembley by any stretch of the imagination, but it was their Wembley. The ground itself could only seat four thousand at full capacity. It wasn't going to be full today, but that didn't matter to them at all. This was their final and they were going to enjoy it. As they were ushered into the players' area by numerous security men on the gate, Jamie and his teammates were shown into the changing rooms.

The excitement was intense as they changed. They put their possessions into the lockers beneath their own personal booths. Jamie decided against this and ensured that the orb was carefully hidden in the pocket of his blazer that he zipped up and checked, twice! For some reason though, he had an unnerving sensation that somebody was watching him. He turned round quickly to try and catch someone out. All eyes were elsewhere, and he shrugged it off feeling slightly paranoid.

As he took off his shirt, the feeling returned and he turned again. Like before, no one appeared to be paying him any attention. He turned once more and again the sensation returned, but he was reluctant to spin around in case anyone suggested that he was going mad! But the nagging feeling that someone was watching his every move remained and the hairs on his neck refused to go down. He turned around one more time just to be sure and standing at the door was one of the opposition eyeing him curiously. The visitor coughed to get Fitz's attention.

"Yes laddie?" smiled Fitz warmly.

"Ah, hello sir. I've been sent in to wish you luck on behalf of The Deacon."

"That's very kind of you," he replied, "please do return the favour," he responded, finishing the conversation. The boy continued to stand there, studiously looking around the room at everyone.

"Thank you young man, you may go now, we've got tactics to discuss." And with that Fitz ushered the boy, who was still unwilling to depart, out of the door shutting it firmly behind him.

A final team talk ensued. A brief but intense huddle and words of encouragement from Tommy before they trooped out and onto the pitch. As they jogged out the crowd cheered them on. The partisan crowd numbered about a thousand parents, friends and classes from each school. Not enormous numbers, but their enthusiasm more than made up for their lack of size! It was noisy enough to make Jamie's legs wobbly!

They took up their positions on the pitch and observed the opposition carefully. They looked supremely confident and not a bit nervous. With a blast of his whistle the referee got the game under way. In terms of possession, both teams shared time on the ball and neither had the ascendancy in the first half. That was until the last couple of minutes when some sustained pressure by The Deacon resulted in a lovely flowing move and a terrifically taken goal. Jamie was bitterly disappointed, but Tommy gathered everyone in and urged them to remain calm. The opposition, sensing an advantage, pressed for a second goal and it was only through some resolute defending and some thumping tackles from the twins that they survived until half time.

Fitz tried to calm their nerves during the break with some wise words. He tinkered with the formation a little, substituting Alex Raspin to a huge round of applause from the rest of squad and bringing on the popular Eddie to slot into the right side of midfield. The team loved bringing him on. He was a magical player.

The second half played out in similar fashion to the first in the initial exchanges, but as time wore on The Deacon became more anxious, desperate to hold onto their slender advantage. Jamie and his teammates were calm and assured, taking comfort in the fact that their coach maintained a composed stance on the side-lines. He'd reassured the team at half time and suggested that they needed to be patient in order to break down a well-ordered and resolute Deacon team. Their patience was beginning to pay off as they exerted a sustained period of pressure upon the opposition.

The crowd gasped as Spencer shot just wide after a flowing move down the right flank. Then, Tobias slammed a powerful header into the cross-bar from a corner. Things were getting interesting and it seemed only a matter of time before Marsh Green equalised. Finally, with just over five minutes to go, the breakthrough came and it was the indomitable Eddie who provided the moment of genius! He intercepted the ball after a half-hearted and tired Deacon attack and played it to Tommy who controlled it and spotted Daniel free on the left. He threaded an inch perfect pass into his accelerating path. A defender attempted to block Daniel's run, but he played the ball cheekily through his legs.

"NUTS!" came the excited cry from the crowd who were on their feet sensing something special. Daniel looked up and stopped suddenly, leaving another defender for dead. Spencer had moved into space on the edge of the box and frantically called for the ball. Daniel obliged, Spencer received the ball and passed it into a space behind the final two defenders as he'd glimpsed Eddie making a late run from midfield. The pass was perfect and without even looking up he sent a thunderbolt of a shot past the keeper into the far corner.

1–1.

The crowd went wild. Eddie was mobbed. The next five minutes were mayhem! Whilst Jamie and his teammates were still revelling in their equaliser, The

Deacon attacked from the kick-off, catching Marsh Green off guard and in the ensuing melee, both Francis and Charlie, who sandwiched him with a painful crunch, flattened the Deacon's striker in the penalty area! The referee had no option but to blow his whistle for a penalty. This silenced one set of supporters who only moments ago had been celebrating and sent the other into rapture!

Jamie couldn't believe it and glanced nervously at Fitz who was pacing angrily up and down in his technical area and muttering ominously to himself. Tommy was having a quiet word with Calum, whose face gave nothing away. Francis and Charlie were glaring angrily at one another and it looked as if each was blaming the other. Jamie knew that it was now or never. If Calum saved this, then his work was surely done. Despite the situation, he was strangely calm.

In the lead up to the match, Fitz had primed the team for this very eventuality. His reasoning was that if the opposition missed the penalty, or Calum saved it, the opportunity for a swift counter attack whilst the opposition consoled the penalty taker was one that could be exploited!

Everyone took their places and prepared for the worst. Only a couple of minutes were left in the match! The crowd were on their feet. The Deacon striker, a formidable goal-scorer, looked confident as he placed the ball on the penalty spot. He looked up and winked at Calum, who for a moment looked as if he might buckle under the pressure. Frowning, he smacked his hands together three times and stood, knees bent, poised like a snake ready to strike.

The referee blew his whistle and the striker began his run up. He paused deliberately just before the ball in an attempt to deceive Calum, which worked sending him diving the wrong way. He threw himself to the right as the striker passed the ball into the left of the goal to make it 2–1. Marsh Green couldn't believe it and The Deacon were beginning to wildly celebrate when the referee blew his whistle. Unbelievably, he disallowed the goal. A brave, brave decision under the circumstances and under howls of protest, he ordered that the kick be re-taken.

Pandemonium!

The referee could sense a mutiny and it looked as though things might get ugly. Charlie and Francis had rolled up their sleeves and looked ready for a fight! He stopped his watch to go and discuss his decision with the coaches from both schools. The Deacon's coach looked unhappy but agreed with the pronouncement and had a quiet word with his striker, who shrugged and prepared himself to take it again. Jamie couldn't believe their luck. What would happen this time?

The whistle blew again as the striker began his run up and struck the ball sweetly. It was placement, not power and it appeared to be a sure thing. The crowd watched as incredibly Calum guessed correctly and was diving full stretch in the right direction. Everyone held their breath.

A roar went up from the crowd, but it was difficult to see just what had happened because the ball had disappeared! Everyone looked about frantically, the ball wasn't in the net, it hadn't sailed clear of the goal, which could only mean one thing. Calum had saved it.

Marsh Green rapidly moved into counter-attack mode as a triumphant Calum got up from the ground with the ball safely cradled in his huge hands. A despondent Deacon team gathered around their forlorn and devastated striker, momentarily caught unawares as Calum spied Jamie who'd made a run clear. Calum threw a beautiful pass to his feet and Jamie set off, dribbling the ball.

The Deacon had only left two defenders in their own half and he had two options, take the defenders on and risk being tackled or ply a one-two with one of his teammates. He opted for option two and passed the ball to Eddie in midfield and carried on with his run. The return pass was perfect and he sprang the off-side trap leaving the remaining defenders in his wake. He only had the keeper to beat.

The Deacon's keeper looked to be in a quandary. He was looking desperately for help from his defenders, but they were at least five metres behind. He made his decision and came off his line to intercept Jamie. Everyone in the stadium watched mesmerised. One correct decision would win the game; a mistake would send it into extra time.

Jamie watched as The Deacon's goalkeeper came off his line. He looked determined and seemed to have only one thing on his mind, take out the threat by whatever means available. Aware of the danger he was in, Jamie decided to go it alone and, in Hollywood style, the world appeared to slow down imperceptibly. He could hear the thumping of his feet on the grass, but not the roar of the crowd. His heart was hammering in his chest as he instinctively struck the ball with the outside of his left foot and the ball curled ever so slowly passed the goalkeeper who despairingly stuck out a hand.

The ball appeared to touch his outstretched fingertips but it didn't affect the trajectory of the ball. The ball carried on one way, but his momentum flattened Jamie, taking him out in a painful exhalation of breath from both boys as they landed in a heap of tangled limbs and mud.

It was obviously a foul, but the referee allowed the game to carry on as the ball continued unabated towards the goal. Jamie peeked out hopefully from under the keeper as the ball edged closer to the empty goal; his teammates were beginning to celebrate as it finally sailed majestically into the top corner of the goal and with it sent Marsh Green into wild celebrations.

The referee blew for a goal, and then checked his watch. He put the whistle to his lips once more and blew for full time. They'd done it! They'd won the cup! Jamie had scored the winning goal! They'd beaten the mighty Deacon! The Deacon's keeper eventually extricated himself from on top of Jamie and begrudgingly helped him up, shaking him by the hand, before he was flattened again by his exuberant teammates.

"Oi, you lot," laughed Francis and Charlie, last to arrive as always, "get off him. We want a go!" The crowd got off and together the twins hoisted him up with whoops of delight. They plopped him on their shoulders parading their hero to the crowd. A few of the others followed suit with Calum, and Fitz joined the throng as they made their way to the half way line where a temporary stand was being erected for the cup presentation.

Jamie looked into the crowd searching for his family, when he caught the eye of his father who was waving to him happily and shouting, "Well done!" Grandma gave him a wink and Mum was grinning broadly despite her conflict of interests.

The rest of the proceedings went by in a bit of a blur. They were debriefed and congratulated by highly satisfied Fitz, then the obligatory shaking of hands with the deflated opposition and finally, finally, the presentation of the cup. They all shook hands with the local mayor and collected their winners' medals, taking their places excitedly on the stage.

Jamie was beside himself with excitement and everything felt slightly surreal. He'd scored the winning goal and here he was collecting the cup. Only last week three of his teammates were trying to inflict real physical harm on him! How things change he mused as they jigged up and down, beside themselves with exhilaration, as Tommy finally appeared to collect the cup. He shook hands with the mayor, the official bit over with, and received the cup. With shouts of excitement they held it aloft. The crowd erupted as a blast of green and gold fireworks went off behind the stage. It was some moment.

Once Tommy had finished with the cup, he handed it over to Calum and Jamie who gleefully held it aloft. A photographer for the local newspaper stood in front of them, snapping shot after shot, with them both grinning away, as the supporters came down pitch-side to join in the celebrations and commiserations.

Jamie's family were quick to find him, a manly handshake from Dad quickly turned into an excited 'to hell with it you're just a kid' bear hug and kiss on the cheek, followed by more hugs from the ladies in his life. It was a real partisan atmosphere. Excited parents were congratulating Fitz on a job well done and hugging all the triumphant players. Miss Bareham, the headmistress, was there too, chatting to each team member in turn with a kindly smile and a promise of rewards yet to be received back at school. Mum was talking excitedly to Jamie, when she caught the eye of The Deacon coach, and called out to him.

"Robin!" she waved, walking over to him with Jamie firmly in tow. "Robin. Gosh, what a spectacle. You must be so proud of the boys for such a pulsating game. I'm delighted with them and will tell them so when I get a chance."

Instead of a resigned smile and an invitation to see the boys he surprised Jamie by frowning and snarling, "I see you're consorting with the enemy."

"The enemy? I don't know what you mean?" Dad, sensing a fight, had sidled up quietly to watch. Jamie could see his mum tense and she gripped his hand firmly, making him wince. He decided to take control of the situation.

He pried himself from his mother and held out a hand introducing himself. "Good afternoon sir." Mr Thomas begrudgingly held out his hand and loosely gripped Jamie's, avoiding eye contact. Jamie knew this was the height of bad manners, so gripping the offered sweaty palm as tightly as he could finished, "My name is Jamie Lomax and I would just like to congratulate you on producing a fine team and being part of a game I will never forget." His reaction was quite extraordinary.

"Jamie who?" he muttered all colour from his cheeks draining away.

"Jamie Lomax sir."

"You have the same surname as, as, as?" he stuttered.

"As my mother, yes sir."

"Do you mean to tell me, that Mrs Lomax, Deacon employee, Head of year ten and colleague of mine, is, is, your mother?" he spluttered his face now as white as a sheet.

"Oh yes sir," Jamie grinned "and this over here is my proud father and my rather amused grandmother." Jamie released the teacher's hand and gave him his best smile. Mr Thomas' face fell as he slowly put two and two together.

"But, but, but…" he could barely manage, looking from Jamie's mum to Jamie and back again, "he scored the winning goal against us, he can't be your son, that wouldn't be fair!"

Mum came and put a loving arm around Jamie's shoulders and said, "Absolutely Robin. I am extraordinarily proud of him!"

"But, but, but..." Mr Thomas was speechless. Mum gave him her best smile and told him she'd see him back at school, but she'd quickly pop into the changing rooms to chat to the boys. They all turned to go leaving the bemused master still spluttering and shaking his head in disbelief.

"Wonderful, just wonderful," crowed Grandma.

"Hilarious," agreed Dad, "how will he be at school darling?"

"Awful," countered Mum, "but nothing I can't handle. Looks like all I have to do is mention Jamie's name to send him into a spin. He'll never get over it." She chuckled and then turned her attention back to Jamie. "Go and get changed and we'll see you at home as soon as you get there. Celebratory takeaway tonight?"

"Yes please Mum, terrific, see you later." And with that, he trotted contentedly into the depths of the stadium to find the changing rooms and join his triumphant teammates.

Theft

The scene when he arrived was not the party atmosphere Jamie was expecting. Quite the reverse. The cup stood, pride of place on a table in the centre of the room gleaming and real, very real, but the mood of his teammates didn't reflect the gleaming surface of the cup. It was dulled and people were looking around anxiously. Jamie's heart began to sink. He sidled up to Tobias to ask what was going on.

"We've been done over mate," was the reply. "Someone's nicked our stuff. My new phone is gone."

"That's awful!" exclaimed Jamie as he began to walk to his locker, dread beginning to mount with each step. Each person he passed was missing something.

"My money!"

"My new Parker pen with my initials on it from Dad."

"My sunglasses!"

"My watch!"

"Someone's even stolen my shower gel!"

"That's a shame, you'll need it!"

"Oi!"

Jamie reached his locker and with shaking fingers stretched into his blazer pocket. Nothing. Perhaps it was in the other one. He slumped down heavily into his seat, head in hands, beside himself with anxiety and grief. The orb. Someone had taken it. He couldn't believe it. Who would do that? More importantly, without it how was he possibly going to be able to fulfil his part of the bargain?

He sat slumped in his seat with head in hands panic beginning to set in. He took some deep breaths and tried to calm himself. Suddenly, he had some clarity in the mixed emotions flowing through him and a flash of certainty took him by surprise. Something had happened before the game. Now what was it? He sat up remembering the curious episode and stood up.

"Listen everyone, I think I've got an idea who may have done this, but I'm going to need my mum's help. She's a teacher at The Deacon."

"Typical!" muttered Spencer, but Jamie ignored him, taking charge.

"Shut up Spencer! Tommy, can you write down a list of everything that's gone missing and I'll be back in a moment."

"No worries Jamie," replied Tommy looking puzzled as Spencer stared at them. "Did you lose anything?"

Jamie gulped down hard, "Just a whizzy toy that helps me to relax."

"Whizzy toy it is then," remarked Tommy raising an eyebrow.

Jamie rushed out of their changing room in search of his mother. He looked frantically left and right, but could hear nothing. There were quiet murmurings behind the door of The Deacon's changing room, so he tentatively knocked on the door and went in.

The atmosphere inside was not unlike theirs and he scanned the room quickly. He caught the eye of the curly haired blonde boy who'd come in before the match. The boy lowered his eyes for a moment, and then looked up and winked at him. A wink! Was he being friendly or were Jamie's suspicions correct? He frowned at the boy and caught sight of his mother. He coughed politely.

"Um, Mrs Lomax. Could I have a word with you please?"

Jamie's mother turned around and looking at her son replied, "Of course, young man," maintaining their teacher–student relationship for the benefit of everyone else. "Let's step outside."

She closed the door quietly behind her and smiled, the teacher in her disappeared and Mum returned. "What's up? Do you need a lift home?"

"No nothing like that Mum, it's pretty serious and I'm not sure what to do."

Mum's expression changed and she switched back into teacher mode. "Go on," she encouraged.

"We've been robbed Mum and I'm pretty certain I know who did it," Jamie said carefully.

"Wow, that's a brave accusation. What evidence do you have to suggest that someone has done this and I presume that by talking to me you think it might be someone from The Deacon?"

"Mum, there has been the odd spot of trouble at Marsh Green, but believe me no one would steal from each other on a day like today. It just doesn't make sense. I thought I'd talk to you to see if anything like this has happened before and try to sort it out before Fitz calls the police."

"Go on," she encouraged.

"We had a visitor before the game." Jamie watched his mother carefully and although she tried her hardest to hide it, her expression changed ever so slightly and she raised an eyebrow. She said nothing more and allowed Jamie to finish. "He came into our changing room to wish us good luck. Said Mr Thomas had sent him, but he just hung around looking at all of us in turn without expression, almost as though he was taking mental pictures. It was weird!"

"Could you describe him for me please?" Mum asked looking slightly dejected.

"He is a little smaller than me, smiley face, but had distinctive blonde curly hair."

"Oh dear!" exclaimed Mum looking crestfallen, "Oh dear, oh dear." She thought for a moment and then spurred herself into action, decision made. "Leave it with me. I'll chat to Mr Thomas and see what I can do. You tell Fitz that I'm on the case and will talk to him at match tea. I'll need a list of all the things that have gone missing. Everyone needs to behave as though nothing has happened, okay?"

"Okay!"

"I was going home, but I'll think I'll send Dad and Grandma back and join them later. See you at tea."

Aware of what was going on behind the scenes, Marsh Green changed into their uniform for match tea and made their way to the official presentations in the players' dining room. As they entered, all eyes were on the conversation between Fitz and Jamie's mum. Mr Thomas interjected every so often, obviously unhappy at the situation, but it was quite clear who was in charge. Fitz listened carefully and nodded in agreement, a grim look on his face. All the teachers looked as though they'd been sucking lemons. They were grimacing and the whole episode looked to have left a sour taste.

Match tea and the presentations were largely uneventful. The captain of the local club stood up to give a brief chat about the game and life as a professional. Fascinating stuff, but Jamie's thoughts weren't on football at this moment; he was too worried about the orb and more importantly losing his soul. He shook his head in disbelief at the situation he found himself in. When the professional finally finished, a couple of people at a time were allowed to ask questions and pop up for an autograph or two. Jamie was momentarily startled when his mother popped up her hand.

"Would you mind signing the match programme as a memento for our school?" she asked.

"Of course, I'd be delighted," returned the

professional with a broad smile.

She got up and started walking to the podium when she rather dramatically clutched her head and murmured that she didn't have a pen. She looked around and caught the eye of the curly blonde haired boy from The Deacon. She gave him her best smile and walked up and asked if he had a pen he could borrow. He opened up his jacket to reveal a whole range of pens in his inside pocket, but obviously trying to impress Mrs Lomax and without thinking, chose a particular one. She thanked him as she took it and continued on her way.

The professional footballer made a great show of signing the programme.

"Nice pen!" he remarked.

She took it back to her seat and popped on her glasses. To Jamie this was a sure sign that something was up. She studied a piece of paper intently, sighed and passed them over to Mr Thomas, who looked furious.

The room went silent as Mr Thomas, went up to the curly haired Deacon boy and asked him to follow them to the changing rooms. Jamie's Mum led the way out of the dining room a grim expression on her face. A stunned silence quickly turned into an excited discussion all across the room. Fitz put up with it for a couple of minutes before calling for quiet and gave a little speech of his own to fill in time.

Jamie's mum finally appeared with a sports bag and a grim expression upon her face. She glanced quickly at Jamie and nodded as if to say "We got him, thanks for the info" and then held a final conversation with Fitz, obviously apologising profusely, before dismissing the rest of her team to trudge back to their changing room.

In the relative quiet of the Marsh Green changing room five or so minutes later, the stolen items were returned to their rightful owners. Fitz didn't say much, but it later transpired that the Deacon boy had confessed to everything and it wasn't the first time that it had happened either! He had a bit of a problem, kleptomania Mum called it, and he was in a lot of trouble.

Jamie breathed a sigh of relief as the items were handed back one by one, but to his horror, the orb didn't materialise! Everyone else's items had been returned, but his was still missing. He counted to ten slowly in his head and tried hard not to panic. He closed his eyes and concentrated hard, reaching out to the orb. He was convinced there was a connection between them both so perhaps it would answer him in some way.

Nothing.

He concentrated harder and he felt a tingling sensation creeping up his neck as if the orb was answering. He stopped and the sensation went away. He tried again, and the sensation returned, much stronger this time and an image of someone in Marsh Green uniform started to materialise. He knew who it was going to be as the image began to focus.

Spencer! Angry thoughts began to swirl in his brain and he clenched his fists ready to go and confront him. Jamie opened his eyes carefully, unwilling to show his emotions. He was tempted to go and thump Spencer and could feel real anger building inside. He thought back to what happened in the warrior's tent on their first meeting and tried to calm himself, scared of what he might do. He looked around for Spencer; hoping no one had noticed his panic. The team was getting ready to go, the atmosphere fantastic again, relief that their possessions were returned and finally able to celebrate the result. Spencer, as if aware that Jamie was watching him, turned to speak. His hair was behaving strangely, as if it was affected by static electricity and he had a weird look on his face.

He smirked at Jamie. "Lost anything? I saw you looking in the bag. Did you find it?"

"I think you and I both know the answer to that!"

"I really don't know what you're implying," remarked Spencer with a grin reaching into his pocket to touch something.

"Is that a fact," countered Jamie taking a step closer, "I thought you and I were okay? I've done nothing to offend you and if you've got my property, which I'm guessing you have, then I'd like it back. Please."

"Well, if that's how you feel, you'll have to physically get it from me."

"I'm not interested in fighting with you Spencer. If I wanted to, I'd really do some damage."

Spencer laughed, "That's a shame, as I'd like to see what you can do." He paused for a moment, studying Jamie to see how he'd react, and then appeared to make a decision. "Somehow you're behind what happened the other day."

"Don't be ridiculous Spencer, you and I know that would be impossible."

"Well, whatever. If, I have your thing, if, then I'm keeping it unless you want to do something about it." And with that, he picked up his stuff and followed the others out of the changing room. Jamie wasn't sure what to do, but he was certain where the orb was and followed Spencer onto the bus smarting with anger. He was unsure how to get it back with actually hurting Spencer.

Spencer turned and waved, which made up his mind. He felt his anger return with a flash and he dropped his bag ready to engage Spencer. He was oblivious to the genial atmosphere of the team. Spencer was going to get it. He took a step forward fists

136

clenched when the world stopped, shifted and he felt himself falling, falling…

Training of a sort

Until…

He fell with a thump to the floor.

Feeling slightly dazed and disorientated, Jamie looked about him but he wasn't surprised, he knew where he was. Shaking his head he got to his feet and staggered for a moment before his equilibrium centred again. He was back in the warrior's tent. Nothing had changed from his last visit, except it was perceptibly lighter; possibly earlier in whatever day he'd materialised in. He looked around but couldn't see anyone. Suddenly a roar of noise from above him made him dive to the floor covering his ears. Whatever it was screamed overhead and exploded far enough away for him not to be in any danger, but close enough for his ears to ring.

He got to his feet again and shook his head to clear the buzzing in his ears. Despite the tinnitus he could hear hoots of maniacal laughter from outside and then orders being shouted in a language he couldn't quite understand. He hurriedly calmed himself and readied for whatever was coming next, as a large flap in the front of the tent opened wide and the warrior strode in followed by a slightly more diminutive figure. The other person quietly made their way into the shadows as the warrior strode forward still laughing.

"What was that?" Jamie asked.

It took a moment for the warrior to compose himself. "Just a few tests we are doing on a new weapon. The picture on your wall jogged my memory somewhat and my trusted scientists are doing their best to produce something that might fly. It makes a lot of noise when ejected from the catapult, but then explodes quite dramatically. It does make me laugh, although

I've lost ten of my finest men." The warrior shrugged. "All part of their duty."

He held out his hand but Jamie was unsure of how he should react. "Don't keep me waiting," the warrior snarled.

"Sorry," stammered Jamie, before offering his own hand. The warrior clasped it and gave it a squeeze. Jamie winced slightly as the warrior held on. Beads of sweat sprung out on his nose as the pain intensified, but the warrior quickly let go. Jamie tried hard not to react.

"Good to see you again my young friend," he said. Again the mask covered his face, but the voice rang out clearly through the room as if they were in an amphitheatre and his eyes shone with amusement. "You made it here on your own this time."

Jamie was amazed. "You mean you had nothing to do with it?"

The warrior snickered not unkindly. "All your own doing."

"Wow!"

"Indeed." The eyes changed as the warrior obviously frowned. "Where is the orb?"

Jamie shrank back frightened by the intensity of the warrior's voice. "I've lost it!" He managed to stammer.

"You've done what?" the warrior roared.

"I've lost it," Jamie repeated scared now.

The warrior took a step forward. "That was foolish," he growled. "I presume that your nemesis has it?"

"Yes. Somehow, he managed to get it from me."

"You should have been more careful. But," he added brightly his anger gone as quickly as it had appeared, "it does mean that you'll fail in your quest and that your soul will be mine."

Jamie stamped his foot and his voice echoed around the tent. "No! I will not be staying here!"

"Excellent. You are angry again. You could just

139

take it back you know. It wouldn't be hard, but everyone would see you as you really are."

"Which is?" said Jamie angrily. He was without his version of the orb, but he still felt power beneath the surface of his anger.

"A warrior. Like me. You could take anything in your world if you so wished."

"That's not would I wish for."

"You might," the warrior goaded.

Jamie exploded again and his voice bellowed in the tent. "I WILL NOT!"

The warrior snorted nastily, venom in his voice. "I might just send you back now and watch proceedings unfold. In your present state you would easily get the orb back, but you would definitely lay waste to whosoever got in your way. That would be most amusing. Quite brutal I should imagine. I'd love to see that sort of power unleashed on your world." The warrior thought for a moment then began to wave his hands. Jamie could feel the air begin to shimmer and his reality began to shift. "I think that's what I will do."

"No! Please!" pleaded Jamie. The warrior's eyes glinted with amusement and the world stopped spinning. He forced himself to calm and took deep breaths. "What alternative do I have?"

"You stay here with me!"

Jamie sank to the floor in despair and sobbed, "So I have to stay here then?"

"Well it's that or potentially murder your entire team to retrieve the orb."

Jamie cried out. Tears of despair poured down his face. "I couldn't do that. I'll have to stay."

The warrior patted his shoulder and put a hand under his armpit hoisting him up. Jamie looked him in the eyes. "There is an alternative. I was just testing you."

Jamie dared not hope but with a shaking voice pleaded. "Anything."

"Be careful what you agree to."

Jamie sighed heavily and held his head in his hands saying nothing. He desperately wanted to go home, but figured silence might be the best policy. Hear what the warrior had to offer.

"Stand up and stop feeling sorry for yourself." Jamie did as he was asked and looked the warrior in the eye. "Better," he said. "Now, it appears that you have helped the second person on your quest for the wish. I suppose begrudgingly this needs some congratulation." The warrior started to clap slowly and sarcastically. "Oh well done. The orb, it seems, wishes to reward you."

Jamie perked up at this. The orb? Was it here? Had the warrior sorted out his mess for him? Had he read the situation all wrong?

The warrior seemed to read his mind. "Not your version of the orb but mine." He held his in his hand and it glowed with an icy blue intensity that reflected off the obsidian material of his armour.

Jamie's hopes were dashed in an instant and his face made no attempt to hide it. "Oh" was all he could manage.

"You are beginning to try my patience with your attitude." The warrior glared at Jamie. "You have one more chance to be more appreciative or this whole charade will end." Jamie stood to attention and nodded. "Better. The orb in your time and in mine is one and the same. At the moment I am resisting, but it wishes to reward you with more power."

Jamie finally found his voice. "Power?"

"Have you not noticed? The fireball you produced here is its most raw and destructive element. You could produce that at any time which is why sending you home would be most interesting." Jamie nodded and he continued. "You can levitate, a most calming attribute, and you have mastered the art of possession it seems."

"Possession?"

"Please stop repeating me." The warrior snapped. Jamie hung his head as the warrior composed himself. "Putting a suggestion into those sporting gauntlets was most ingenious. I am quite impressed. That boy you helped will change dramatically as a result. His original destiny has changed and he will live a longer more fruitful life as a consequence. His life will not end at the base of a cliff as before."

Jamie was horrified at the suggestion that his friend would have chosen to have done such a thing. The warrior watched Jamie and added. "That will not happen now, thanks to your intervention. His perception of himself is now different. He has confidence, which was not there before. The orb too, is impressed. I am sure you are beginning to realise that it has an identity of its own."

Jamie nodded not wishing to aggravate the warrior further. "I often wonder whether the orb controls me at times, but I am struggling to stop it from granting you more power." The warrior's eyes glinted. "It definitely likes this game and it likes you. There has been no one quite like you for generations and it won't allow me to just destroy you."

The warrior paused to allow his words to sink in. "You are no match for me and besides I am enjoying the challenge that someone as young as you is posing. Most intriguing. Your world too is one I had forgotten existed and it is most," he paused for a moment thinking, "barbaric." He laughed.

He shuddered for a moment and concentrated hard as the orb attempted to leave his hand. "Not so fast little one. I will allow you both your moment, but only if you agree to return. That is the bargain. It would do me great harm, but I could still stop this little reunion and you would stay here with me forever."

Jamie thought furiously. Should he take his chance that the orb might break free? He glanced at the warrior's gloved fist as it closed on the orb and decided against it. He nodded in agreement.

"Good. There is much that you and I should discuss and I know you will be needing me again."

Jamie began to protest, but the warrior held up his hand warning against such insubordination. "As I said before, the orb will grant you more power. I have a feeling that if used properly it may help you with the dilemma you face. If not, well…" The warrior left that phrase hanging in the air for effect and Jamie shuddered.

"Ready?" the warrior asked.

"Yes," replied Jamie.

"Did it hurt last time?" asked the warrior.

Jamie shook his head.

The warrior grunted. "That's a shame. Oh well! It might this time. Be prepared." He held out the orb, which shone with a piercing blue. It began to revolve slowly on its axis and floated to a space between them both. The warrior folded his arms and tilting his head with interest, watched in silence. Jamie stood and waited. The final comment of the warrior startled him a bit. Painful? Last time it was peaceful. Wonderful.

Jamie eyed this other orb with trepidation. The fact that it wasn't his, but was the same thing was utterly baffling, but he had to accept that this was real. Just in another time and space. It begin to spin with more urgency and blue, iridescent sparks flew off in all directions. He readied himself and breathed deeply but the blast of energy that shot from the revolving sphere and into his chest still took him by surprise and he cried out.

Jamie's body shook as energy from the orb invaded his whole body. Involuntarily his arms raised in a V and he could feel his toes lift off of the floor. He cried out. This felt entirely different from last time! His whole body felt as though invisible spiders were crawling through it anaesthetising him with incapacitating bites. He continued to lift off the floor and he shook violently until one final blast of energy pulsated through his whole body. It was so intense he thought his head would explode and then it left him. He cried out again and crumpled to the floor in a heap.

He lay on the floor literally tingling. A distant part of him mused that this must be how people who were struck by lightning must feel. He was reluctant to rise just yet, thankful he'd survived and he explored his mind to see if anything was different. He searched for a clue that might give him some sort of advantage over the warrior. He remained quiet and searched. He definitely felt different. Invigorated, as though fresh from an icy cold shower he felt more positive and an inkling of what he now had the potential to do was tantalisingly close. He had no more time to explore this as the warrior's voice brought him back to reality.

"How do you feel?"

"Terrific." Jamie couldn't lie and he got up.

"So you should. That was most enlightening."

"Did that happen to you?"

"Yes it did. I remember it well."

"So what happens next?"

"We try to harness your new talent."

"Do you know what it is?" Jamie asked and the warrior nodded in assent.

"Do you have any idea?" he asked.

Jamie thought about this and an understanding began to dawn on him. "Does it have something to do

144

with seeing or not seeing?"

"Good, allow it to take a hold." The warrior's gaze bored into him and he had to look away.

Jamie closed his eyes and concentrated. A flash of inspiration jolted through him and he frowned. "How will that help?" he asked.

"Being able to evade your enemies and move around unseen is a most favourable skill to have."

"You mean I can become invisible?"

"Not as such, but it will alter other people's sight. They will look at you, but they will not see what is really there."

"But I will still be there?"

"Oh yes, and if someone walks into you they will get a surprise."

"Wow! Can you show me?" Jamie asked a now empty tent. Despite himself he laughed out loud. "Where are you?"

"I am still here," came the warrior's voice from the spot where he was just standing. "I haven't moved. Tell me what you see."

Jamie squinted and then opened his eyes. "I see the tent, but where you were standing is slightly out of focus. It's like I can see through you. If I didn't know you'd been there a second ago I'd be none the wiser."

"Very good," said the warrior as he materialised. "You try."

"How?"

"Think about being somewhere else with one part of your mind but never forget with the other where you are. If you can master that you will remain out of sight to others. Try it with your hands."

Jamie did as he was asked and tried to pretend that his hands were at home stroking Duster. He concentrated on them and he thought he saw them shimmer slightly. He peered hard but they certainly

145

didn't disappear. Suddenly the warrior laughed and exclaimed. "A good effort. You learn quickly."

Jamie lost the connection with home and frowned at the warrior. "But nothing happened."

"You will never see the results. In your mind's eye, you will remain where you physically are. It is others that lose the perception that you are there with them."

"So what happened then?"

"Your left hand and three of the fingers on your right hand vanished from my sight. You will need practice to perfect it, but a good start nevertheless."

Jamie felt quite satisfied. It was the first real time that the warrior had shown any real admiration that wasn't heavily scented with sarcasm. He shook off this feeling quickly, not wanting to come attached to this frankly scary and unpredictable person. He tried again and pictured his whole body at home at his desk doing his homework. He watched fascinated as his body shimmered and looked at the warrior, whose eyes widened. Jamie nodded and moved away from the warrior. The warrior's eyes stayed where they were, but then recognised the movement in the air and followed Jamie's progress. He clapped his hands.

"Excellent work. Be careful of your legs. They kept appearing, but with practice you will remain invisible to others." The warrior nodded again in appreciation. "If you master the art you can extend the illusion to objects and even to other people. Watch."

The warrior clapped his hand three times in quick succession and a figure approached carrying a jar. Jamie gasped as the figure came into the light. Dressed in simple armour, the figure held the jar in front of her with long elegant fingers. She was the same height and age as Jamie, with medium length jet-black hair. Jamie couldn't shake off the feeling that he was looking at his own reflection in a mirror. Her features appeared to emulate his own. She acknowledged neither of them and placed the jar carefully on the ground before disappearing back into the shadows. He was aware of the warrior studying him as he watched the girl leave.

"Who was that?" Jamie managed to say.

"Did you like what you saw?"

"I thought she was familiar."

The warrior laughed out loud dismissing the notion. "We'll save her identity for another time. Now watch the jar."

Jamie was too perturbed by the appearance and familiarity of the silent girl to concentrate wholly on the jar until it vanished.

"Can I do that?"

"You could try, but for the moment this will be beyond you."

Jamie nodded. "Can I go home now?"

"Yes it is time. Remember if all else fails you can still take the orb by force," remarked the warrior as the now familiar feeling of displacement began to make Jamie's stomach turn.

I should be used to this he thought as he struggled to keep the contents of his stomach in check. The world shifted away from his feet and he found himself back outside the school mini-bus. His legs wobbled as the world started again and he stepped carefully onto the bus, anxious to hide his feelings. He knew he had to remain as calm as possible. If he lost his temper, things would get really nasty. He breathed deeply and took a seat away from everyone else on the bus.

Surveillance tactics

On the noisy bus ride home, Jamie did his best to join in the merriment, but his mind reeled with conflicting emotions. The visit to the strange warrior and the receiving of the power still made his skin tingle. He looked over at Calum who was laughing and joking with the twins and felt real satisfaction. The thought that his friend would lead a happy life now was excellent news, but it really frightened him to think that it could have been so different. He shuddered and tried to think about something else.

The appearance of the girl had shocked him. Who was she? The fact that he thought she resembled him in some way added to his unease, but he dismissed it quickly as he launched into another song on autopilot trying to be like everyone else. He tried affecting the same air of jocularity as the others until he caught Spencer grinning at him in triumph.

The anger that he felt at the loss of the orb and Spencer's continued harassment irked him. The orb wasn't in Jamie's possession, but he knew that he could lash out catastrophically if he was pushed. He ignored him as best as he could, but it was really hard. He had to get the orb back.

Thankfully Jamie managed to avoid any more eye contact with Spencer and the journey ended. He breathed a sigh of relief. As they stepped off the bus Jamie said his goodbyes to the others. He knew he'd be walking home alone, but he looked around to see if anyone was there to pick up Spencer. He watched as his ever-apparent foe looked around for a minute or two, before he appeared to sigh and then started to trudge home. Before he did, he turned and gave Jamie a cheerful wave. Jamie felt sparks of electricity crackle from his fingers, but he forced himself to be calm, and as he was guided, began to imagine himself elsewhere. He pictured himself in the warrior's tent as he followed Spencer at a safe distance.

Despite the distance between them, Jamie felt connected to the orb. He thought of the girl in the tent and her mysterious appearance. He was aware of the light around him behaving differently and he hoped that he was now undetectable to the retreating Spencer.

He wasn't entirely certain, but he felt different. A tingling sensation crept from the floor enveloping him till it reached his head. His nose itched and he scratched it, curiously. He couldn't be invisible could he? There was only one way to find out. Spencer set off home striding purposefully through the village, with Jamie a safe distance behind. He didn't bother to look back.

At one point Jamie, tripped over a bump in the pavement with a loud clatter and jumped up certain that he'd been caught, but Spencer hadn't even faltered in his stride. It was twilight and gloomy, but his feeling of invisibility grew stronger and his nose itched again almost making him sneeze. He stifled the explosion, he might be invisible, but that would definitely give him away. The sneeze died away and he crept closer to Spencer, gaining in confidence.

When Spencer reached the edge of the river close to both of their houses Jamie was only a couple of metres behind. Where is he going? Jamie thought to himself. Despite his apparent invisibility, he took no chances and slid behind a tree to watch. This time Spencer did look around to ensure that he was alone and appeared to gaze straight at Jamie. He froze. Had Spencer smiled knowingly? Whatever the case he made no attempt to hide the fact of what he was planning and there was nothing Jamie could do to stop it without revealing himself. He was tempted to attack, but again he held himself back.

He took out the orb from his pocket and casually tossed it from hand to hand, before taking aim and throwing it into the middle of the fast flowing river with a resounding splash. Satisfied, he slapped his hands together as if ridding himself of something dirty and with a jaunty skip disappeared off into the gathering gloom.

Jamie waited a minute or two to be sure Spencer had gone before he ran to the edge of the river. He was desperate to jump in, terrified that the orb was lost forever as he tried to peer into its depths. He looked around frantically, but couldn't see it. He wasn't sure he'd see it in the daylight and distraught he fell to his knees.

In desperation, he held out his hands and called out to it. Instantly, the water in the middle of the river glowed brightly in answer. It was safe, thank goodness. His breathing returned to normal. He called again to make sure it wasn't being swept away and the same bright glow appeared in reply in the same position.

He tried once more and again the effect was the same, but this time an image flashed into his mind. It was of a rock and Jamie knew instantly that the orb was stuck and Jamie wasn't yet powerful enough to move a rock by sheer will. He was tempted to ask the warrior for help, but was determined to do things his way.

He thought for a minute panting with exertion, his head ached with a dull throb. He realised that now was not a good time to clamber out into the river, because it was far too deep and really he needed his wetsuit and goggles. He found a distinctive stone which he placed a metre back from the water's edge and used the church tower and the tree he was hiding behind to tri-angulate his position. He resolved to get up early and rescue the orb in the morning, as it was Saturday. He just hoped

150

the orb would still be there. He stood up and calmed himself and nodded satisfied. It was safe for the moment. He had to trust his instincts.

He didn't like it, but it was the best he could do in the situation and with mixed feelings about a quite extraordinary day, traipsed home to reluctantly celebrate with his family.

Problems with water

The radio clicked on and a faint hint of jazz brought Jamie out of his reverie. With a contented stretch he yawned. He was about to swing his legs out of bed and start a well-deserved weekend when the seriousness of his dilemma slammed into him like a punch in the face from a heavyweight boxer. The orb! It was still dark outside and he knew now was no time for relaxing as the gravity of his situation dawned on him.

Jamie checked his clock. It was early, good. His mind cleared quickly and he went over the plan he'd made the night before. The supper had gone well and he'd tried hard to join in but he was pre-occupied. His mother had asked if his eyes were all right at one point. He'd forgotten about that as he now studied them in the mirror. They'd changed again and now had a hint of green about them. He'd dismissed this as tiredness and he'd caught the look his grandma had given him, but he was too worried to sit up and discuss it with her. Once he'd retrieved the orb safely, he'd share all his latest news with her. If he got through it that is.

He'd retrieved his wetsuit from the top shelf of his wardrobe before he went to sleep last night and it lay on his chair. Duster, sensing an adventure, had jumped off the bed and was snuffling around the wetsuit, tail thumping loudly against his desk. He knew that it meant a watery quest of some kind, as Jamie only wore it if he went body boarding or out in the rowing boat during the winter.

"Shh!" admonished Jamie, calming the dog down with a frown and a ruffle of his fur. "Be quiet! We mustn't wake up Mum and Dad."

Jamie popped on a pair of swimmers and pointing his toes struggled into the wetsuit. The neoprene material squealed in protest, but finally he squeezed both legs in. He pulled up the suit to his waist, the top half still to do. He took a deep breath and encouraged his left arm into the hole. His torso ached in protest after yesterday's game.

With a sigh, he managed to get his right arm into the other hole, only the zip up the back remained. Jamie reached around, caught the zipper and slowly began to zip it up, fearful of getting it tangled and having to begin the whole process again. Slowly, slowly, slowly. Duster watched him, tail thumping, encouraging him on, but disaster struck as the zip became caught. He tried to force it back down again, but it was jammed. He cursed silently. He was in, but not completely. It would have to do, a bit of wetsuit was better than none at all.

He opened his door and avoided the creaky floorboards as he made his way silently downstairs. He opened the kitchen door allowing Duster to follow and closed it again. He walked over to the fridge and retrieved an apple for his breakfast.

"Morning Jamie," said a quiet voice behind him. Jamie dropped the apple with a start and it bounced across the kitchen floor towards Duster. Never one to say no to food, he snaffled up the present in his mouth and disappeared out of the dog door, leaving it flapping back and forth, to eat it in private. Jamie turned around and faced his grandma. "Where are you off to this early in the morning?" she asked.

Jamie knew there was absolutely no point lying to her. He quickly told her about yesterday's events with Spencer and urged her not to tell Mum and Dad where he was if they got up before he returned. He told her there was more, but that would have to wait until later. She looked unsure of this but Jamie pleaded with her that he had to go now. She agreed with reluctance and

153

she helped Jamie sort out the mess he'd made of his zip. She gave him another apple, insisting he wore his wet weather gear over his wetsuit, and ushering him out the door telling him to be careful.

"I will Grandma. Please don't worry." She smiled as she shut the door, but he could sense she was concerned. The weather had been bad overnight with heavy rain and high winds. The river would be high and Grandma was concerned about its power today. Jamie was also anxious about the orb and whether or not it would actually still be there. He'd spent a good hour worrying that he'd made the right decision as he lay in bed last night listening to the rain. He decided to just trust his instincts. He'd done all right so far.

Jamie fetched the oars from the garden shed. He gave a low whistle and Duster trotted up happily. Together, they walked along the sodden garden path to the back gate. They passed through, clicking it gently closed behind them and walked down to the river's edge and the private jetty where their rowing boat was moored.

The moment Jamie spied the river, he knew it was going to be difficult. The water was brown and flowing much faster than it did usually. The level was high, not treacherously so, but enough to warrant extra care. Under normal circumstances he wouldn't actually have gone on the river, but this wasn't a normal situation. He worried for a moment that the boat had been swept away as he couldn't immediately see it. The rope that held it moored to their small jetty was gone too. Duster was completely unbothered by the state of things and was busily snuffling in the undergrowth, presumably for a stick for Jamie to throw into the river, a regular game for them both. He whistled again and Duster appeared instantly, ears cocked and head on one side, stick in mouth ready to play.

"Not today boy. Too dangerous to throw in the river today." Duster seemed to understand, dropped his stick and trotted down to the jetty. He peered over the edge and barked a couple of times. "What have you found?" Jamie asked, as he joined his dog carefully at the edge of the soggy wooden platform. As he looked over he saw the rope submerged in the water, stretched to near breaking point. He followed the line and presumed that the boat was safe judging by the tautness in the rope.

He stepped off the jetty and began to walk downstream along the river bank. Duster ran around him nearly tripping him up, getting more and more excited. There was nothing he liked more than a trip on the boat.

Jamie had spied a large willow tree ten metres away, with its fronds gently tickling the water. The rope appeared to disappear into it and as he reached the tree, he carefully pushed aside some branches to peer inside. Nestled in the gloom was the boat, but his heart sank. The cover had been torn and judging by the weird angle it was in, it looked to have taken on water. The river's current under the willow was not strong, but it did look quite deep.

Jamie came out from the depths of the tree and thought for a moment, panic beginning to set in. He forced himself to calm and made up his mind. Decision made, he ducked back in and jumped in the river. The water was freezing and it took his breath away. He shivered instantly. He wasn't looking forward to swimming later, but he may not even be doing that if the boat was in trouble. He splashed over to the stricken boat and when he reached it, his worst fears were realised. The boat had sunk overnight. It had taken on so much water that one edge had obviously dipped into the river allowing more water to flood in. It also looked as though one of the bungs was missing. It was obvious that this little craft was going nowhere. He clambered out from underneath the willow tree and kicked out at the bank in frustration. Duster was waiting.

"What do we do now then boy?" he muttered. Duster barked a couple of times and started to run back to the house. "Where are you off to?" he called following. Duster turned and ran back. He barked again and grabbed Jamie's laces in his teeth tugging them urgently. "What is the matter with you?"

An excited Duster made it back to the garden gate and not bothering to wait, sailed straight over it in one giant leap. "Show off!" Jamie muttered impressed, following him back into the garden through the gate. Duster raced up to the shed and nudged the door open. Jamie wasn't far behind him and when he went inside he found Duster sitting with his nose pointed up into the gloom of the roof. "What on earth?" said Jamie as he turned on the light, puzzled at the behaviour of his dog.

As the strip light flickered on Jamie looked up. Fastened to the ceiling was the family's rubber dinghy. It was a good quality one with reinforced sides and a wooden seat. It wasn't all that big, but it would accommodate them both. It would be a squeeze, but Duster was definitely not going to be left behind! Jamie gave him a pat and wondered idly if the orb had affected the dog too!

It took a couple of minutes, but Jamie soon had the dinghy down, pumped a little air in and squeezed the inflatable through the door of the shed. It wasn't going to be nearly as good on this type of water as the rowing boat, but in the circumstances it would just have to do and he knew that he had to hurry.

The dinghy was light enough for Jamie to carry above his head and he commandeered it down the jetty where he plonked it down. Duster jumped up and down, whining with anticipation. "Couple of minutes more boy, then we'll be gone." Duster woofed in acknowledgement as Jamie ran down to the stricken rowing boat to retrieve the anchor.

"We'll definitely need this today boy." Jamie tied the anchor, which was on a ten-metre length of rope, to the front of the dinghy and then carefully ran some of the rope around a cleat on the jetty, so the inflatable wouldn't float away. Crossing his fingers, Jamie carefully launched the boat into the river where it quivered in the river's strong current.

The change in vessel didn't deter Duster and he jumped in excitedly, happy and confident in boats. Jamie followed him more carefully with the oars. He sat down in the boat facing the stern and put the oars at his feet. He then picked up one oar and slotted it snugly into the rubber hole on one side of the boat and then repeated the process on the other side.

Satisfied that they were in and able to move about, he made sure that he had the anchor attached to the boat one more time before untying them from the jetty. He wasn't too worried about the fast flowing current sweeping him away the moment he untied them, as they had to go down-stream anyway, but he was going to need all his rowing skills to keep them in the centre of the river away from the more dangerous water at the banks.

He released the dinghy and pushed gently away from the jetty. The boat immediately reacted, almost excited to being on the fast flowing river. It was real shame they weren't in the rowing boat; a beautifully made vessel, with sleek lines and designed for moments such as this.

It didn't take them long to row to the markers Jamie had left the night before. He found the large rock quickly and manoeuvred the dinghy so he was in line with the church steeple on the other bank. He now had to row quite hard against the current, using each oar alternately to keep the nose of the inflatable into the current. He rowed back up stream for a few metres, knowing that the time it took to throw in the anchor the dinghy would zip downstream into the position he wanted to be in. Happy with the dinghy's position he popped the oars on the floor and threw the anchor off the front. It sank to the bottom quickly and became rigid almost instantly. They wouldn't be going anywhere for a while.

Duster barked excitedly as Jamie put his goggles on his head. He cleared his mind of all thoughts and then tried to connect with the orb, the way he had done the night before. No response. He tried once more and looked into the water hoping to see its comforting glow. Again nothing and the first feeling of dread began to creep into Jamie's thoughts. He was now sure that it had been swept away overnight.

He tried to clear the anxiety from his brain and then reached out as far as his mind would allow. He waited patiently trying desperately to remain to calm. The orb wasn't here, it must have been swept away. He cursed his decision to wait until morning and urgently tried to think of what to do.

He hauled up the anchor and instantly he and Duster were floating rapidly down-stream. After a minute or so he rounded a bend in the river and found some calmer water. He closed his eyes and concentrated hard trying to connect with the orb, but there was still nothing.

Utter despondency began to settle in, but in desperation he nosed the craft back into the current. It was beginning to pick up speed now, but Jamie no longer cared. A roar in the distance brought him back to reality. He blanched. The weir! The one place on the river he was forbidden to row anywhere near! He was floating quicker than he would have liked now towards it and he threw in the anchor.

The boat took another ten metres to stop and for one horrifying minute Jamie thought the whole thing was going to capsize when the anchor attached itself to something on the riverbed. They were thrown to the side of the dinghy as the whole vessel threatened to be literally flipped over. He threw himself to the other side to right it and finally it stopped bucking in the current. He sat back and breathed a sigh of relief. He tried to connect with the orb for one last time before he gave up completely.

This time there was success and Jamie cried out in relief. He concentrated hard and scanned the water around him. Slightly to starboard, he saw a faint glow under the surface of the water. His hands shook nervously as he attempted to put on his goggles. He told a fidgety Duster to sit still and then pencil-jumped into the water as close as he could to the rope attached to the anchor and surfaced clutching it. The water was pretty murky, so he couldn't see a great deal; he would have to be quick. He tried to connect to the orb again and frantically he began to search.

A faint glow indicated it had moved with the current, but this time closer to the inflatable. Jamie was a strong swimmer, but he wasn't sure he could swim up-stream, dive down and manage to get back to the dinghy without being a victim of the strong water himself. He took a deep breath and kicked away hard.

Being under the water was like being in another world. It was silent, but all around were signs of a maelstrom. Millions of bubbles of trapped air attacked him from all sides. It was if the river itself wanted to want to kill him and forcibly batter his body to bits. Added to the murderous nature of the river was flotsam and jetsam from upstream, which he tried to avoid without much success. He didn't have time to appreciate the sort of mortal peril that he was in and swam, or rather battled, in the direction of the orb.

He could see it. It was tantalisingly close and he reached out an outstretched hand to grab it, but at the last moment it shifted in the current. He momentarily lost sight of it and kicked up to the surface out of breath. He let the current take him, resting for a moment before grabbing the rope. He took a couple of deep breaths and kicked off again. The underwater world was just as menacing the second time and if anything, getting aggressively worse. Despite the battering of his senses he connected with the orb that glowed more brightly than before. He swam towards it as powerfully as he could and reached out with his hands.

The tips of his fingers brushed its smooth surface. It appeared to be nestling in some riverweed. It moved away from him as he dislodged it and looked about to be swept away when he made one last desperate grab for it. His fingers closed around it, but something bumped into him and he let it go. It swirled around him caught in an eddy of water and it took all his reserves of strength to keep from being swept away himself. The sphere hovered tantalisingly close, until he grabbed it and held on tight. He was rapidly running out of air and didn't waste any more time on the riverbed. He quickly spun round, kicked off the bottom of the river and shot up to the surface.

Jamie burst out of the water, gasping for air. He took a few deep breaths before he sensed that something was wrong. He didn't have time to assimilate the information as he grabbed the rope again with some relief and popped the orb safely into the dinghy. He began to haul himself into the boat unsure of why he felt so uneasy, when the truth of the situation hit him like a hammer blow. Duster was gone! Another bad decision! He shouldn't have brought him in the first place.

Stupid, stupid, stupid.

There was no time to berate himself now. Duster had been on the river many times before. That's why he'd brought him. He was a strong swimmer and he had to be close. Jamie looked upstream but shook his head. That shouldn't have happened, but Duster must have jumped in after him.

Jamie switched his attention to down river and thought he glimpsed a head swimming strongly for the far bank. He had no time to waste. He hauled himself into the boat as quickly as he could, donned a life jacket, grabbed the orb putting it in a secure pocket and threw himself into the river. He lay on his back, pointed out his toes, crossed his arms over his chest and rocketed along the current in pursuit.

It didn't take Jamie long to reach the corner and he swept around it. He slowed himself down marginally, by pushing his weight forward, and attempted to tread water whilst at the same time scanning the river. The noise of the weir was loud now but there was no time to be frightened. He suddenly caught sight of his dog, clearly struggling against the current and trying to make his way to the riverbank.

Jamie reached inside his wetsuit and put a hand on the orb. He felt its warmth and appealed to it for help to rescue Duster and to survive the danger of the weir. The connection was immediate and he felt the now familiar surge of magical power take over every cell in his body. He calmed and felt literally buoyed. He felt light and was sure that if he took off his life jacket he'd float! His mind cleared quickly and a plan formed in his mind; an insane and dangerous plan admittedly, but one that just might work. He looked around for Duster

161

again and whistled as loudly as he could. Duster's ears pricked up. He'd heard.

"Keep swimming Duster, I'm coming," Jamie shouted. He swivelled around so he was on his back and pointed his toes using them as a rudimentary rudder. The water was incredibly powerful as it was being sucked toward the weir. In his calm like state, he began to remember watching kayakers on days such as this use the weir in the past as a high-octane white water training facility. But he knew the dangers that low water dams such as these represented. The fast flowing water over the weir caused all kinds of problems.

Jamie had studied weirs at school. They were very powerful mini-waterfalls known as 'drowning machines', deadly traps of moving water. The only real way to survive these traps was to avoid them altogether, which is why going over them as the kayakers often did was seen as irresponsible. There had been many fatalities they'd been told by their Geography teacher.

Jamie eyed the weir with horror as he recalled how the water flows over the dam. It creates a circular pull of water towards the bottom of the weir called a hydraulic. This is what pulls a person back towards the dam, drags them underwater and repeats the process over and over. It's like being in a massive washing machine and once you're caught in it it's almost impossible to escape!

Jamie squeezed his arms into his side to make himself more aero dynamical and rapidly caught up with Duster who was tiring quickly. He called out. Duster looked at him vaguely, barely recognising his master. He urged him on. The dog responded and paddled the last few inches so Jamie could grab hold of his collar.

The adrenaline was pumping through his veins, and he easily heaved the sodden dog onto his chest, nose pointing at his chin. First part of the rescue achieved, now for the hard part. He took a deep breath and began to swim on his back towards the bank and away from the mayhem of the weir.

At first he was going nowhere, but another surge of energy gave him more power in his legs and he began to make progress to the riverbank. Suddenly, they were both hit by something hard. It ricocheted off them leaving Jamie slightly dazed and unsure of where he was for a moment and he stopped swimming. His senses came back quickly as Duster began to struggle in his arms and he realised that it was the dinghy that had hit them. He tightened his grip on his dog as he watched in dismay as the inflatable capsized and was swallowed up by the terrifying power of the weir. He didn't have time to think about what might happen to them, as the crest of the mini-waterfall was upon them with a terrifying roar.

They rocketed feet first over the weir at frightening speed. People would have paid good money to achieve such a mad experience if it was a ride at a theme park or at some water park in sunny Spain, but fun this was not and both Jamie and Duster were in mortal danger. They disappeared into the churning water and under the surface. They were buffeted like balls in a pinball machine, thrown around at will. Jamie's breath was about to go and a desperation began to set in, when they were both flung out of the water.

Jamie took a deep and welcome breath of air and Duster licked his face before they were sucked back into the churning water. Again they were pummelled and battered in the weir's awesome power. Jamie clung on to Duster, hooking his fingers into the dog's collar. Suddenly they found a calm column of water, not unlike the eye of the storm and Jamie had a moment to think.

They sank quickly to the bottom, whilst around them the water churned itself into a frenzy. Jamie's feet touched the bottom of the weir and with a silent admonishment to the orb for the expected and as yet unforthcoming help, kicked with all his might to the surface. The effect was extraordinary.

They both popped up to the surface like the cork from a champagne bottle. Jamie felt the power of the orb flow through him once again and it was as if he was riding a jet of water. The feeling was immense and if he wasn't out in the open, he would have been tempted to see if he could control the direction he was going in. He decided against it and allowed this strange force to fly them over the maelstrom and into the calmer water away from the weir with an enormous splash.

Again, Jamie went under the water, but this time they were not being sucked back into a terrifying vortex and were floating peacefully away downstream. He allowed himself a self-satisfied smile, but he had to admit that his exertions had exhausted him. He looked down at his dog, still held tightly in his arms and loosened his grip. He reached down to ruffle Duster's ears, but worryingly there was no response. He called out his name, adrenaline beginning to pump again through his veins, as he realised that something was dreadfully, terribly wrong.

Jamie tried to rouse the dog once more, but again there was no response. His heart sank with fear. He couldn't lose his dog, he just couldn't. He was so immersed in this fresh panic attack that it took him a while to realise that people were calling his name from the bank.

"Jamie! Jamie!" called one voice.

"Over here you flipping madman! What are you

like?" shouted another.

Jamie shook his head to clear it a little and looked over to the bank.

"We're here, on the other bank. It's us, Tommy and Calum. Swim over."

Despite his exhaustion and his panic, Jamie managed to swim with difficulty to the bank where his friends jumped into the shallow water to help pull them both out.

"Is your dog...?" Calum didn't really want to finish the question, unsure of the answer he might get.

"I don't think he's breathing," replied Jamie, dread evident in his quavering voice. Tears began to well up and he couldn't think straight. Tommy came over to have a look and confirmed his worst fears. Duster wasn't breathing.

"What are we going to do?" Tommy asked uncertainly. The orb vibrated strongly in Jamie's pocket and immediately there was clarity to his thoughts. He could breathe properly again and he instinctively knew what he had to do. He laid Duster on his side on the flattest surface he could find. The others watched with growing amazement.

Jamie watched Duster carefully. There was no rise or fall of his chest and he put his face close to his dog to feel for any breath. Nothing. He checked the dog's gums, which were blue, a sure sign of oxygen deprivation. He extended Duster's head and neck and opened his mouth to check for any foreign object. That wasn't the problem, so he began the rescue breathing. He lifted the dog's chin to straighten out his throat and used one hand to grasp his muzzle and hold his mouth shut. He put his mouth completely over Duster's nose and began to blow gently.

Duster's chest expanded with his breath, so he knew he had the right pressure. He waited for the air to leave

165

the lungs before he did it again three seconds later. He kept going for a couple of minutes before he felt a twitch of movement below him. He placed Duster's head gently on the grass and watched carefully.

Suddenly and without warning, Duster jerked violently before vomiting out a significant amount of water from his lungs. Jamie was about to start the artificial respiration again when Duster opened his eyes and began to wag his tail weakly. Tommy and Calum cheered and high fived each other as Jamie lay down next to Duster and gave him a hug. He was rewarded with weak lick. He was alive. Jamie had saved him.

He was still worried about Duster, but the relief of saving his dog and the magnitude of what he had just done hit him hard and his head began to spin. He wobbled about on his feet as he suddenly felt queasy and he sat down with a thump. He allowed his head to hit the floor and he passed out.

Jamie wasn't sure if he was awake or not, but he was aware of a bright light enveloping him in a cushion of harmony and serenity. As the light intensified, he knew for certain that he'd activated another facet of the orb's power. He'd achieved the third part of the quest by saving his dog. Unlike the previous occasion, this was more peaceful and he felt the power rejuvenating his tired body as it coursed through his veins. He allowed it in and in his dream-like state felt more beatific than at any other time in his life. If this is heaven he thought, I like it! He enjoyed the sensation for a while longer, but didn't have time consider what he might now be able to do when he felt someone shaking his shoulder.

"Jamie," he heard a concerned voice calling. "Jamie, are you all right?"

Jamie groaned, not wanting the sensation to stop. He opened his eyes experimentally. Peering over him was the concerned face of Tommy. "Yeah, I'm fine," he said sitting up.

"What's happened to your eyes?"

"My eyes?"

"Yeah, they look a bit weird. I don't remember them being that colour."

Jamie laughed. "Nah mate, they've always been this colour."

Tommy shrugged. "Are you sure you're okay? You were thrashing about there for a moment. I tried to touch you, but got a bit of a shock."

"I have that effect on people," he answered. "Static I think."

"Oh, okay."

"Where's Duster?"

"He's over here," Calum called. "He's fine. Come on boy. Over you come." A bedraggled Duster came and lay down with a thump next to Jamie who squeezed him gently.

"What were you doing anyway?" asked Calum.

"It's a long story. I was trying to retrieve my winner's medal from the river. Spencer stole it after yesterday's match and threw it in." The other boys frowned ominously. "I wasn't expecting it to be such an adventure getting it back. What happened?"

"Well, Tommy and I went for an early morning bike ride. We were still buzzing after yesterday and for some reason we rode down to check out the weir.

"We were watching the water crash over taking some footage on our phones, thinking how cool it would be to kayak over it, when we saw this dinghy fly over. Talk about an action shot! We didn't have time to think about that when something else came hurtling down the stream towards us. As soon as we realised it was a person, we just knew it was you. You flew over it like a torpedo and then vanished!"

"Yeah, mate," Tommy continued, "we thought you were a goner for sure. We were desperately trying to spot you when you appeared, but then disappeared again. I was about to strip off and dive in when incredibly you came flying out. How on earth did you manage that?"

Jamie thought for a moment, torn between lying to his friends and revealing the truth. He felt a lot better and Duster was now wagging his tail almost normally and was beginning to move around without too much trouble. He made his decision and thought it was better to keep them in the dark. The less people close to him were involved the better. He didn't trust the real motives of the warrior.

"I've no idea," Jamie lied. "I just kicked out and felt myself lift off. Perhaps a current caught hold of me and my momentum carried me out."

"Some current!"

"Yeah. Wasn't it? Lucky it was there. Think we had a lucky escape."

"Did you get the medal after all that?"

Jamie patted his jacket and nodded. He gave his dog another pat and changed the subject. "Come on, I think we should get Duster checked out by the vet."

Calum and Tommy looked at each other and Tommy raised an eyebrow. "Sure pal."

Calum scooped Duster up into his arms and received a friendly lick for his troubles and together they made their way back to Jamie's.

What would you wish for?

Jamie and Tommy had retrieved the bikes and quickly sped along the river path looking for the dinghy. They didn't look for long and found it nestled on a shingle beach. Jamie jumped down and pulled it up, securing it safely to a tree to pick up later. They caught up with Calum who was struggling with a squirming dog.

"I think he wants to get down, Calum," Jamie said. Calum allowed him to jump down and although not his usual energetic self, he was soon snuffling about for rabbits.

Reaching the Lomax house, they'd clattered into the warm and inviting kitchen and thumped themselves down noisily at the table. They watched as Duster flopped into his bed beside the Aga and within seconds was asleep on his back with his legs in the air.

"Breakfast for three is it?" smiled Jamie's grandma good-naturedly as she came into the room.

"Yes please," came a chorus of voices.

Jamie's Mum came in. She bade them all good morning and asked where they'd been. Jamie couldn't lie to his mum, but he was economical with the truth as he told her about the early morning trip in the boat. They'd all agreed not to talk about the weir incident, but Jamie felt that Duster needed to be checked out by the vet, so he told her about fishing him out of the water and the artificial respiration. Like Jamie's friends, she was amazed and a little puzzled.

"How on earth did you know how to do that?" she asked.

"I read about it somewhere," he fibbed, "and it must have lodged firmly at the back of my brain."

"Well whatever or however you knew, you're my little hero." She grabbed him and gave him a huge hug.

The other boys started to snigger as Jamie attempted to release himself.

"Mum!" he protested, "Get off." She let go of him, only to grab him again and plant a smacker on the top of his head for the benefit of the others.

"You're still my little boy," she teased. "Well done though. I'll give the vet a ring," she said as she got on all fours to check on Duster. She rubbed his tummy and his back legs began to move at the same time. She laughed. "He seems okay, but it's definitely worth having him checked out."

It was as they were tucking in to bacon and eggs that the vet arrived to give Duster the once over. The story was repeated and the vet, not usually prone to admiration, whistled in appreciation at Jamie's decisive and life-saving action as she checked Duster's vitals. Apart from a slightly damaged throat caused by retching up all the river water, Duster was given the all clear. The dog, as ever, took this good news with dedicated doggy grace, turned three times in his bed, scratched behind his ears and promptly fell back to sleep.

With breakfast over, the boys cleared the table and Grandma brought over three steaming cups of hot chocolate leaving them to discuss the morning's exciting events. They trooped upstairs to Jamie's bedroom and sat on the floor. Jamie asked if they had any footage of the weir incident. Tommy nodded and showed him.

"Wow!" exclaimed Jamie nervously, as they watched the terrifying recording. "I was so lucky to have survived that."

"You're not kidding," agreed Calum, "did you see what it did to your dinghy? I'm still amazed you're okay."

"It's all Spencer's fault," grumbled Tommy.

"Not much we can do about him," Calum murmured. "At least he's less of a menace at school."

"Let's not talk about him. Thanks for your help today," Jamie said. "Can we talk about something else?"

"What about yesterday's game?"

"Great idea!"

All three boys replayed the game in every detail. Calum talked about the save and revealed he'd been scouted for a local team.

"That's brilliant."

"Awesome."

"Bet you wouldn't have wished for that a couple of days ago."

"True. Hey, here's a question. What would you wish for if you could?"

"Now there's a problem."

Jamie watched his friends with interest. He'd spent no real time thinking about this, not daring to dream for fear of ever fulfilling the prophecy. He was interested in what his friends had to say, although a part of him wanted to share more.

"Another three wishes, obviously," decided Calum with finality and crossed his arms.

"No way!" spluttered Jamie. "You can only have one wish!"

"But that was my wish," countered Calum.

"No genie would accept that," laughed Tommy.

"Why not?"

"It's not very honest is it?"

Calum thought about it for a moment and shrugged. "Okay, just the one wish then."

They were all quiet for a moment until Tommy suggested, "Fame and fortune. More money than you could know what to do with."

"Tempting, very tempting, but again it doesn't quite

feel right," argued Jamie.

"What's the matter with you?" Tommy goaded punching him lightly on the arm. "You could buy whatever you want. Clothes, cars, houses, even a flipping football club! Mate, you could even leave school, you'd be so wealthy and get some young yummy tutor to look after you."

Jamie smiled thoughtfully at that, but then frowned. "Even so, but all that money would mean I could have whatever I want, whenever I want it."

"Duh! What's wrong with that?"

"Well it's just the same as asking for more than one wish. You could get what you want without ever having to lift a finger. Where's the fun in that? The best bit about getting something you want is the fun in saving up for it in the first place."

"You're seriously weird."

"Maybe, but think about it for a minute. Say you want something desperately, a new bike perhaps, and you get it by hassling your parents, or they simply buy it for you because they can afford it. How do you feel?"

There was a pause as the boys thought about it.

"Good point. I'd hate that," confirmed Calum with a frown.

"Me too, it wouldn't feel quite right. I don't think I'd enjoy riding it quite so much."

"And if you'd saved up for it yourself?"

"Totally different. You'd have earned it."

"Okay, we've gone off the point a bit," said Tommy. "I'd wish to be able speak any language on the planet so I could work in any country."

"Good choice Tommy," agreed Jamie. "Calum?"

"I think I'd like to pick up any instrument and play it at expert level."

"Useful for impressing girls Calum. Excellent thinking," said Tommy. "Jamie?"

"Um, world peace?" Jamie ventured knowing it would wind up the other two.

"You what?" spluttered Tommy.

"Who are you trying to impress?" laughed Calum.

"JC obviously," teased Tommy. "I've seen the way you look at her."

"How I look at her?"

"Yeah. A bit like this." And they watched as Tommy, pursed his lips and fluttered his eyelashes. "Jamie loves JC."

Calum doubled over with laughter.

"I do not."

"I think you do."

"Right that's it!" Jamie stated as he picked up a pillow. "You need to shut up now or Mr Pillow is coming to meet your face," said Jamie, playfully thumping Tommy with the nearest cushion. Tommy responded and within moments the conversation was over and a pillow fight had broken out. Just as the fight was beginning to escalate, Jamie's Dad walked in with Duster close behind. He just raised an eyebrow and smiled.

"Morning boys."

"Morning Mr Lomax." The boys stopped instantly and hid their pillows behind their backs. Jamie's Dad came over to his son and ruffled his head affectionately.

"Mum told me about your heroics with the dog. Great job. He seems okay now." He bent down and nudged Duster with his head. Duster immediately rolled onto his back. "Nothing wrong with him then," chuckled Dad as he scratched the dog behind his ears. "What are you guys up to for the rest of the day? Game of football?"

All the boys groaned and Jamie's dad laughed. "I guess not."

"If you're not busy Dad, the rowing boat has been damaged and has taken on water. It needs rescuing."

"I tell you what boys, there's some extra cash in it for you guys if you manage to get it back to the garden and then I'll help you fix it. What's the river like today? Should we go fishing?"

All the boys looked at each other and groaned again.

"What did I say?" said Jamie's dad puzzled.

"Nothing Dad. We'll see you outside. Any chance we could go to the cinema instead?"

Duster looked up at them both and barked once, loudly.

"Cinema it is then. See you all outside in a bit." And with that, Duster yawned, jumped onto Jamie's bed and went back to sleep.

Later that day an exhausted Jamie flopped melodramatically at the kitchen table and frowned at the calendar he'd brought down from his room. The movie at the cinema had been an action movie and it was only the amount of successive explosions and gun battles that had kept him awake. Dad had come home and whisked Mum off for a drink at the pub, so he had an opportunity to chat with his grandma. He really only wanted to go to bed. It had been a gruelling last couple of days and he couldn't wait to go to sleep.

His attention returned to the calendar and with some satisfaction he noticed that he'd helped three people in a week. Seven days were crossed off. At this rate he'd have it all sorted by next Wednesday. He laughed grimly to himself. It definitely wasn't going to be that easy was it? He felt sure that the warrior wouldn't let him win this easily! He looked at the calendar and sighed. Next Saturday was his fifteenth birthday. For most teenagers this would have been a good thing, but birthdays, especially his, in this household were torrid affairs.

His mother, despite her initial bonhomie, would collapse into a wreck at some point in the day. Jamie's birthday also represented his twin sister's anniversary and despite her best efforts to enjoy his day, his mother, usually strong, never failed in getting terrible upset. Dad too was generally quieter and Jamie suspected that when he was older and moved out it would be better not to celebrate this day with his parents at all. Besides, they never really got him a significant present. Mum revealed that it didn't feel right, so he had to ask for the bigger presents at Christmas. A voucher for an online bookstore and a cake was all he generally received.

Jamie sat at the table staring at the date wondering what she'd have been like, his sister. He thought back to the strange girl he met the last time he was with the warrior, which in hindsight he felt sure had been orchestrated. The similarities between them in the briefest glimpse he'd had was unnerving. But it could only have been a coincidence. They couldn't have been related, it just wasn't possible, but in this, the strangest of weeks ever, anything was possible.

His grandma sat down next to him and asked if he was okay. He smiled and said he was fine and just feeling tired after the events of the past couple of days. She took one of his hands and squeezed it tightly.

"You didn't tell me everything when we last spoke," she prompted.

Jamie told her about the aftermath of the football final and his next encounter with the warrior. For some reason he omitted the bit about the strange girl. She was dumbfounded by how he'd made himself invisible.

"That's incredible," she said. "What happened next?"

He recounted following Spencer, but didn't linger on his anger issues at the time! "The rest you know."

"And the weir? How did you survive? I assume you

175

harnessed some of the orb's power."

"Yes. It allowed me to have the most amazing strength in my legs and I felt I could float. Desperation I think. But I kicked upwards and we jettisoned out."

His grandma whistled. "And Duster?"

"I just knew what to do." Jamie shrugged. "I read about it somewhere and with a clear head I just did it."

"I'm proud of you. You've helped two people in under a week. You're well on the way."

"Three actually Grandma."

"Three?"

"Duster counted apparently. It happened again. It's a bit like a power surge. Look at my eyes."

Grandma popped on her spectacles and took an intake of breath.

"Oh gosh yes. They're a greeny-blue now. Very different to the brown of before. Have your parents noticed yet?"

"They haven't said anything."

"Good. Might have to try a bit of simple suggestion with them. I'll have to check my books. I haven't done it in a while."

"Hypnotism?"

"Sort of yes."

"I could try," suggested Jamie.

She squeezed his hand again. "You've got enough on your plate. Leave them to me. Simple parlour tricks I can manage. Now, are you going to show me what you can do?"

"I'd love some help."

"Good, not too tired?"

Jamie was tired, but the opportunity to experiment a bit with someone he totally trusted was too good a chance to dismiss. "Sure. Can we go to my room?"

"Of course."

"I won't bring anything this time!" She shuddered

remembering the incident with the netsuke. "I don't know how you've coped with your encounters with him."

"Nor do I!" Jamie agreed.

They entered Jamie's room and Grandma suggested that they sit on the floor. Jamie picked up the orb from his desk; it reacted in its usual effervescent manner.

"I never tire of that, Grandma."

"It is impressive, I agree."

Jamie sat down opposite her and placed the orb between them, where it continued to glow.

"Does it always do that?"

Jamie nodded. "More and more this week. If I have it in my pocket, I'm afraid others will see it glowing!"

"Perhaps you should wrap it a glasses bag. A black one."

"Not a bad idea."

His grandma nodded. "Now let's recap. You've managed a bit of suggestion, levitation, possession and now invisibility."

"Not really invisibility, more of an illusion."

"Okay, an illusion. Try it now for me."

Jamie picked up the orb and bright light within it swirled as Jamie began to concentrate. Like before he pretended he was elsewhere and he pictured the local pub where his parents were. He felt himself shift away, as though his visual shell had actually left the room. The air shimmered around him and he watched the reaction of his grandma. Her eyes opened wide and she watched amazed. Dumbstruck and unable to speak, Jamie watched her begin to smile and then laugh. Tears began to roll down her face.

"Are you there darling?"

"I'm here Grandma." She started astonished for a moment before bursting out into joyous laughter once more. Between her laughter, she managed to splutter,

"That…is…amazing!"

Jamie allowed his shell to return to his body and he 'reappeared'. "Good eh? I managed to fool Spencer."

"That is astounding," she managed wiping away her tears. "Quite brilliant."

"Shall we see what else I can do?"

She nodded. "Why not trying to move objects with your mind. I've seen that done by people before."

"Really?"

"Yes and it wasn't a trick either. She could actually do it. Spoons off the table, that sort of thing. Let's try something on your desk."

Jamie picked up his pencil case and placed it between them. "How do you think I do it?"

"She told me that the trick was to be allow the object to become an extension of your hand, as if you were holding it."

"Okay." Jamie held the orb in his left hand and concentrated hard on the pencil case. He imagined he was part of the material and that it had melted into his hand. They both watched as the pencil case began to shake ever so slightly and it turned on its end for a moment before falling to the floor. Jamie breathed out.

"A good start," nodded his grandma in appreciation. "Have another go."

Jamie breathed deeply and tried again. The orb glowed brighter than before and he felt the pencil case merge into his hand. He moved his right hand into the air and the pencil case floated. His Grandma nodded and Jamie noticed how she watched him carefully.

Without warning a voice inside his head whispered, "*Oh, you can do better than that. Let the orb show you.*" Jamie nodded and agreed as he sat bolt upright and a bolt of light shone from the orb straight between Jamie's eyes. His head was thrust backwards and an ancient knowledge became clear, like the solving of a mathematical problem.

The light returned to the orb and Jamie moved his head forward and spoke in a voice that terrified his grandma.

"Hold out your hand and join mine," he ordered holding out his hand as the pencil case clattered to the floor. She did as she was told, unable to resist, as Jamie's eyes glowed with an ancient power. Jamie's powerful voice was to be obeyed and shaking with fear she took his hand.

He smiled not unkindly. "Don't be afraid. I will not hurt you."

She smiled back looking at his eyes that seemed to burn with fire. The orb also burned with an orange glow as if it too were in flames.

The orb lifted gently out of Jamie's hands and floated between the two of them, spinning slowly and glowing fiercely as they joined hands. The moment they were joined two shafts of energy flowed into each of them. His grandma cried out elated, as all the hair on her head stood to attention.

The energy continued to surge into them and they were filled with an unimaginable power. Tears streamed down Grandma's face. As one, they began to lift gently off the floor and started to spin around the orb. As they did so sparks of electricity jumped from each of them in turn, cascading into everything electrical in the room. All the lights flickered crazily and they watched as first Jamie's television sprang into life broadcasting a programme in Spanish, then his radio clicked on and flicked from station to station indiscriminately.

Jamie looked toward his old toy box in an old tea chest next to his wardrobe door. It wobbled and then fell with a clatter to the floor, scattering the toys of his earlier childhood everywhere. Jamie smiled and concentrated on the toys. Slowly, they began to moan and groan audibly and stretch their once inanimate limbs into motion. He felt his grandma gasp in astonishment as his toys took on a life of their own and began to chase each other around the floor.

Both Jamie and Grandma continued to spin slowly and they watched old teddies wrestling with a couple of Action Men. Two units of plastic soldiers, one painted red the other grey, prepared for a battle across the bedroom, as a once discarded plastic trumpet called everyone to battle.

Jamie frowned slightly, suddenly bored of this seemingly childish display and looked up at his Union Flag on the ceiling. His grandma watched as the flag began to flap at each corner and ridding itself of its drawing pins fluttered down like a red, white and blue butterfly, gently covering the battlefield to cries of disgust from a thousand toy soldiers and their teddy commanders who'd defeated the Action Men.

"Enough!" commanded Jamie and gently they both stopped spinning and returned to the floor. The orb did the same and suddenly extinguished and severed the tie between them. The commotion beneath the flag ceased instantly. Jamie closed his eyes and felt the power diminish within him, but his new abilities nestled somewhere in his brain ready to be used if needed. He opened his eyes to see his grandma shaking visibly.

"Are you all right Grandma?"

"Is that you Jamie?"

"Of course," he replied. "It was always me."

"You should have heard yourself." She could barely look at him.

"It was definitely me, Grandma." Jamie reached out a hand again and she took it shuddering slightly. "It's me."

She looked up, the fear beginning to leave. "You

were so scary. The power in your eyes was unlike anything I've ever witnessed and I've seen some very strange things. There was no way that I could disagree with you. The display you produced was incredible."

"It seemed like the right thing to do."

"What suddenly happened?"

"It was like a light going on in my brain. A voice told me to open my mind."

"Our mysterious warrior."

"I suppose so. And then it was like, boom!"

"Boom indeed. Your eyes." She shook again. "I don't want to see them too often. There was an ancient power there. If I wasn't worried before, I am now."

"It's okay Grandma. I think I'm getting more control over it. The trick is not to allow myself to get angry."

"I can see why. You could do a lot of damage. I know you've talked about your levitation and I think you should concentrate on that." She got up to go. "I've got a book on meditation that you need to read." She got to the door and turned round.

"This is serious, it's not a game Jamie." She seemed to have returned to her normal self.

"I know."

"Good. Don't get overconfident and whatever happens you must tell me everything."

Jamie agreed with a nod of his head. "Sorry I scared you."

"That's okay. It has showed me that my help is definitely important. Now come on, let's find that book."

Things go viral

After the first full on week of his so-called quest, Jamie was disappointed and a little alarmed to find that nothing was happening. It was Wednesday, four days after he had managed to bring the toys in his bedroom to life and no matter how hard he tried he couldn't replicate it. It was really frustrating. He could now move things around on his desk when the orb was close by, but the dramatic scene of the other day was becoming a distant memory.

In the privacy of his room, he continued to practise the other skills he'd learned. The illusion of disappearing seemed to work most effectively, but he couldn't make other objects vanish. He'd attempted to put some suggestions in Duster's collar and he'd been amused by the results. The dog had managed to pick up various objects and bring them to Jamie, but he felt a lack of spelling knowledge had let the dog down as he appeared with Dad's smart phone instead of the remote control!

But as yet, the utter calm he'd felt before could only be achieved by floating around. He'd explained this to his grandma who had taught him some calming exercises away from the orb. Grandma had found a book on meditation and although it was a bit old fashioned he'd read bits of it and done some calming exercises with his her. He had to admit to feeling a sense of peace, but it was not nearly as tranquil as when he was floating, which wouldn't help if he lost his temper with Spencer.

Jamie thought about Spencer as he made his way downstairs for supper. It had been a normal week at school so far. Spencer had, for the most part, ignored him and acted as though the incident with the orb in the river hadn't happened. The odd barbed comment and insult came his way if they passed on the corridor, but in the general scheme of things this seemed quite light. He wasn't sure whether he was pleased with Spencer's general lack of interest or whether he should be wary of it.

On the plus side, JC kept finding opportunities to hang out with him and they'd agreed to meet up on the following Saturday for a walk with the dogs. He hadn't mentioned it was his birthday and he was pleased that this might prove to be the best part of the day.

The general adulation of the school had taken him by surprise as well. In assembly on the Monday his headmistress invited the triumphant team up to the stage and Tommy had held up the cup to tumultuous applause. Jamie had never heard noise like it. Even the staff were on their feet inciting a standing ovation and the whole school cheered for ages. Despite his frustrations at home, school was pretty good. People stopped from every year group to say hello and which part of the game they had most enjoyed. Even some of the teachers halted their lessons to chat about the game.

After the applause had died down in assembly, Miss Bareham declared that some very exciting news was in the offing. Jamie got the feeling that she'd said too much and she didn't reveal what it was entirely, but suggested that his year group had an adventure planned and that the whole school might get an extra day off. She looked mightily pleased with herself as the school, led by the head boy, gave an impromptu three cheers.

Jamie ate supper and was trying to plan where he was going to take JC on their walk when the doorbell rang. Duster charged to the door woofing in excitement. Dad was still at work, a late meeting had kept him in London, but Mum was home and chatting away with over-enthusiasm to his grandma about plans for the weekend. Jamie sighed. His birthday wouldn't be any different from normal he felt sure.

"I wonder who that could be?" remarked Mum. She pushed back her chair with a squeak and walked into the hallway.

He took another mouthful of his grandma's homemade tomato soup as she popped more rolls from the oven onto the kitchen table. He could hear his mother admonishing Duster as she opened the door, telling him to behave and to get down. He didn't bother to listen any more, as it was obviously grown up business and he tore apart another hot roll and dunked it into his soup.

His mobile phone buzzed in his pocket indicating a message, but he ignored it not wanting to upset his grandma and left it for later. The front door closed after a few minutes and a rather ashen-faced Mrs Lomax walked back into the kitchen. She looked at Jamie darkly and muttered the words no teenager likes to hear.

"Wait till your father gets home!" Jamie swallowed his mouthful carefully, so he didn't choke and looked evenly at his mother, trying to read the situation. Duster had crept under the table and lay on his feet, a sure sign of trouble.

Jamie thought long and hard about what he might have done, the only thing that crept to mind was last week's episode with the weir and the dinghy, but they'd all covered their tracks hadn't they? Jamie gave his mother his best, 'I'm listening carefully, but I've done nothing wrong, honestly' look and sat up straight waiting to receive the news, which was obviously bad.

"Could you pop the kettle on please Mother?" she said wearily flopping into her chair with a heavy sigh. She pushed her soup away, obviously not hungry any more. Grandma said nothing, knowing the moods of her daughter in law and did as she was asked. Finally, she stated simply, "We just had a visit from a newspaper reporter."

"Really?" offered Jamie as innocently as he could after pausing for as long as he dared.

"Yes, really," countered his mother, again looking at her son with an element of disbelief. "Apparently, someone who didn't want to be named, suggested that she looked on ViewTube and type in 'Weir'd Events'. Any ideas Jamie?"

Jamie's blood ran cold. "Um, no?" he ventured hopefully.

"Apparently, it shows an amazing rescue of a dog from a raging weir by a young man of approximately your age. This boy appears to not only rescue the dog, but escapes the weir miraculously and then resuscitates the said dog, bringing him back to life.

"She informed me that she had taken a little walk around the area today and suggested that the weir in question was none other than our very own one, and that the video was dated for last week. She was impressed, very impressed. All she needed to finally make it to our front door was a little help from her unidentified caller. I wonder who that could have been?"

Yes indeed, wondered Jamie, as he mentally hung, drew and quartered a number of individuals, but one person definitely came to mind. Spencer! But how would he have known? None of the others would have told him, unless the warrior had pointed him in the right direction. But for what purpose? To make life as difficult as possible he supposed.

Jamie sat stunned, unable to think clearly. He obviously had a huge decision to make. Should he come clean? Always a good thing where his mother was concerned. She was an old school mum. Firm, fair but ferocious if pushed. She was one of those sorts of parents whom you could never lie to.

Being a teacher, she had some sort of in-built lie detector technology. She could spot a fib a mile off and if you carried on with the charade she'd get mad, really mad. She had that look about her at the moment and she'd made the Dad threat, which generally was a bad thing. He'd jump up and down and break things when he got cross, which was rare, but Mum was a far more frightening prospect.

He came clean.

"All true Mum," he confessed.

"Explain please."

For the next ten minutes, Jamie carefully explained how the events had transpired. He still wasn't ready to tell the whole truth about the orb and he glanced at Grandma nervously as he dodged that particular subject. She nodded conspiratorially as she sat sipping her tea at the table. He explained that he hadn't wanted to worry them, that Spencer had stolen something of his and he'd wanted it back. Hence the early morning and treacherous journey in the boat that morning to rescue the said item, which he claimed was his winner's medal.

He truthfully told her that he hadn't wanted to make a big thing of the theft and carefully added that she'd always taught him to try and solve his own problems. She nodded in agreement to this, but continued to glare at her son. He carried on with the tale and admitted that he had been wrong to take Duster with him on the river, but never expected the dog to jump out whilst he was in the water. Besides they'd been on the river many times before and he'd never jumped out before, plus there was no way on earth that he'd muck about near the weir. He'd promised them that he wouldn't and to this day would never attempt anything like that again.

He explained that in his heart, he knew he just had to rescue the dog. He couldn't let him die could he, he argued. As for surviving the weir, he explained that he didn't know enough about how they worked to clarify his spectacular escape.

"How did you know about the resuscitation?" his mum asked.

Again he claimed that he'd read about it and he offered to show her.

"Not on the dog!"

"No!" Jamie replied. Can I borrow your teddy bear from your office Grandma?"

"Sure," she agreed. "I'll just pop and get it."

His mother stayed silent, still fuming as Grandma left the room and Jamie avoided her gaze. When she returned Jamie repeated what he'd done to the large teddy bear.

"I think it survived, Jamie," said his grandma in an attempt to break the ice between mother and son.

Mum sat quietly for a long time pondering and disseminating the information. Jamie could tell that she believed him, it was how she'd react to the dangerous situation he'd put himself in that appeared to be the main issue. Finally she spoke.

"I'm really cross with you Jamie. Really cross. Your father will feel the same. I think ultimately you should have told us about the theft. I'm going to ring Spencer's parents."

"Mum!" objected Jamie, but one look on her face told him that silence at this point was the best course of action, but he blundered on. "Mum, please listen. I can handle Spencer, really I can." Mum looked sceptical, but gestured for him to elaborate. "He's an old fashioned bully with an axe to grind when it comes to me. I am not scared of him and never will be. If you get involved, there's every possibility it'll only make the situation much, much worse." Mum looked offended. "Mum, please. Let me deal with it."

She thought about it and then spoke. "I'll see, Jamie, once I've spoken to your father, but in the meantime I'd like you to go to your room and think seriously about your conduct over these last few days." Jamie cleared up the remains of his lunch, his appetite gone, put the detritus in the dishwasher and trudged mournfully upstairs, cursing his luck and the persons responsible for uploading the video onto the internet.

Jamie opened the door to his room with Duster trotting behind and threw himself onto his bed burying his head into the pillow in frustration. Moments later, his phone buzzed again. Another message. He rolled onto his back and fished out the phone from his pocket. The screen registered two messages. The first was from Calum and read:

"Sorry mate. My sister got hold of the weir video somehow and uploaded it to ViewTube to impress her friends. Sorry, sorry, sorry. Call me!"

Jamie sighed as he read it; he couldn't be cross with his friend for too long. He texted back:

"No probs. Call you later. Not angry, but Mum is – OUCH!"

He was about to close the phone, when he remembered the older message from lunchtime. It was from an unavailable number and as he read it his blood grew cold. It simply stated:

"I know what you did and how you did it. I'm onto you."

It could only be from one person. Spencer. Jamie sighed and thumped the pillow in frustration. Duster whimpered and hid under Jamie's desk, unused to his master's bad mood. Things just couldn't get any worse, could they? He texted back:

"Let's talk. You name the place," and sat back awaiting a response. He didn't have to wait long when a cryptic retort arrived.

"You'll know when. Enjoy the limelight, loser."

Limelight? Jamie sat up, understanding slowly dawning on him as his phone buzzed once, twice, three times. Paused then continued to buzz without stopping and the phone rang downstairs along with his mother's and his grandma's mobiles. Jamie buried his head in the pillow as Duster groaned under the desk echoing his master's distress.

By the time Dad returned from work, the story had escalated to the point where Dad had seen a snippet of the video himself on the train. He breezed in through the front door and informed Jamie that he was in trouble, but this wasn't the time to sit and discuss it. Interest was definitely out there and the story looked as though it might go viral.

A decision was made to contact the original reporter and the local television news who had also enquired about the story. News, it appeared did indeed travel fast. Jamie sat in the kitchen watching his parents as they discussed what to do.

Mum was adamant that the weir video should be taken off the Internet, but Dad wasn't so sure. He asked Jamie to show him the video again. Dad watched it without speaking and without emotion. He raised an eyebrow when Jamie shot out of the weir clutching Duster and clapped his hands when his son resuscitated the family dog.

"Come here lad!" he said. Dad leapt up out of his chair giving his son the biggest hug, much to his mother's disgust. "My hero!" he laughed whistling for the dog who came bounding in and threw himself at Dad with a delighted woof. Dad let go of Jamie and started wrestling with the dog on the floor. Duster growled happily as Jamie joined in as well and within seconds the three of them had engaged in a full scale wrestling match. Mum stood there with her best 'I'm not amused face' and soon decided enough was enough.

"Time to be serious now!" she ordered. "Let's work out what to do about this mess." Dad sat back at the computer and watched the video once more.

"Jamie? How on earth did you fly out of the water like that?"

Jamie shrugged his shoulders and repeated the story he'd told his friends and his mum earlier. "I'm pretty certain that as we went down, I hit the bottom and kicked away from the river bed as hard as I could."

Dad seemed satisfied with this explanation. "I assume that these numbers next to the video signify how many hits the video has had?"

Jamie looked at the screen. "That's right."

Dad whistled in appreciation. "So what you're saying is that this video has been watched twenty-four thousand three hundred and twenty-two times?"

Jamie stared at him. "That many?" He looked over his dad's shoulder.

"Interesting, very interesting." Jamie could see a plan forming in his dad's head. "What do you make of it Mum?" said Dad turning round, but Mum had rushed out of the room.

"Stay where you are both of you, I'll be back in a moment." Dad refreshed the page and the counter now read twenty-four thousand, seven hundred and sixty-five. He scratched his head thoughtfully as Mum came bounding back in visibly excited by something and clutching a supplement from last week's Sunday paper. She flipped through noisily until she got to the article she wanted.

"Aha. According to this, Internet video sensations can be incredibly lucrative to the owner of the video. The owners of ViewTube will not disclose how much money people can make, but if the video tops six figures in terms of hits then they can reward the video owners. Some parents claim they've made enough money to get their children through university."

"Blimey Jamie. Refresh the page again." Jamie did as instructed and the counter now read twenty-five thousand and eighty-seven. "This video has had nearly a thousand hits in under five minutes. Get on the phone to Calum quick," ordered Dad. "Have you spoken to Calum?"

"Only by text Dad."

"Is he planning to take the video down?" Jamie shrugged. "We've got to keep this video on the website. Can you ring him for me?"

Jamie did as he was asked and passed his mobile over.

"Calum, hi. It's Jamie's dad. Great game the other week. Is your dad at home? No don't worry, you're not in any trouble. I think you boys may have struck gold!"

The story, it seemed, was going to be big news for a while and after another phone call, the reporting team were around the house within half an hour. It was getting late, but the story should make tomorrow's bulletins they were reliably informed. Jamie watched from the window as the local reporter, a rather swarthy lady named Penelope Gladstone, appeared to argue and gesticulate rather angrily at another lady, who he later found out was called Jenny Swing, from the local television news.

Dad walked out to meet them both, in a business-like fashion as he shook hands with first Penelope and then Jenny. He could not see what he was saying, but it was obvious that he was clearly laying down the ground rules for exclusivity to Jamie and the weir story. Penelope looked as if she wanted to argue, but Dad raised a hand in warning, obviously insisting that it was on his terms that the interview was going to happen. She nodded sulkily in agreement and shook his hand.

Dad closed the door behind him and came back into the kitchen.

"I've agreed to let you be interviewed tomorrow after school at the weir. Okay?"

"I'm not sure Dad. I might make a fool of myself."

"Don't worry. I've told work I won't be there tomorrow afternoon. They owe me some time. Your mum and I will be there."

"What will I say?"

"What you've told us."

Jamie wasn't so sure, but he thought he might have the orb in his pocket for a little extra reassurance.

One minute of fame

As Jamie made his way with his parents to the weir the following day, a crowd had begun to gather. Jamie had done his best to keep a low profile at school, but after scoring the winning goal to win the cup and now this, he had gone from a nobody to a minor celebrity in a very short space of time. Despite his best efforts and one or two avoidance manoeuvres, it had been quite a stressful day. Added to that his nerves were shredded. The thought of being interviewed in front of a camera made him want to crawl into a big hole until it was all over!

The sound of the weir was getting louder as they approached and it was clear that the interview would take place further down the river with the levee being used as background. As they approached Jamie could see a small crowd being kept back by some burly looking security guards. Jamie's dad caught the eye of the reporter and she waved back. She walked down to the guards, who made a path through the crowd to allow the Lomax family through. Duster trotted alongside them, as he was the miracle people were interested in.

The odd camera flashed as they walked through, adding to Jamie's general feeling of unease and a few questions were fired at him as he tried to look confident. Dad had primed him beforehand recommending that he kept quiet. The path closed again and Jenny led the Lomax family to an area where a camera and sound equipment had been set up. She took one look at Jamie and frowned.

"Oh dear," she said. "You don't seem very happy with this?"

"I'm really, really nervous," Jamie replied. "I was

on stage once. I learned all my lines and was fine in rehearsal, but as soon as the curtains opened, I forgot them all."

Jenny laughed. "That happened to me once. I had the main part too. Good thing someone else had learned the lines. My stage fright was so severe I had to be helped off the stage."

"You're kidding!" Jamie smiled relaxing a little.

"I kid you not."

"But how come you can do it now?"

"Hypnosis!"

"Hypnosis?"

"Well suggestion really. My mum was a bit 'out there'. A bit of a new age alternative lady, bless her. She embarrassed me loads as a kid, but she sat me down one day and helped me relax. Looking back, I was so relaxed that I almost went to sleep."

Jamie watched Jenny as she continued with her story.

"She worked on my anxiety, and made the most amazing suggestion that I should just imagine that the audience were naked."

"No way!"

"True. I got on stage the next day and never looked back. I had to learn to get rid of my grin, but thinking that the audience were undressed, worked then and still works today."

"I've seen you on television and you always look so cheerful. Is that why?"

"Indeed so."

Jamie laughed out loud.

"That's better Jamie," she said putting a reassuring hand on his arm. "Look I'm not suggesting that you do the same, but what I am saying is that you're not alone in feeling this way. I hear you're a good footballer."

Jamie nodded. "Well if you can play in front of loads of

194

people, talking to me in front of a camera will be a doddle."

"Okay."

"Good lad. Just ignore the camera, don't look into it, just answer my questions. If the naked thing works for you, then go for it."

"I don't think so," Jamie answered.

"Just me then," Jenny laughed. "Come on, we roll in five minutes. I just want to go through the questions I'm going to ask you."

With the cameras rolling, it was a nerve-wracking experience, but Jenny's professionalism carried him through. Jamie tried to smile as he answered her questions and if he faltered she filled in the gaps for him. Her skill in interviewing was impressive and as the questions went on, he felt himself answering without stammering too much and he thought he gave a good account of the incident. Jenny gasped dramatically for the camera as he told how they'd been flung out and when he explained about the resuscitation she bent down and gave Duster a cuddle. Jamie was impressed. It was good footage and when the director called time, the production team gave a round of applause.

"That's a wrap everyone," he called. Jenny reached out a hand to shake Jamie's.

"A good job Jamie. Well done. That'll make a great segment for the news tonight."

"Thanks Jenny. I didn't feel nervous at all."

"Good, neither did I. Oh and Jamie. That thing about imagining people naked."

"You made it up?"

"Yup."

"Figured that was the case. Thought it would do the opposite and put you off!"

Jenny laughed. "But it worked though. Helped you

195

to relax."

"True."

She shook his hand once more. "Got to shoot back to the office to edit this in time for the news at nine this evening. Be seeing you kid."

"Thanks."

"No problem." She bent down to ruffle the hair on Duster's head before turning and heading off.

Jamie breathed a sigh of relief and looked around for his parents. Dad was chatting to Tommy and Calum, but he couldn't see his mum. They bounded over.

"All right?"

Calum shuffled his feet nervously. "I thought you'd be mad. I didn't see you at school today."

"It all got a bit crazy. I kept having to hide in the toilet."

"Oh no," Tommy cried. "Not a nice way to spend your day."

"Hopefully now this interview has happened, people will leave me alone."

"Who let the cat out of the bag Jamie?" asked Tommy.

"Well it was Calum's sister who released the video, but it was Spencer who reported it to the press." replied Jamie wearily.

"Spencer?" Tommy grumbled. "Why won't he leave you alone?"

Jamie shrugged. "Dunno. Just doesn't like me I guess."

"Is he here?" asked Calum looking around.

"He was over there!" pointed Jamie. As if on cue, the small crowd now dispersing parted to reveal Spencer, arms folded, looking smug, staring right at them.

"Don't give him the satisfaction of letting him get to

you Jamie," suggested Tommy. "Let's give him a wave."

All three boys waved at Spencer and shouted hello. He wasn't expecting this and started looking around nervously. Jamie's mum appeared suddenly and had also spotted him. She was making her way over. Spencer spotted her, retrieved his bike from behind a tree and sped off before she could intercept.

"I wouldn't like to be in Spencer's shoes when your mum catches up with him!" commented Calum drily. He gulped and added as an afterthought. "She's not after me is she?"

Jamie thought about it for a moment and pretended to look worried as his mother had turned her sights on him and the boys. "I've had it in the neck today. She may decide to take it out on you two as well." Both boys looked to turn tail, but before they got the chance a decidedly grumpy Mrs Lomax was barring their way.

"Ah, I suppose I should be thanking you two for all this!" she remarked tapping her foot and glaring at the boys. They remained silent, not sure what to say.

"Well what do you know?"

"Is that the time?"

"We'd better be off. Nice to see you Mrs Lomax."

"Say hi to your dad Jamie. Tell him I'll keep an eye on the video hit rate."

"See you on telly later."

Jamie tried not to smile, not wanting to antagonise his mum further. His mum, generally still fuming about everything, muttered "Boys" under her breath and stomped off to find Jamie's dad who was chatting amiably to Jenny. This was until he saw the look on his wife's face and saying a quick farewell intercepted her on her way over.

He gave her one of his cheekiest, goofy grins and dropping his head, hoisted her up fireman style onto his shoulder. There was a shriek of indignation as Jamie's father spun his angry wife around on the spot. Jamie watched with amusement; this was his father's failsafe manoeuvre to make her smile, although it didn't seem to be working. She slapped him on the back and ordered to be put on the ground at once. His father did as asked and put out his bottom lip, like a child, pretending to be sad. She took one look at his ridiculous face and smiled.

"That's better," teased his dad, "stop being such a grump-bag and come and have a coffee with me."

"Don't want to!" pouted his mother, echoing her husband's babyish behaviour just a second earlier. Jamie cringed as his parents reverted to tickling each other and talking in babyish voices. This was all rather embarrassing. Jamie patted his side so Duster would follow and they wandered back to the village, whilst his parents continued to flirt and behave like teenagers.

"Honestly, get a room," he muttered.

Later that evening, the Lomax family were sitting in the living room waiting for the local news to begin. Mum had forgiven Jamie to an extent. She lay on the sofa next to Dad with her legs draped across his lap. Duster lay at their feet and Grandma was in her armchair flicking through a book.

She put the book down and tipped Jamie a wink. "Are we going to videotape this?" she asked her son innocently. This was a common game she played on him and it never failed to rile him.

"Videotape?" countered Jamie's father, oblivious to the trap he'd unwittingly fallen into. Again! "Mother. Honestly."

"What pray tell, is wrong with videotape? You'll be telling me next that we can pause live television and record two programmes at once."

Dad had just taken a sip of water at this point and

spluttered it over the dog. Duster sat up in disgust and moved away.

He narrowed his eyes and pointed at his mother. "Are you playing tricks on me? A spell maybe?"

"A spell? Next you'll be accusing me of being a witch!"

"But you are a witch."

"Are you suggesting that I am some evil, nasty female that rides a broomstick with a black cat in tow?" At that point, as if by magic, Bob the family black house cat strolled confidently in, bopped Duster on the nose and jumped up into Grandma's lap, staring intently at Dad with its pale yellow eyes.

"Hah, I rest my case!"

"Be quiet you two!" ordered Mum as the national news ended.

"Now over to the news team in your local area." Jenny appeared behind her news desk looking every inch the serious broadcaster and led the local news with Jamie's story. A still picture of Jamie and Duster flying out of the weir came up behind her and he gulped. Mum swung her legs around and sat upright as Dad pushed his glasses up his nose and Grandma put down her book. The orb vibrated reassuringly from deep within the pocket of Jamie's hoodie.

"We start this evening's news with a remarkable story of bravery, involving a fourteen year old boy and the amazing rescue of his dog…" Jenny then proceeded to tell Jamie's story and the slightly shaky video shot by Calum played as she talked over the images.

"…And if that was not amazing enough, look what happens next." Jamie's resuscitation attempt was then played to cheers from Dad. Jamie smiled shyly.

"We asked Jamie just what happened and how he knew just what to do." His interview with Jenny came up next and after hiding initially under a cushion in embarrassment, he eventually watched and nodded in appreciation. Jenny had done a good job. What came next however was a bit of a surprise to them all.

"After my interview with Jamie Lomax, his head teacher from Marsh Green College had this to say:"

"Well, we are all immensely proud of young Jamie. I have seen the footage of their miraculous escape and the subsequent lifesaving heroics." She paused for maximum effect. "It's fair to say that here at Marsh Green College, we teach the students all about common decency and expect them all to help others." The camera focused on a gleaming, freshly polished trophy behind her as the Lomax family heard Jenny comment on the cup.

"What this little thing? Ah yes, well our hero Jamie scored the winner in the football county cup just recently. The team were superb, but it was Jamie's cool head that saw us through in the end." Jamie groaned. This was all he needed. If the news item weren't bad enough, he now would have to contend with jibes from everyone else about being teacher's pet. "And I'd like to take this opportunity to say that the school and donations from the parents of Year Ten have paid for all of the boys and girls in the year group to go on an Outward Bound trip to the Lake District. They will be visiting a centre in Ullswater next week instead of school as a surprise."

"And what about the rest of the school?" Jenny asked.

"The rest of the school will be getting the day off next Monday." She smiled magnanimously at the camera as Jenny gushed about what a nice dénouement to the story this was and then as quickly as it started, the segment ended.

"Well, well, well," remarked Grandma as she got up and turned off the television. Mum and Dad both

200

looked a bit put out and rather surprised by the announcement and they looked guiltily at one another. "Did you two know about this?"

"Well..." Dad spluttered.

"What your father means Jamie is that yes we did know about it. It was meant to be a surprise, but it rather seems that your headmistress has rather stolen everyone's thunder."

"What do you think?" asked his dad.

Jamie grinned. "Fantastic. Just fantastic. It's going to be awesome."

Possession

Jamie woke up with a start just before his alarm clock was meant to wake him. He looked around his room blearily half expecting someone to be sitting in a chair or mysterious messages adorning a bedroom wall, but all seemed to be all right for a change. He shook his head, but couldn't dismiss the notion that something was going to happen today. He'd slept fitfully enough, but he'd experienced one of those almost conscious dreams in which he really, really tried to wake up, but couldn't. In his dream he'd woken up, only to go back to sleep and continue with the same dream.

He sat up and struggled to remember the dream itself. The facts were disappearing fast, but he was left with a deep sense of unease. He reached across to touch the orb, which reacted the moment he touched it and he was surprised to see it glow with a green hue. It hadn't done that before, and it only added to his general feeling of disquiet.

He showered, dressed and breakfasted as normal. Nothing was any different. His parents and grandmother were the same. He watched them carefully as they went about their usual morning routines. They hadn't been taken over by aliens like the characters from his favourite film *The Invaders from Mars*, which he'd watched last night. Perhaps it was this that had given him the bad dreams. He didn't think so, as he'd watched it scores of times, but he did check the back of his father's neck for puncture marks just to make sure he hadn't had his mind swiped!

Instead of being cold and hostile like the protagonist's father in the film, Jamie's dad was more enthusiastic than was normal for a Friday morning. He had checked ViewTube and the hits were still rising, but not as quickly as before and the story had made one or two of the national papers, albeit taking up minimal column space. Penelope's story in the local paper however was a full front page spread and Dad was in the process of deciding whether he should frame it or not.

Grandma was busying away and chatting away about nothing in particular, but his mum was freaking him out a bit. She was smiling sweetly enough, but she kept looking at him and touching his hair as she passed. She often did this before his birthday and despite himself he was beginning to feel a bit irritated. The mix of differing emotions in the room wasn't helping his own mood, so he quickly excused himself and saying goodbye made his way to school.

The temperature outside was cool and Jamie thrust his hands into his pocket to keep them warm. The orb he knew was glowing away, but it gave him no warmth, nor did it do anything to ease his state of mind. He tried to connect with it, but whether it was his frame of mind or something else altogether he couldn't access any of his newfound abilities. The television interview had been a welcome respite from a frustrating week and the promise of an adventure week in the mountains was an enticing one. However, he'd be the only one with a quest to complete and he rather doubted that anyone else had the threat of losing their soul hanging over them.

With two people left to help, time was fast running out and although he'd try his best to enjoy himself, this serious threat to his future was really beginning to make him seriously nervous. Adding to the sense of foreboding he felt today, he was not in the best state of mind. Even the lure of the wish, which normally excited him, could not shake him from the lethargy he felt. He sighed in frustration and bowed his head against a wind that had picked up. It gusted around him picking up crunchy autumnal leaves and in curious eddies created by passing cars swirled around his head like bothersome flies. He swatted a couple away in irritation.

The moment he walked through the school gates, he knew something was wrong. Instead of the usual cacophony of noise, the school seemed devoid of pupils practising their instruments, hailing each other in the playground, kicking footballs, laughing, fighting or desperately finding someone to copy their homework from. The wind was even stronger on the playground and it howled around everyone attempting to whip away paper they were holding and ruffling their uniforms in an attempt to unsettle them all.

Something was going to happen. Jamie wanted to run away, but he didn't have the energy to do it. He followed a group in through one of the entrances and was relieved when the door closed behind them. He had to forcibly shut the door, as the wind tried to rip it open again. He looked up hoping to catch a conversation with someone he knew to see if they felt the same as him, but the atmosphere appeared no better inside the school corridors. It was eerily silent.

It was weird. No one was talking. The school should have been celebrating. Year 10 got to go on a trip and the rest of the school got a couple of days off. Why weren't people jumping about and getting excited? It looked and felt as though they were all walking through treacle. Jamie felt it too. An ominous presence, weighing down on them all. Crushing their enthusiasm like a blanket of fog. Jamie harked back to his science fiction movie from the night before. Surely not? Enough weird stuff had happened recently, he hoped this subdued atmosphere didn't have anything to do with him or the orb, but he suspected that it might.

He popped his bag in his locker and followed everyone silently as they trooped into the school hall for assembly. Jamie caught Tommy's eye as they took their places, but it was a fleeting glance and he looked away quickly. He noticed that the rows of children, himself included, were of uniform size. Ten to a row with a gap in between like soldiers.

Like soldiers?

The door slammed shut with a crash.

Jamie tried to break from the line he was in but couldn't move. His feet were anchored to the floor. A chant started from somewhere at the back of the room, quietly at first but getting louder as it moved from the back to the front of the hall.

"Hail, hail, hail. All hail. Hail, hail, hail. All hail."

Jamie felt the temperature drop and groaned. He watched as everyone around him began to thump their feet on the floor in unison whilst chanting "All hail". He took the orb out of his pocket for protection, no longer bothered that someone might see. It was obvious that no one knew who he was, they were waiting for whoever, or whatever was to emerge from the door. The orb glowed brightly, illuminating the darkening hall as the light from outside extinguished leaving the school in relative darkness. The lights in the hall flickered on, but only at half power like lanterns.

Jamie knew what was happening and he concentrated on connecting with the orb to protect himself. He felt a flicker of recognition; it was as if the orb itself was affected by this stupor that had afflicted them all. Suddenly, the chanting increased in volume and together with the stamping, the noise in the room was deafening.

"All hail, all hail."

Then silence. A silence so profound and thick you could have cut it with a knife. The door opened and their head teacher appeared. Not, definitely not, what he was expecting. She was dressed in her normal dowdy outfit, a brown blouse with brown matching cardigan, and brown stockings with brown brogues that she clomped across the stage in. Her pince-nez spectacles perched on the end of her nose and her hair was tied in a bun on the top of her head. She looked like she normally did.

She raised a hand then the other and Jamie almost cried out. In her left hand she was holding a metal softball bat about three feet in length. She appeared surprised to have it in her hand and she twirled it around experimentally. An appreciative roar went up from his assembled peers and despite the security of the orb he was very scared. She held a hand up and the noise stopped instantly and from somewhere one of the spotlights in the ceiling illuminated the stage with an audible clunk. Her shadow on the back wall towered above her, but it wasn't her shadow.

Somehow it was the shadow of the warrior and Jamie feared for everyone in the room, distraught that they were all caught up in this. When she looked up it was him and him only that she stared at and she gave him an evil smile. When she spoke it was the warrior's voice that carried throughout the room.

"Well, well, well," he boomed. "It seems I have another army to control. How strange young Jamie, that these children are so in awe of this body I have borrowed. She must be most powerful. I could do with someone like this as a captain." The warrior headmistress nodded appreciatively. "Shame about the armour, it's a bit, well brown! However, I do like this weapon." The warrior headmistress slammed the bat against the lectern with a resounding smash. "Nice!"

With a wave of the hand they sat down in unison and kept their heads bowed in reverence. The only person left standing was Jamie himself and the possessed figure of his head teacher made its way down off the stage towards him, thwacking the bat into her borrowed hand with every step.

"I forgot how amusing your time was Master Lomax." The warrior headmistress stopped in front of a line of girls and studied them intently. Jamie knew without thinking who he was looking for. He tried to keep calm and attempted to speak, but no words came out. The orb bounced erratically in front of him and the centre of the sphere itself was as black as night. No matter how hard he tried he couldn't utter a word.

"An interesting phenomenon, don't you think?" The warrior headmistress paused awaiting an answer and then laughed maniacally. He raised a hand and a deathly, humourless laughter emanated from everyone else in the room. He lowered it again and as quickly as it started it ceased.

"You may think that I have no power in your world, but I do. The orb doesn't like it, but as you can see it is in my control at this point. It won't last, but the collective consciousness of everyone in this room gives me a distinctive edge over what you can do. Shame you can't speak. Cat got your tongue? Now, where was I? Oh yes. You!"

He pointed to someone in the row and a figure got up and moved towards him. The fact that it was the usually amiable Miss Bareham behaving in such a way made it utterly terrifying and sensing this, another evil laugh echoed around the room. Jamie didn't dare breathe, hoping upon hope that the warrior headmistress wouldn't hurt anyone. His heart skipped a beat as JC, head bowed, stepped into the aisle.

"What a lovely young girl," the warrior headmistress said as he used the tip of the softball bat to raise her chin.

Eyes that didn't focus looked at the possessed headmistress and she chanted quietly, "All hail, all hail."

"Oh how sweet, such adoration and complete and utter devotion. Friend of yours?" The possessed headmistress swished her bat over the top of JC's head making Jamie wince. "It appears so. More than just a friend it seems. I could knock her head off with one blow. You know that don't you Jamie?" The warrior headmistress looked at Jamie. "Speak up! Oh sorry you can't do anything." He started to stroll about the room with JC following helplessly behind. "I could destroy everyone in this room and then blame it on you if I so desired. You know that too don't you?"

Jamie could feel his anger rising, but he was powerless. The warrior's control was too great. He concentrated harder than he'd ever done before. A severe pain in his head threatened to knock him off his feet, but it had the desired effect. The orb stopped oscillating and the black mist dissipated slightly. The lights came back to full brightness for a couple of seconds as everyone in the room raised their heads. This stopped the headmistress warrior and she turned to face Jamie.

"Oh bravo my young protégé. A little fighting spirit." The warrior headmistress started to clap his borrowed hands slowly and in an instant everyone in the room followed suit. He stopped and they did. "It won't work though. I could turn this collective mind here on you in an instant. Give it up!" With one wave of his hand the pain intensified in Jamie's head and it took any strength he had left to remain standing. The orb returned to its blackened state and the chanting began again barely audible above the voice of the warrior.

"Now, the reason for my visit before you pass out.

208

Thought I'd let you know that time is running out for you. Three down, two to go. Thought I'd give you a little helping hand with number four." The room started to applaud. The warrior headmistress took a bow.

"Thank you, thank you. You are too kind." The applause ceased. "I've enjoyed your efforts thus far and decided to show you how powerful I am and what potentially awaits you if you fail. Pain, torment, sheer hopelessness to name but a few of the emotions you will experience once you fall. Thought I'd just remind you. I was getting bored waiting."

A cheer rang out through the room and the warrior headmistress laughed out loud. "Look how your world loves me. I had forgotten how easily minds here could be controlled. I must come back more often. Maybe even put it on my list of dimensions to conquer!"

Jamie used his last ounce of energy to look the warrior in the eye and shake his head. "Defiant to the last. Good lad. Perhaps I will spare this world. Depends on how you get on really. Take care my friend and keep a close eye on those that you cherish."

The pain in Jamie's head was excruciating, but he managed to watch as the warrior headmistress took her place on the stage once more. Behind her the shadow of the warrior loomed above her and giving a final wave disappeared. The lights came on full and the darkness outside gave way to light.

Everyone came to, as the headmistress bade everyone a cheerful good morning.

"Let's start with hymn two hundred and one."

Jamie just had time to put the orb in his pocket before he passed out.

He woke up and tried to move unsure of where and who he was. The pain in his head was still there, but the intensity of the earlier pain was fading. He tried to sit up and winced.

"Oh, good. You're awake," said a kindly voice.

"Where am I?" asked Jamie as his vision blurred for a moment.

"You're in the school infirmary. You fainted in assembly."

More than just a faint thought Jamie miserably. His vision swam again and the larger than life figure of the school matron came into focus. "Here drink this," she said.

Jamie sipped some of the offered water and feeling better sat up. "Careful. Don't be too hasty. You might feel sick."

"Thanks, I'm feeling better."

The school nurse was distracted by a knock at the door. "Excuse me a minute."

He watched her open the door and discuss something with someone Jamie couldn't see. She nodded finally, obviously not entirely pleased with the decision and allowed JC to walk in.

"Hello," she began, smiling. "Are you all right?"

"Never better," joked Jamie.

"Yeah right. You passed out rather dramatically. Gave me a fright."

"Sorry. Got a bit hot and felt sick. Before I knew it, everything went black."

"Do you remember anything about assembly?" Jamie asked. JC looked at him strangely. "Anything weird?"

"No weirder than normal," she laughed.

"Excuse me young lady," ordered the bustling school nurse as she barged past JC and popped a thermometer between Jamie's lips.

Jamie tried to protest, but she shushed him. She waited a minute and then taking it out examined it closely. "No temperature, but I'm still sending you home."

Jamie groaned and began to protest. "But what about all the details of next week's trip?"

"I'll get them and drop them round tomorrow," offered JC.

"Good," said the nurse. "No more arguments. Now lie down. Anyone at home today?"

Jamie nodded. "My grandma."

"Number?" Jamie struggled to remember. "Never mind. I'll get it from the school office."

JC reached over and squeezed Jamie's hand. "I'm glad you're okay. Get better all right? I still want that walk you promised me tomorrow. I'll bring the details of the trip and you plan the walk. You hadn't forgotten?"

"I hadn't. Looking forward to it. Come over at about ten, if that's good?"

"Good with me." She squeezed his hand again and smiled. "Get better. See you tomorrow."

Jamie watched her leave, torn between screaming "No, stay away from me!" to actually really looking forward to her company. Surely the warrior wouldn't try that trick again would he? Jamie vowed to be doubly on his guard just in case.

Birthday presents

His grandma had fussed over Jamie all afternoon. She'd made him a day bed in the living room and he'd watched movies feeling a bit of a fraud. He didn't feel ill, his head throbbed a bit, but that was all. He'd told her about the frightening events of the morning and the feeling of unease that had so unsettled him on the way to school.

"Gosh!" she'd exclaimed. "I felt it too. I just thought it was the weather. You poor boy, to have gone through that!"

When he got to the moment of the assembly itself she cried out holding her head.

"That's not possible."

Jamie assured her that it was more than possible and told her of the threat.

"Have you tried using the orb this week?"

"I have Grandma, but with no success."

She thought about this and frowned. "If you feel up to it later, I think you should."

Jamie finished another movie and sat up with orb in his hand. He tried to connect with it, but every time he tried his head felt like it might explode. All it did was exhaust him and finally he'd had enough and took himself off to bed hoping he'd feel better in the morning.

He barely had time to get under the covers before he blacked out again and when he came to, it was a wet lick that brought him back to life.

"Thanks Duster," he groaned.

"Morning sleepy head." Jamie opened his eyes and saw his dad in his dressing gown sitting on the edge of his bed. "Happy birthday son."

"Is it morning?" Jamie was surprised.

"Yes. Grandma told us you went to bed at three in the afternoon yesterday and it's now eight the next day. You had your mum and I worried, but Grandma assured us it was just sleep you needed. A chance to recharge your batteries. It's all been a bit hectic recently hasn't it?"

Jamie nodded blearily. "How's Mum?"

Jamie's Dad frowned and shrugged his shoulders. "Who knows? Unlike you she tossed and turned all night and checked on you at least ten times."

"Will she be okay today?"

"I think so. She was too worried about you to think about your sister."

"Dad?"

"Yes son?"

"Did she have a name?"

Dad smiled sadly. "Yes. We called her Ginny. Seems a bit weird never having told you that."

"'S okay. It's a nice name. Do you think Mum will be happier this year?"

"Let's see shall we? Come on. Get yourself dressed and come down for your birthday breakfast." His dad kissed him on the top of his head and left Jamie to get up. His felt so much better and his head didn't hurt. It was clearer than it had been for days. The energy he'd used trying to combat the weird spell the warrior put over his school had obviously take its toll. He reached out for the orb and instantly the sphere sprang into life and he connected with it in a way he hadn't been able to all week.

"Amazing what a bit of rest and recuperation can do for you eh?" Grandma had brought him a cup of tea. "Happy birthday." She popped the steaming cup next to his bed and kissed him on the cheek. "Feeling better? You look it."

"Feeling terrific Grandma. Never better."

"Good. Just cooking breakfast. Bacon and eggs suit?"

"Perfect. Thanks."

His Grandma left the room and he attempted to throw the bedcovers off using thought alone. The duvet whipped off the bed enveloping the dog who fell to the floor with a yelp. Laughing, Jamie jumped out and untangled Duster, who looked thoroughly irritated.

"Sorry boy. Let's go walking later. I've got someone for you to meet." The word 'walk' pricked up his ears and mollified, he trotted out of Jamie's room in search of the smell of bacon.

Jamie entered the kitchen to be greeted by his mum who jumped from her chair and enveloped him in a bear hug. "Happy birthday my boy. You had me worried." She squeezed him tight.

"Mum!" Jamie protested.

"Sorry." She released him from the hug, but held onto his arms staring at him with tears in her eyes. "My fifteen year old son. Who'd have thought it? Are you feeling better today?"

"I'm fine honestly."

"Good." She hugged him again and then released him, wiping tears from her eyes. Dad passed her a tissue.

"Come on Mum. Let the boy sit down and open his cards."

Jamie looked at the table. No big presents then. Never mind he thought as he sat down and gave everyone his best smile. "Thanks everyone."

A plate of bacon and eggs with some fresh toast appeared and he tucked in. He was hungry! It was only when he was half through with his meal that he looked up and saw his family staring at him.

"Slow down," laughed his dad. "There is more if you want it."

"Sorry," smirked Jamie. "Bit hungry." He put down his knife and fork and reached for an envelope with his mother's spidery handwriting on the front. He opened it and for a change the card was quite funny. It had a picture of two mushrooms on the front. Their hoods were overextended to look like Mexican sombreros and the caption read "To a Fun Guy!"

Mum smiled. "Dad thought it was funny."

"Good choice Dad. I get it. Very good for you."

"Excellent. I haven't lost my touch then. I can make fifteen year olds laugh like fourteen year olds then."

Jamie opened another envelope and inside that was a voucher for a hundred pounds to spend on Jamie's favourite online store. Jamie's dad looked a bit sad.

"Sorry my son. Not very inspirational, but you know how it is."

"It's great, both of you and I do understand. Honestly." Jamie pushed back his chair and went over to give his dad a hug and then sidled over to Mum. She hugged him tightly sighing as she did so. She looked up at him and stroked his face saying nothing.

Jamie smiled at her. "Thanks Mum. I love you."

"I love you too," she managed before bursting into tears. She knocked her chair back onto the floor with a clatter and fled from the kitchen sobbing.

Jamie was distraught and looked over at his dad. "Sorry," he mouthed.

Jamie's Dad nodded and smiled indicating that it wasn't his fault and left the room to find her. Jamie sat down with a thump and absent-mindedly pushed the rest of his breakfast around his plate.

"What a to-do," stated his grandma. "I knew your mother found your birthday difficult, but I didn't think she was this bad." She tutted. "Oh well. Open my card Jamie."

Jamie did as he was told and opened his grandma's

215

card. It was a typical card, with a picture of a racing car on it, but inside were three tickets to the Formula One qualifying session at Silverstone.

"Thanks Grandma." Jamie beamed. She came over and gave him a squeeze.

"Something to look forward to when this is all over."

Jamie smiled grimly. "Let's hope so. I'd like to go and do something fun without anything hanging over me!" He caressed the tickets with his fingers and smiled broadly despite himself. "Thanks Grandma."

She winked at him. "No problem Grandson. Can't wait to go myself. Spin in the beast later?"

"Yes please." Jamie's appetite returned and after a few minutes Dad poked his head around the door. "Mum's in the living room. She'd like to see you."

Jamie's face fell and Dad smiled reassuringly. "It's okay. She's recovered."

"Okay Dad." Jamie got up and padded into the living room. Mum was sitting on the sofa with her feet tucked underneath her. Her eyes were still red, but she'd stopped crying. She clutched Dad's hanky with one hand, but with the other she patted the sofa. Jamie sat next to her.

"Hi Mum."

"Hello my darling." She sniffed and blew her nose. "I'm so sorry about my behaviour. I should be celebrating, not mourning your sister. It's not fair on you."

"It's fine Mum, really it is." Jamie eyed his mother carefully. This was a regular birthday scenario and he knew he should tread with care. She was so level headed for the majority of the year, but on his birthday, she always had a mini collapse. She'd be fine tomorrow, but for now he had to watch what he said. Without warning though a thought came into his head

216

and he asked her a question he'd never considered before.

"Why haven't you and Dad tried for another little girl?"

He felt his mother stiffen for a moment, but then relaxed. "What did you say?"

"Um, I don't mean to be rude and I do know enough about it to know you're still young enough for another child. You had me at twenty-three, which would make you…"

"Thirty-eight this year." She laughed surprising herself. "Thank you for reminding me." She reached for Jamie's hand. "We, I, thought you wouldn't like it."

"You never asked, Mum."

She sighed at this. "Your father and I have rather thrown ourselves into our careers haven't we?" Jamie said nothing. "You're a good boy."

"I wouldn't mind you know Mum."

"Mind?"

"Having a baby sister, or brother," he added quickly.

She sat up and looked at him. "Really?"

"Really. It would be fab."

She sighed again. "The doctors at the time did warn us that it might never happen again."

"Aren't there tests you can have?"

His mother laughed and opened her arms. Jamie lay on her lap and she stroked his hair. "Maybe I will. Thank you."

"What for?"

"For never complaining. For being so level-headed. I know you must think us too driven in our jobs and all the nannies we've had. You've liked some of them haven't you?"

Jamie nodded. "Some."

There was a pause. "And here?"

217

"I like it here."

"Me too. Perhaps I'll make that appointment for next week."

Jamie sat up. "Really?"

"Definitely," she replied. "Now I'll try not to ruin your birthday any more."

"You haven't Mum and you don't. I just want to help."

She smiled again and wiped away a tear. "You do, my son," she sniffed. "Right, I'm not going to start again. What have you got planned for the rest of the day? A ride in that infernal machine of your grandmother's no doubt."

Jamie nodded. "Plus a walk with a friend."

His mum's eyes sparkled. "A friend?"

"Yeah, she's called Jane-Claire, but we call her JC."

"Is she nice?"

"Mum!" Jamie protested.

"Will you introduce her to us?"

"If you promise not to be embarrassing."

"I can't vouch for your father, but I'll behave. Promise."

"Good. I'm going to get ready. She'll be here soon."

"Don't forget to wash under your armpits."

"Mum!"

A walk in the woods

The doorbell rang. Jamie was torn between charging down the stairs to wrench the door open or playing it cool. He didn't have a chance to decide, as his parents opened the door together. Jamie had warned them earlier that she was bringing her dog, so Duster was in the garden waiting to be introduced and he could hear him barking in the garden.

"Hello," he heard JC say. "I'm Jane-Claire."

"Hello," he heard his parents say. "Jamie should be here in a sec. Who's this with you?" Jamie saw his father bend down and a chocolate Labrador thrust his nose in the house sniffing furiously.

"This is Murphy. Murphy," she commanded, "sit and say hello." Jamie watched as he came down the stairs as Murphy sat and raised his paw for his dad to shake.

He chuckled. "He and Duster should get on famously. Come in." Dad closed the door behind them as Jamie reached the bottom of the stairs.

"Hello JC."

"Hi Jamie. How you feeling after yesterday?"

"Great thanks."

Jamie had to admit she looked great. She wore a red hooded top and a pair of simple jeans. Her hair was tied back and she wore a pair of walking shoes.

"Should I take these off?" she asked politely.

"Thank you JC. That would be great."

Jamie felt a bit nervous as she took off her shoes so he introduced himself to Murphy who gave him a big lick. "Shall we get the dogs together?"

"Good idea."

"This way. Carry your shoes though 'cause we'll go out the back gate."

Jamie's parents watched in amusement as he led them into the kitchen. Grandma had popped out so it was one less person to potentially embarrass him. As they padded through the kitchen he saw JC eye the birthday cards on the table.

"Whose birthday?" she asked.

"Mine," answered Jamie.

She raised an eyebrow. "Happy birthday."

"Thanks," Jamie replied changing the subject. "You ready?" JC nodded. "If you get Murphy to sit, I'll bring Duster in."

"Will they be okay?"

"Definitely. Trust me. Duster loves everyone. Well nearly everyone."

Jamie opened the back door. Duster was waiting, head cocked. He knew something interesting was about to happen. He wagged his tail. "Sit there boy. I've got someone for you to meet." Duster sat obediently and Jamie called for Murphy. Murphy trotted out and paused for a moment upon spying Duster. Duster stayed put, but his tail thumped against the floor in excitement. JC followed him out.

"Sit Murphy," she instructed. Murphy did as he was told and the two dogs sat facing each other noses almost touching. Duster licked Murphy's nose and Murphy licked him back. Duster whined and barked once and that was it, they both tore off down the garden leaping about and barking madly at each other.

"Best friends."

"So it seems."

"We'd better go quickly though," warned Jamie. "Grandma will take a dim view if they tear up the garden."

"Sure."

As JC retrieved her shoes Jamie slid into his wellies and put on a fleece. JC did up her laces and saying goodbye to his parents they closed the door behind them.

"Lead on MacLomax!" she grinned putting an arm through his.

Jamie whistled and Duster came running, tongue lolling out of the corner of his mouth. Murphy appeared seconds after and both dogs sat by their feet. Clipping on the leads, they sauntered out of the garden and after a short walk through the village entered the woods.

It was crisp autumnal day. The wood they were walking through was made up of beech trees and their leaves had turned to a golden brown. The sun shone brightly illuminating the different shades of red and brown on the trees as they crunched noisily through the woods. The dogs careered everywhere zigzagging across the path and scattered the last few remaining birds from the trees with their good-natured game of chase.

JC kicked through the leaves. "I used to collect leaves."

"Me too," said Jamie, "but there was never quite as many of these where I lived in London."

"Where was that?"

"Brixton."

"I've heard that's a scary part of London."

"Nah. The twins are far scarier than anything or anybody I met in town," Jamie answered.

"Weird how they changed isn't it?" she asked innocently.

"Certainly is. Quite pleased about it, have to say."

She stopped for a moment picking up a leaf that was almost red in colour. "I'd have loved this one for my scrap book a few years ago."

"Do you still collect them?"

"Not any more. Other things occupy my thoughts now," she replied looking at Jamie with a twinkle in her eye.

Jamie didn't know where to look and blurted out. "Do you know what they call holiday makers who go to New England in the USA to look at the trees?"

She giggled and said. "No?"

"Leaf-peepers!"

"Leaf-peepers?" she echoed affecting an American accent.

"Sure."

They carried on walking pretending to talk in American accents. Jamie was really enjoying her company. He stole a look at her as she tried to do other accents and was struck by how alike they were and how funny she could be. She was popular with her friends, the alpha girl, and leader of the pack. He hoped she was enjoying his company too. Mustn't try too hard he thought to himself. He cringed inwardly as he did a rubbish Scottish accent.

"Kiwi?" she teased.

"Shut up," he retorted picking up a pile of leaves and chucking it at her.

"Oi!" she cried. "You can't do that to me. I'm a defenceless girl."

"You don't look defenceless to me. I've heard you're a judo black belt."

"Why don't you come here and find out?"

"No fear!" shouted Jamie as he picked up speed and ran up the hill. The dogs gave chase as did JC with a pile of leaves in her arms. The path they were following reached the top of a small incline and the trees cleared leaving a fantastic view over distant hills. Jamie stopped, distracted by the view forgetting that he was being pursued. A shower of leaves exploded all over him as JC caught up.

"Got ya!" she cried in triumph.

Jamie spluttered theatrically. "Thanks JC," he said

wiping leaves from his shoulders. "Don't you just love this view?"

"Never tire of it," replied JC joining him. "There's a good log over there. I need a rest." They sat down side by side and she sidled up close to him. "Why didn't you tell me it was your birthday?"

Jamie squirmed a little, unused to female attention and scrutiny. "Birthdays in my house can be a bit traumatic."

"Why?" she instinctively said, but added quickly. "Sorry. That's rude of me."

"No it's fine." Jamie told her about his twin sister and how his mother reacted every year.

"Poor you," she said and kissed him on the cheek.

Jamie blushed and managed to splutter. "Thanks."

"No problem. I like you."

"I like you too."

"Good. Let's do this again."

Jamie brightened. "I'd like that."

"Excellent." She kissed him again and he nearly passed out. She jumped up. "Come on. Race you back."

They ran back through the woods, hooting and laughing whilst the dogs charged off in front. Before they knew it they were panting by the edge of the woods, holding their sides.

"That was fun," Jamie said managed between breaths.

"Same time next week?" JC asked trying to get some air into her lungs.

"You're on," replied Jamie.

Recovered finally, they came out of the woods and clipped the leads on the panting dogs. As they approached Jamie's house from the woods, JC spied Grandma's Jaguar out the front of the house. Her eyes widened.

"Wow. What's that?"

"What's what?" goaded Jamie, knowing full well what she was referring to.

"That!" she urged pointing at Grandma's car.

"A car I think," Jamie answered.

She hit him playfully on the arm. "It's not just any car. Look at it."

"It's a green one?" offered Jamie.

She biffed him again. "Philistine. It's a fantastic looking sports car." She looked again. "Hey, it's outside your house."

"Yeah, it's Grandma's."

"You're kidding."

"Nope."

"Come on!" she urged breaking into a run. "Let's see it."

With the dogs barking alongside them they reached the Lomax house where the Jaguar sat waiting. They let the dogs into the garden and JC walked around the car whistling appreciatively. Jamie looked on in amusement. The gate clicked shut and Grandma appeared.

"Hello dear. I'm Jamie's grandma," she introduced. JC shook her hand and said hello. "What do you think of the car?"

"It's amazing. Beautiful. Jaguar E-Type, with its original Dunlop tyres. Series 1?"

"Correct." Grandma raised her eyebrows and looked at Jamie.

"Wow. Three point eight or four point two litre engine?"

Grandma was impressed. "Four point two."

"Cool. That must make it a 1964 model."

"Sixty-five dear, but spot on."

JC whistled and trailed her finger down the bonnet. "That must mean it has two hundred and sixty-five brake horse power, right?" Grandma nodded. Jamie's mouth was open in astonishment. JC continued. "The four point two had the same power as the three point eight, but the later model had a much better throttle response." Grandma nodded again. "Top speed approaching one hundred and fifty miles an hour."

"Correct. Managed it once with Jamie's grandfather on an old airfield in Lincolnshire."

"Brilliant. Does she still go that fast?"

"Haven't tried it recently, but Jamie can testify to her speed, right Jamie?"

Jamie nodded and asked. "How do you know so much about cars?"

"My Dad races old bangers. I've always loved engines. Been to loads of events, Dad even taught me how to drive."

Jamie was impressed.

"I can't let you drive this though, but would you like a ride?" JC's eyes lit up.

"Oh yes please."

"Hop in then. Jamie you don't mind do you? Ladies first."

Jamie waved graciously. "After you JC, but hold on tight, she thinks she's Jenson Button."

"Stirling Moss my dear. Less facial hair!"

Jamie watched JC slip into the passenger seat of the two-seater and buckle herself in. His Grandma tied her hair back, slipped on her leather driving gloves and eased herself into the driver's side shutting the door with a satisfying clunk behind her. Just as she did so a cloud passed over the sun. Jamie looked up and was momentarily startled. The sun illuminated the cloud's shape and if he wasn't so used to strange events he would have sworn that it was shaped like the warrior's distinctive helmet. A shiver went down his spine despite the temperature and he remembered the warrior's warning.

"Keep a close eye on those you cherish."

Jamie barely had time to register a warning when the orb buzzed urgently in his pocket. The Jaguar roared into life and sped off leaving him waving frantically. Both girls waved back assuming he was sending them off and he watched hopelessly as the Jaguar sped off into the distance. He didn't know what to do. There was no point in giving chase, he'd get nowhere near them. He reached for his pocket and was about to text a warning to JC, but thought better of it. She'll think I'm insane he figured.

He hopped from foot to foot as he listened to the car leaving the village and winced as it picked up speed. He felt the orb vibrating strongly in his hand and he connected with it, allowing its power to envelop him. Keep them safe he urged strongly. His body shuddered and he felt energy leave him. It swirled around him for a moment before it shot off in a shimmering haze in pursuit of the car.

The next ten minutes were the most anxious of Jamie's life. He kept looking at his watch and frantically kept trying to remember how long the journey usually took. He put his watch to his ear to check it was still going, but felt silly suddenly. It was digital! It didn't tick. He wasn't thinking straight.

Stay calm he kept telling himself. Stay calm. He strained his hearing and thought he could pick up an engine noise in the distance. It sounded like a car, but it sounded wrong. He listened again and this time he was sure it was the Jaguar. He heard a gear change and its distinctive roar and knew they were close. He nearly cried out in relief. They were okay. Come on, come on, he kept telling himself. Be fine, be fine.

The noise increased and suddenly round the corner came the car. Something was up with the engine and it sounded wrong. Grandma pulled up next to the kerb and switched it off. She looked bothered and drummed her fingers on the steering wheel.

"What's wrong Grandma?" Jamie asked. He glanced over at JC, who looked disappointed.

"She's not firing properly. We left the village nicely enough, but without warning the engine misfired and we lost power. Every so often she'd come back to life, but then there'd be another misfire."

Jamie tried to put on his best concerned look knowing it may have been his fault, but at least they hadn't gone fast enough to have an accident. Jamie was sure that was what would have happened. The orb had been pretty insistent after the cloud passed over. He was sure that evil things were afoot.

Grandma reached across and patted JC on the knee. "Never mind dear. Once she's fixed we'll go for another spin okay?"

JC nodded and got out of the car. She smiled at Jamie. "What a car!"

"Jamie smiled back. "When she goes, she really goes. Next time eh?"

"Sure."

Grandma looked at her watch and said. "Jamie, tell your parents that I'm going to drop this round to my friend Dave. He'll know what the matter is and he should be in."

As she said this, another shadow fell across the car and Jamie had to rub his eyes. No surely not. He could have sworn he saw the warrior sitting in the passenger seat. The sun came out again and he shook his head. The seat was empty. His nerves were at breaking point and the orb vibrated strongly in his pocket.

"I don't think you should go," he said.

"Don't be silly," she answered. She looked at him. Jamie couldn't say anything in front of JC, so he made up his mind.

227

"I'll come with you," he declared.

"You've got a visitor. I'll be fine."

"Grandma!" Jamie was insistent. He turned to JC. "Can I call you later?"

JC looked bemused. "It's your birthday. You go with your Grandma. Course you can ring me later. Don't forget. Okay?"

Jamie nodded gratefully and jumped into the car. He waved JC goodbye as Grandma started up the engine again. She was right it didn't sound like it normally did. She popped it into gear and with a couple of bunny hops and loud bang from the exhaust she gingerly nosed the big car into the road.

She had a grim look on her face, obviously worried about the Jaguar. "What's up with you?" she asked.

Jamie assumed she was talking to the car and didn't answer. "Jamie?"

"Oh sorry. Look I couldn't talk then. The car. I did it. The warrior is here!"

She didn't have time to register this when the car suddenly began to speed up. "What's happening?" she yelled as it accelerated away.

"He's here Grandma. He's going to try and kill us!" Jamie yelled. He held on for dear life and clutched the orb in his hands.

"Not bloody likely," shouted his grandma over the noise of the engine. "Let him try."

The car was picking up speed as it left the village. She tried to brake, but nothing was slowing the car down, the accelerator was jammed. Jamie watched as she tried to engage the clutch pedal, but it too was jammed. She tried to slip the gear lever into neutral without the clutch, but the cogs ground in protest. Giving up, she placed both on the steering wheel.

They approached a bend in the road and she yelled, "Hold on tight!" as the big car, tyres screeching took

the curve far faster than it should. The back end started
to slide and Grandma struggled with the steering wheel
trying to bring it under control. The car fishtailed from
side to side and Jamie saw in horror that another car
was coming in the opposite direction. The other driver
flashed their lights and the horn blared but the back of
the old Jag clipped the oncoming car with a terrifying
crunch of metal, which sent them into an uncontrollable
spin.

Jamie could barely hold onto the orb, but despite his
world spinning he managed to connect with it. At this
speed and in this flat spin, they'd be killed instantly. He
imagined that all the latest crash protection was fitted to
the old Jaguar, inspired by the tickets his grandma had
given him that morning. There had been no casualties
in serious motor racing for years and he imagined them
in a Formula 1 car. He felt rather than saw the result as
a powerful protective bubble seemed to envelop the car
and he had no time to hope it would work as the Jaguar,
tyres squealing, left the road and slammed into a brick
wall.

The impact was incredible. One moment they were
flying round in a circle and the next they met a solid
object. He could feel his body being thrown sideways
and then back in the other direction. His head slammed
against the side window and the glass exploded
outwards, but he felt no pain. The breath in his lungs
was forced out as the seat belt tightened and then all
was still. He quickly checked himself. He was still
breathing and he could feel a trickle of blood rolling
down his cheek. He tried to move his arms and legs. A
quick check confirmed nothing was injured. He silently
thanked the orb and put it into a pocket.

The old car hissed and crackled and he looked over
to his grandma. She was unconscious, head slumped on
the steering wheel, but she groaned audibly. Thank

goodness, Jamie thought. She's still alive. He could smell smoke and petrol fumes and hurriedly unclipped his seat belt. He had to get Grandma out of there now. He could hear concerned voices shouting from somewhere as he opened his door and stumbled slightly, his legs turned to jelly.

He leant against the battered car allowing his head to clear for an instant before he tried to run around to the driver's side. The car had come to a rest with its bonnet against the wall, allowing enough space to open the other door. Smoke started to billow from the engine now and the petrol fumes were more distinct. There was every possibility that it was about to go up in flames.

He scrabbled with the door handle, hands shaking. He willed himself to calm down and tried again. It opened and he reached across his groaning grandma to unclip the belt. He pressed down on the button release, but it was jammed.

"Come on!" Jamie shouted as he saw the first flicker of flames lick the front of the bonnet. He only had a minute or so before the petrol leaking from the tank ignited. He tried again, harder and this time it released. He unravelled the prone figure of his grandma from the belt and had no time to assess for any life threating injuries. He had to get her out of their now, or there would be a fatality!

He reached under her armpit and started to pull her out of the car. She slid agonisingly slowly out of her seat and he was worried that her legs were caught in the crumpled front of the car. He paused, panting hard before he tried again. He was aware that the voices were closer now but had no time to cry out for help as he could see the flames staring to catch hold. He breathed deeply and then with all his effort pulled his grandma. Suddenly her legs came away and they

230

tumbled backwards out of the car.

Another pair of hands picked him up. "Quick!" said a male voice. "Let's get you both away from here, that's going to go up any second." Together they dragged Grandma groaning more loudly now and obviously waking up as far away from the now burning Jaguar as they dared. They gently leaned her against a tree.

"Thank you," Jamie panted and looked up. Standing next to Jamie was a tall man in glasses. The car they'd hit was up the road with both doors open. Jamie could see Spencer leaning against the car watching him, arms crossed. It had to be Spencer's dad.

"Wowee you were lucky." He didn't seem angry, just concerned. "What happened? You clipped us at at least seventy miles an hour. The spin was pretty dramatic."

Jamie's grandma coughed and croakily said, "The accelerator jammed!"

Jamie cried out. "Grandma! You're okay!"

She smiled bravely. "I think I've broken my ankle; it's pretty painful. Head hurts, but otherwise fine and dandy." She looked up and only now noticed the car. "Oh my god! Look at the car."

The car was now smoking badly and the flames were flickering over the front of the windscreen. Grandma looked at Jamie and patted his arm. "Thanks for getting me out of there."

Mr Rogers turned and shouted at his son. "Spencer. I left my phone in the car. Ring 999 and let them know we need a fire engine and an ambulance, quick sharp." Jamie watched, as Spencer didn't move. This irritated his father who shouted out "NOW!" This seemed to get him moving and to no one in particular he muttered, "I don't know what's with that boy half the time!"

A sound like a sigh went up as the leaking petrol

caught fire and instantly engulfed the car in flames. Jamie felt sick. That could have been Grandma in there he thought. He felt his anger rising, but calmed himself. This wasn't the time to face the warrior. He didn't have the energy now; he'd hope to deal with him later.

He bent down to check on Grandma and tears were pouring down her face. "You brave, brave boy," she sobbed. "Goodbye, my wonderful car."

Jamie fished his phone out of his pocket and he rang his parents to let them know they'd been in an accident and they were just outside the village. He told them to hurry. They were okay, but badly shaken. Within a couple of minutes Dad pulled up and both he and Mum jumped out of the car and ran over.

"Mum, Jamie!" Dad cried out. "Are you okay?" He saw the burning car burning viciously. "Is that the Jag?"

Grandma nodded.

"Blimey."

Jamie's Mum said nothing but kissed her mother in law and gave Jamie a big squeeze. Sirens could be heard in the distance and Jamie sank down into the grass exhausted, but alive. For the time being anyway.

Repercussions and revelations

Jamie sat in the kitchen sometime later nursing a bowl of hot soup. Some birthday he thought to himself. The fire engine had arrived to put the fire out and the police questioned the both of them over the accident. Spencer's Dad was happy to accept that the accelerator had jammed open and it had happened so quickly that Grandma had had no time to stop the car safely. He wasn't going to press any charges.

There wasn't much left of the car once the fire brigade had finished with it and the police very much doubted that they'd be able to verify the story one way or another and seemed satisfied. JC had appeared breathless and worried as Grandma was being loaded onto the ambulance. She'd thrown herself into Jamie's arms quite unexpectedly giving him a hug. He'd winced slightly as he was a bit bruised but he certainly hadn't complained! Jamie smiled at the memory.

Grandma was going to be all right, she'd broken a couple of ribs, her ankle and suffered a serious concussion. Dad was with her now and the hospital had insisted that she stay in for observation for a couple of days. The paramedics had given Jamie the once over. He was quickly given a clean bill of health and told to rest. He might suffer from shock later he'd been told, but nothing that a good night's sleep wouldn't solve.

He finished his soup and washed the bowl up in the sink. Mum had barely left his side the rest of the day and she looked up from her marking.

"Hello darling. How are you feeling?" she asked for the umpteenth time.

He didn't want to hurt her feelings, but he was beginning to feel a bit trapped by all the attention. "Mum, I've told you that I'm fine. The accident was

233

frightening, but I'm okay and Grandma is too."

"She drives too fast," Mum snapped. "It was always going to happen."

Jamie sighed. "Mum, Grandma is an excellent driver, you know that. The accelerator got jammed on the old car. It happened, it's over and maybe she'll buy something more sensible now to drive to bridge and her golf."

Mum managed a weak smile. "Maybe. Well, do you need anything else?"

"No thanks." He kissed his mum on the cheek. "I'm going to go to bed, it's been some birthday." She got up to come with him. "Mum," he warned. "Please! I'm going to have a shower then go to bed."

She looked reluctant to let him out of her sight, but sat down again. "Sleep well. Just shout if you need me."

"Night Mum."

"Night."

Jamie trudged wearily up the stairs and shut himself in the bathroom. He turned the shower on and allowed the steam to build up whilst he undressed. He stepped into the shower and the moment the hot water blasted down onto his head and his shoulders he felt better. It had been the most unusual, frightening and downright strange two weeks of his life.

So much had happened during this time that it made his mind ache at times. He was proud of how he'd helped everyone so far and doubly honoured that he'd rescued his grandma from a certain fiery end. He knew that when he was ready, the orb would acknowledge that. This meant he had just about two weeks left to help the final person. He suspected that might happen next week in the Lake District and was a bit nervous about being away from the support of his grandma.

As he rinsed out the shampoo, he thought about the

warrior and how underhand he'd been these past few days. To involve his grandma had made him mad. He was angry, really angry and he was doing his best to keep that particular emotion in check. A confrontation between them was imminent, of that Jamie was sure.

Jamie dried himself and left some clothes by the side of the bed just in case tonight was the night. He sat at his desk and placed the orb in the palms of his hand as if receiving a gift and closed his eyes searching for a connection. A moment of clarity in his thoughts and a jolt of electricity from his hands signalled the connection this time and he opened his eyes. The orb lifted off his hands by a couple of centimetres and started to spin.

Jamie readied himself as the orb released a bolt of energy that flew around the room in exhilaration before diving onto the top of his head enveloping him in an energy he'd never seen before. It surrounded his body, tickling him, caressing his cuts and bruises, before his body welcomed it into him and absorbed the shimmering white light.

A feeling of contentment flowed through him. His body healed from the inside. He watched as the bruises simply disappeared and he could see the blood coursing around his veins in celebration. The feeling was extraordinary and he felt euphoric. Tears coursed down his cheeks and he laughed out loud. He wondered for a fleeting moment if this what he'd be able to do now. To heal himself. It would be a useful skill to have if he had to fight with the warrior. His body arched as the energy fizzled up his spine and he could hear cartilage clicking into place, before it entered his brain zapping neurons and clearing his mind of all his worries.

Jamie felt invincible for a fleeting moment before the energy flew out of his hand and entered back into the orb. The orb slowed its spin before flashing four times and settling back into his palms before extinguishing. He placed it with care on the desk. He felt like going for a run, he was full of energy. He stretched experimentally and endorphins coursed through his veins. On impulse, he did ten press-ups and jumped up eager to release a bit more energy. The orb glowed brightly and as he touched it in thanks, this pent up energy was released and he became tired. Utterly satisfied, but tired beyond belief. He made it to his bed before as had happened so many times when it came to his dealings with the orb fell into an instant sleep.

Jamie woke up at some point during the night, startled and disorientated. He looked at his clock, but it read 12:77. 12:77? He rubbed his eyes and looked again, but the numbers hadn't changed. He sat up and looked for Duster, but he wasn't there. He shivered and breathed out. He could see his breath in the cold of the room; this wasn't right. It was never this chilly in the house. He breathed in deeply. It was time. He was ready.

Jamie slipped his legs from under the bedclothes, got dressed. Despite the warm clothes he'd selected earlier, his teeth began to chatter. He reached out to the metal lamp on his desk and flinched. It was freezing cold and the tips of his fingers almost stuck to it. He switched it on, but it barely illuminated the ghostly gloom of his room. His breath continued to billow from him and he shivered again.

Jamie tentatively reached out to pick up the orb from his desk, unsure of how cold it would be. He needn't have been concerned as it was warm to the touch. His outdoor coat was on the back of his chair and he slipped it on. He put the orb in the inside pocket and zipped it up to his neck. He quickly grabbed a pair of socks from the drawer and put on a pair of trainers. He stepped cautiously into the gloom of his room. He couldn't see anything. As he stepped away from his desk, a cloud seemed to envelope him, blinding him.

Jamie reached inside of his jacket and brought out the orb. It immediately shone like a beacon splitting the cloud in two. His room had begun to shimmer and it took on a translucent quality as if it wasn't there. He stepped towards the window, which as he approached crackled, instantly freezing into a sheet of ice. He looked at it as if in understanding and then looked into it. His own face, distorted slightly, stared back at him and then suddenly, as had happened to him before, the world shifted. He fell, but he was prepared for it this time and welcomed the journey.

"Salutations," said the warrior. Jamie had arrived.

He kept his simmering anger at bay and took a step forward. "That was unnecessary today," he started bravely. "You could have killed her."

"That was the intention." The warrior's eyes bored into Jamie's challenging him.

"But it didn't happen. I saved her and the orb has granted me the fourth part of its power."

"So I see," answered the warrior. "Your eyes have changed again."

"Did you have to involve my family?"

"Thought it might be the kick start you needed."

"I was doing okay."

"Yes, but it was all rather low impact stuff though wasn't it. Your escape from the water wasn't bad, but I felt you needed to understand that this quest isn't a game. There has to be an end result."

"I realise that now. I will beat you."

The warrior laughed good-naturedly for the first time at this. "We'll see, we'll see! Now you are here and you appear to truly understand the nature of our agreement is there anything else you wish to know?"

"Your identity?"

"Is that important? I'm not sure you'd believe me if I showed you."

Jamie nodded firmly. "I'm sure."

"This may send you into a bit of a spin young Jamie. Ready yourself." He reached behind his head and unclipped his helmet. Jamie watched intrigued as the mysterious man took off his helmet and placed it carefully on the floor.

Jamie gasped in astonishment, his senses reeling in shock. He rubbed his eyes, disbelieving what he was seeing. "But, you're, you're me?"

The other man smiled not unpleasantly, "and it appears you, are me, albeit a much younger version."

They looked at each other in sudden understanding. The warrior unmasked, was an older version of Jamie. He had jet-black hair, piercing blue eyes and the same distinctive features of the younger Jamie. The only difference was a tidy beard, flecked with grey that accentuated a wide jaw. Jamie noticed there was a faint line on one side of his chin where no hair grew and he touched the scar on his chin, knowing instinctively that they were the same.

"Wow!" whistled Jamie. "Is this what I'm going to look like when I'm older?"

"It will be so."

Jamie's knees buckled slightly. "I don't understand."

"Probably best not dwell too much on it, because it will drive you to complete and utter distraction. For all intents and purposes, we are the same. I am you and you are me."

"But I don't want power, take over worlds and laugh evilly all the time."

"You have the potential to take over your whole world! You could if you put your mind to it."

"Why would I want to?" he countered bravely.

"You might change your mind."

"I doubt it. Do I turn into you?"

"A good question and one that I cannot answer. But know this, you have the potential to turn into this version of us."

"I am a version of us?"

"Yes."

"But not you?"

"No."

"What if I were to die?"

"I would feel the pain of your death, as I have of the other versions of us across the dimensions of time and space, but I would remain."

"There are others?"

"Indeed so. Many have accepted the challenge as you have done. Many never find the orb in their lifetime, so never have this particular conversation and lead their lives without fear. Those that have activated the orb all come here at some point. All have resisted my help and all have failed in their quest."

"The wish?"

The warrior nodded. "The reason I have intervened so much recently was to test your inner strength. You have power, the orb knows that, I know that. If you were to join me, well, together we would be unstoppable."

"That won't happen. I will succeed," Jamie stated.

"I applaud your bravery, but the last person you will decide to help is always without doubt the hardest. Many have fallen at this point you will do the same. A great challenge, a dilemma will test your resolve. Succeed and the wish will be yours, but fail..." The warrior paused and took a step forward, but Jamie stood his ground. He wasn't scared any more. "...fail, then I'll be there and your soul," the warrior prodded Jamie painfully in the chest, "will be mine!"

Jamie continued to stand his ground and he stared back at his older face. The warrior took a step back and clapped once. The flap to the curtain opened instantly and the strange girl he recognised from before entered.

"You called, Lord." She betrayed no emotion

Jamie stared at her understanding beginning to dawn. "Is she?" he began.

"Our sister?" the warrior finished.

"Yes."

"Judging by the look on your face, you know this to be true."

Jamie was dumbfounded. "Are there many versions of her too?"

"Only one," the warrior answered with the hint of a smile on his face. "I had to hunt high and low for her. Like you I felt the pain of the loss of a twin and as I grew more powerful, I began to search. She is here with me now, not with the version she should be with."

"So in her time, she gets to live?"

"Oh yes, but then cruelly for the mother she gets taken away."

"What happens to her mother?"

"She dies!" The girl took a step forward fist clenched. "Now, now. Look she has our temper."

"Your temper!"

"Are you sure Jamie? Look how your fists are clenched too." The teasing in his voice vanished as he barked at the girl, "Begone." She stood her ground and with great speed he struck her across the face. The sound of the impact resounded in the tent. She stared at him, spat at his feet and left. Jamie took a step forward as the orb began to vibrate in his pocket. The warrior raised a hand freezing Jamie on the spot.

"You will not be trying the same trick you employed last time. I am ready for you now. It is time for you to return. I shall not interfere too much in your last choice, but I may be tempted to throw in the odd bit of mayhem to keep you on your toes. Be seeing you real soon young Jamie. Watch your back now."

And with a second wave of his hand Jamie felt the world swim around him before he fell headlong back into the twenty-first century and back with a huge sense of relief to his ice-free bedroom. Wide awake now, he checked his clock, which read five in the morning. There would be no more sleep tonight, so slipping off his shoes he lay back on his bed and tried to decide who he might help now he knew more of the truth.

Motorway services

Jamie wasn't sure how he felt as he wheeled his luggage towards school early on Monday morning. The sun was gently warming the air and a beautiful early autumn day beckoned, but the promise of fine weather did little to lighten his mood. An Outward Bound week with his new friends and classmates, as opposed to a week at school, was a real bonus. But, despite his determination to defeat the warrior, he still felt a little uneasy about leaving home.

Beside him strolled his dad; Grandma had been released from hospital yesterday, so he had taken time off work to look after his mother, much to her bemusement. Jamie's mum, however, had taken a lot of persuading to go to school herself and she had left the house earlier seriously on edge. To compound her mood, she had come crashing into his room in a real state just after he had returned from seeing the warrior. She woke him up claiming she'd had a bad dream about him and some figure in a black suit of armour. That had really freaked the both of them and it took most of Sunday to calm her down. She was clearly unhappy about him leaving the fold, despite assurances from both of the men in her life.

Jamie had done his best yesterday, but Mum had still fretted and fussed around him as he finished packing. Despite doing his best to reassure her, she buzzed around him like the midges he thought he might have to encounter in the Lake District. He felt like swatting her away, but he knew that would only exacerbate the situation. Dad, sensing Jamie's frustration, attempted to save the day with one of his stories.

"Did I ever tell you that I went on a school trip to

the Lake District when I was at school?" he began.

Mum looked at him curiously, obviously having never heard this particular story before. She folded her arms and sighed theatrically.

Dad smiled. "No need to be like that. You'll like this one." He paused for a moment and looked wistfully into the distance for full dramatic effect. Mum shook her head and sighed again prompting him to continue. "It was during my A levels that we went on a Geography field trip to Windermere. It was a terrific trip and I could tell you many stories about it."

Mum picked up a pillow in warning. "Okay, just the small snippet then. Where was I? Oh yes, I wanted to say something about midges. There was French girl on our trip called Salome. She was rather pretty actually." Mum threw the pillow, which Dad was expecting and he caught it laughing. "No need to be jealous. Anyway, she had heard someone talking about midges during the journey. On our first evening we were all sitting outside, being attacked by the little blighters, when she pipes up quite innocently, 'don't you just hate it when you get attacked by hoards of midgets!' Well as you can imagine, we all forgot about the midges, such was the hilarity." He burst out laughing at the thought of it again and soon had tears rolling down his face. Mum soon was smiling too.

"Come on you," said Dad ushering her out of the room. "Let's leave Jamie in peace." Jamie's dad winked at him as he left and Jamie had mouthed a silent "Thank you."

Jamie smiled as he recalled the story and by the time they reached school he'd cheered up. Everyone was congregating in the playground and they joined the general melee, looking for some instruction as what to do next. They were on time, but the playground was already full of excited teenagers and their overly anxious parents.

Fitz, clutching his ever present clipboard, seemed to be trying to extricate himself from a particularly vociferous parent who appeared to be giving him all manner of unwanted instructions about her child. He nodded in encouragement and tried to walk away, as it seemed the conversation was over, only to be drawn in again as the parent added just one more thing.

There were forty boys and girls going on the trip and four members of staff. Jamie could see two of the other teachers, their form teachers, Mr Andreck and Miss Kabia, attempting to restore some semblance of order to the proceedings, but not having a great deal of luck.

Suddenly, everything changed as the fourth member of staff, the headmistress, strolled decisively out of the main doors of the school. Jamie shuddered for a moment remembering the recent incident in the school hall and watched her carefully to see if it was really her. Like a shark scouting for its prey, she cut through the masses, instructing parents to stand on one side of the playground, boys and girls on the other. He breathed a sigh of relief, it was definitely her. He watched with quiet admiration as she took firm control of the situation, admonishing the twins for some over-exuberance and issuing orders to everyone.

Most of the younger parents had been taught by her and she still held that gravitas that some could only ever hope to emulate. Very quickly, order was restored to the playground, much to the evident relief of the other teachers, and she assembled everyone in for one of her 'quick chats' as she liked to call them.

Thankfully, this chat didn't last long. She emphasised the importance of good behaviour to the children whilst at the same time making the most of the chance to enjoy a well-earned holiday. This was for the benefit of all the parents present of course, whom she reassured that their children were in the best possible hands.

She mentioned, not for the first time, the success of the football team and for one horrible moment she caught Jamie's eye and appeared to be about to launch into a well-meaning invective about his holiday heroics. Jamie had been half-expecting something of this sort and was desperate to avoid any unwanted showering of praise – certainly not at the beginning of this particular trip. The orb was clenched in his hand and he willed his physical body elsewhere to remain invisible to his ebullient headmistress.

She paused for a moment as the orb vibrated quietly in the palm of his hand, and they connected. She looked quizzically at the assembled throng, and appeared to gaze right through Jamie, before shaking off her temporary lack of memory. She did still produce the cup, to wild cheers, and she invited Tommy up to hold it with her.

To further cheers, the coach pulled up outside the school and the headmistress instructed the parents to say their final goodbyes. Jamie's Dad offered his hand for a shake, but then grabbed his son and gave him a hug much to his embarrassment. Looking around him, he could see many of the others enduring something similar.

Jamie finally managed to escape from his dad after promising for the umpteenth time that he'd be good and yes, he had packed everything he needed and no, he didn't need to go to the toilet. He picked up his bag to stow under the coach and tapped his mini-rucksack on his back to ensure he still had it. Satisfied he had everything, he went to report to Fitz who was ticking off their names on his clipboard.

One by one they were accounted for and Jamie was

allowed to board the coach. As he was loading his bag, someone barged into him, nearly knocking him to the floor. He didn't need to guess who it was, as Spencer elbowed his way in front of him.

"Back of the line loser," he growled quietly.

"Fine. After you Spencer," Jamie retorted, unwilling to allow Spencer to get to him. He was secretly pleased, as he could now ensure that Spencer would get on the coach before him and that his bag wouldn't be moved or tampered with. Jamie waited patiently.

Spencer threw his bag to the driver who was in the depths of the stowage area, then attempted the same trick again. Jamie was wise this time and moved swiftly to his left as Spencer lunged 'accidentally on purpose'. He was committed to the manoeuvre and wasn't expecting evasive action. He missed and stumbled backwards, tripping over JC's bag who was behind Jamie and fell with a yell into the school hedge.

He quickly jumped straight back to his feet as though nothing had happened and pretending that he hadn't just made a complete fool of himself, skipped onto the bus without a backward glance. Jamie felt rather pleased with this minor bit of retribution and turned to help JC with her bag.

"Nice move," she said, grinning at him.

"Don't know what you mean?" he said, grinning back.

"Yeah, yeah. Whatever. You knew he was going to do that again didn't you?"

"It was pretty obvious."

"So obvious that I got out of the way too!"

They were both laughing as they got onto the bus and they made their way down the aisle looking for an available double seat. Spencer was at the back glowering at both of them, as they chose a seat far enough away not to be troubled by him and buckled themselves in.

The first stint of the three hundred mile trip on the coach went in the blink of an eye for Jamie. The coach was comfortable, with plenty of space for everyone. A good-natured groan went up as the headmistress put on a Disney movie, 'claiming' that it was only movie she had. Many of the children still plugged their headphones into the seat in front anyway to watch one of four screens on the coach. Others chatted to their friends or plugged themselves into their various entertainment systems.

Jamie spent a happy couple of hours chatting to JC. She had phoned him the day of the accident to make sure he was okay and they had chatted for over an hour. The instant they sat down, they carried on from where they'd left off. She was funny, sparky and intelligent and he was pleased to see that she enjoyed being with him as well. Tommy and Calum sat in the seat behind and after some light hearted banter about 'who's your girlfriend?' and 'does your mother know?' they soon settled into a quiet, but furious, linked battle on their games consoles.

After a couple of hours, the coach pulled into a service station to allow everyone to stretch their legs and go to the lavatory. It was a relief to get off the bus. JC, Jamie, Calum and Tommy chatted away to each other as they made their way into the service station. They clubbed some of their money together to get a bag of pick and mix, which Jamie offered to get as the others went off to explore. Tommy soon appeared to add his opinion to the choice of sweets and soon they had an unnecessarily large bag of candy to share on the coach.

"Better hide those," said JC as she popped her head into the shop. "Miss Kabia has a thing about children and too much sugar."

Tommy saluted her and then grinned broadly. "Right you are, swotty."

"Good thing too," she retorted, "or I'd have to report you for being annoying."

"Oi!" JC laughed and skipped off as Tommy did as he was asked.

Calum was waiting with JC as the boys came out of the shop and began to dish out the sweets. Calum was appreciative and nodded his head in satisfaction. Jamie handed everyone an equal bag of sweets and together they began to amble back to the coach when suddenly Spencer appeared, barring their exit out into the car park.

"Oh look. How nice. Jamie and his little gang of losers!" he snarled. Pointing at JC he added, "Oh and you've picked up miss brown-nose, the year prefect now as well."

No one said anything. For a moment there was an impasse until JC skirted her way around Spencer and exited the building.

"Oi, where do you think you're going?" he shouted, turning his back on the boys and racing after her. Sensing trouble, the boys followed quickly behind. Calum looked around and muttered, "Where are the twins when you really need them?"

Spencer had caught up with JC and unfortunately for her they were out of sight of the coach and their teachers. A heated argument had sprung up between them. Jamie was beginning to learn that JC wasn't the sort of person to back down from anyone, let alone a potential bully like Spencer and she was more than able at standing up for herself. Suddenly, as if he sensed that the odds were stacking against him, he snatched JC's bag of sweets from her as the boys arrived at her side.

"I'd like those back," warned JC. She looked irritated that she'd dropped her guard enough to have

248

the sweets taken from her.

"Or what?" goaded Spencer, reaching into the bag and depositing a fizzy cola bottle onto the end of his outstretched tongue, in an attempt to further provoke her.

"Don't push me, you unpleasant little worm. You've got to the count of three to give those back."

Munching on his stolen cola bottle, Spencer ignored the warning and reached into the bag for a second time. He foolishly took his eyes off the angry JC as she counted. He stood there shaking and pretending to be scared. Jamie watched as with almost inhuman speed, she stepped across Spencer, took the sweets from his hand and in the same movement tossed them to Calum who deftly caught them without spilling the bag. She then grabbed Spencer's jacket, dropped her shoulder and using his weight flipped the surprised boy over and onto his back. Winded and completely surprised, Spencer lay prone on the ground. JC prowled around him on the balls of her feet, fists clenched. He looked up at her in surprise and then remarkably started to grin at her.

"Get up!" she growled.

Spencer got up slowly. He was winded, but obviously not as injured as he was making out. Suddenly, he threw himself at JC, who was expecting such a move. She stepped nimbly out of the way and turned to face him as he turned and slowly started to stalk towards her, hands balled into fists. The boys watched helplessly, unsure of what they should do to help, but curiously interested to see how this whole situation would pan out.

Again, without any real prowess, Spencer attacked. He went to grab JC, who swiftly turned, stepped across the startled boy and flipped him once more onto his back. He landed in a heap and not unlike a turtle, arms and legs grappled for a sure footing. A 'whoosh' sounded, as the air was forced out of his lungs and the others gasped in astonishment. JC slapped her hands together, as if to signify good riddance to bad rubbish, and retreated back to the safety of the group.

"Wow!" mouthed Calum as they all kept a careful eye on Spencer who was beginning to recover. He moaned and then rolled off the path onto the grass. Everyone could see what was going to happen as Spencer's hand came to rest on a discarded stick. His hand grasped the weapon and with renewed menace sat up and tested the stick in his other hand a couple of times to signify his obvious intent. He rose to his feet snarling and his eyes did little to betray the hurt of being felled by a girl. It looked to all of them that had one thing on his mind. Revenge!

Jamie decided it was time to intervene. JC's obvious skills in the art of self-defence shouldn't now be tested against an offence weapon and he took control.

"Boys. Protect JC and back away as quick as you can." The others did as he asked without question as he stood his ground.

Spencer smiled nastily and growled, "Move out of the way loser. For once, it's not you I want. She deserves what's coming."

"Spencer!" Jamie ordered as the orb vibrated in his pocket. He felt the power in him growing. "Spencer! Snap out of it man. Put the stick down, before I seriously hurt you." Spencer looked at him with real fear in his eyes. He spoke again. "You've got seconds to put down that thing before I forcible take it from you. You know I will." Spencer tapped the stick a few more times in his hand and bravely stepped closer to Jamie. Jamie made himself as big as possible and held his ground.

Without warning a voice inside his head spoke to

him. Jamie staggered slightly surprised, but hoped Spencer hadn't noticed. "Attack him. Beat him. His life is meaningless compared to yours. Another chance to release your true power. Kill him!"

Jamie began to feel his anger beginning to grow. A part of him wanted to lash out with all his might, but he didn't want to hurt Spencer. He knew if he did, Spencer would be seriously hurt, killed even.

Mustering as much power as he could in his voice he commanded, "Give me the stick. Walk away. Think about it. You'd forgotten that JC was a black belt in Judo. You know what she can do. You picked on the wrong person. Don't pick on me, I will hurt you," he repeated as he felt his anger begin to abate.

Jamie's powerful words were beginning to sink in as Spencer stopped tapping the stick and let it fall to his side. The black mist was beginning to dissipate and Spencer shook his head as if in disbelief.

"Give me the stick. Please?" Spencer looked at the stick with puzzlement, as if unsure of how it got there, before sluggishly handing it over to a relieved Jamie. His head drooped and his shoulders slumped as he turned without a word and trudged mournfully back towards the direction of the coach.

The others rushed up.

"Are you okay?" exclaimed Calum, "I thought he was going to brain you with that stick!"

"It wasn't me I was worried about. He was after you JC."

"I've never seen him like that before," puzzled JC. "I know he can be obnoxious and full of his own self-importance, but chasing me with a stick?"

"It might have a bit to do with you humiliating him," offered Tommy, "You did put him on his back, not once but twice."

"Yeah, but he stole my sweets."

"Even so, most blokes would find being floored quite so easily by a girl quite embarrassing."

JC's expression darkened as she frowned at Tommy. He put his hands up in mock surrender.

"Hey, don't shoot the messenger, I'm only saying what we're all feeling. We don't doubt your judo abilities."

"Which were pretty blooming impressive by the way!" grinned Jamie, deflecting the situation. "All's well that ends well and all that! Let's hope that Spencer forgets all about it and keeps quiet for the rest of the trip."

JC was still cross but had softened slightly. "I think we should tell the teachers. I don't see why he should get away with being so nasty and not get into trouble."

"I agree," assented Calum. Tommy and Jamie stared at him. "Well, what I mean is he needs to be taught a lesson."

"I think being humbled by JC will do for now," suggested Jamie. "He'll be quiet for a while, but I'm certain he'll be back to his nasty best soon enough."

They boarded the coach again and a still smarting JC glared at Spencer as they sat down. Jamie shared his sweets with her as the coach sped northwards away from the unpleasantness of the service station. He could feel the presence of Spencer glowering in the background but he did his best to ignore it and after a while, the monotony of the wheels on the motorway lulled them into a peaceful sugar induced stupor. It was only when they left the grey speeding snake trail of the motorway and began the ascent into the Lake District that they began to rouse themselves.

The scenery became more rugged, as the first of the mountains came into view. Fitz, quiet up to this point, borrowed the microphone from the front of the coach and began to quote his favourite Wordsworth poem to the groans of his reluctant and trapped audience.

"The world is too much with us; late and soon, Getting and spending, we lay waste our powers: Little we see in Nature that is ours; We have given our hearts away, a sordid boon!"

This soon woke everyone up and a smiling Fitz popped the microphone back into its holder as the coach slowed and turned left into the gates of the Outward Bound centre to cheers of relief from everyone on board. A huge man who stepped out of the front door and ushered the driver into a designated area for unloading greeted the coach driver with a friendly wave.

The coach's air brakes hissed in satisfaction and the door swished silently open allowing this bear of a man to enter.

"Hello and welcome to Outward Bound Ullswater!" he boomed, ignoring the proffered microphone. A couple of girls squeaked in surprise. "My name is Woody and I'll be your lead guide this week up in the Lake District."

Woody was even bigger as he stood at the front of the coach. He was well over six feet tall, with broad shoulders making him nearly three feet wide. He had long curly blonde hair tied in a ponytail and a well-trimmed goatee, the only hint at pride in his personal appearance. He had kind brown eyes and a slightly wonky nose, suggesting a previous career in rugby. He was covered in freckles and had a rugged tan, befitting a man who spent most of his life out of doors. He smiled cheerfully and looked like the sort of man who did that a lot. "Hop off the bus everyone and before you unpack, I'll tell you a little bit more about the centre."

The school party gathered up all their personal possessions and once Mr Andreck had done a sweep of the coach handing various items with a resigned sigh to persistent offenders, allowed Woody to continue. All the children were standing next to a statue on the well-manicured lawn facing an impressive white building. The sun was shining and the scenery was breathtaking. They were surrounded by jagged mountaintops and the green fields rolled gently down to Lake Ullswater.

"As you can see, this impressive building is a Georgian mansion on the north shore of Ullswater near Watermillock." Woody looked at his watch as if expecting something and looked up at the sky. "In the next minute or so, you'll see that this building has another completely different use." Jamie and the others all squinted against the sunlight and looked up at the sky unsure of what to expect. In the distance they could hear a distant sound of planes approaching. Judging by the noise and speed, it could be only one thing. Royal Air Force fighter planes!

Many of them put their hands over their ears as the jets flashed across the sky directly over the main building. Tornadoes! Charlie and Francis jumped up and down and pumped the air in celebration. Calum turned to Jamie, eyes wide and was about to speak when the noise intensified again. Jamie pointed to the distance where the two fighters were turning to begin their mock assault on the Outward Bound centre again. The noise was deafening as the fighters blasted across the sky. As they turned away down the valley, the two planes waggled their wings quickly from side to side and as rapidly as they appeared were gone.

"Wow!" muttered Jamie. "That was amazing." Tommy's hand was in the air. Woody spotted it.

"Yes, young man?"

"Does that always happen?"

"Every single day. You can set your watch by it." He grinned. "Did you see the planes waggle their wings as they left? That's the pilots showing off a little, but it's also their way of saying thank you."

"What for?" someone else asked.

"Well, since World War Two, this building was used in mock bombing raids. New pilots flew along the valley, over Ullswater lake to the end, where they would bank and drop their imaginary bombs on the white building here."

"Luckily it wasn't the Germans then," laughed someone else.

"You may laugh, but the Luftwaffe was aware that this was going on, but decided that negotiating these peaks was more than a little troublesome. To this day, the RAF practise their bombing raids every single day!"

"Excellent. Obliteration every twenty-four hours!" whooped Charlie.

"Annihilation for Marsh Green College!" countered Francis giving his brother a high five.

More of Woody's colleagues came out to say hello and for the next five minutes they ran through the safety measures of the site and where to meet in case of an emergency. They were split into four pre-arranged groups of ten and given a name.

"Each group," Woody explained, "will be given a name. Your school has chosen mountains. So we have Helvellyn, Bow Fell, Skiddaw and Scafell. Each group will do the same activities until the final day, where the groups will be split into varying degrees of adventure for some overnight adventures." Everyone looked at each other, keen to know what that entailed. "For now, we will show you your dormitories. You've got precisely ten minutes to make yourselves at home before meeting back here. Off you go."

Taking your mind off things

Jamie lay on his bed in his dormitory, tired but content. Despite the ticking time bomb of his quest, he had found a little peace for the first time since all of this began. He had tried hard to ignore the days as they slipped past. He had ten days left to fulfil the prophecy, but for some reason he was supremely calm about it. He felt that an opportunity would present itself soon.

He had been allowed to ring home to check on his grandma and once she had assured him that all was well, he had relaxed and engaged in all the activities. He had looked for opportunities to help someone, but no suitable opportunity had materialised. He'd had plenty of quality time to think about what he might wish for and an idea was forming in his head. He didn't want to get too excited or think about it too much, fearing the warrior might find out.

The recent revelation in whatever time the warrior existed still freaked Jamie out a bit, but he read comic books and science fiction. In many stories they toyed with the idea of separate realities and playing with time. He absentmindedly played with the orb, which fizzed and glowed as he did so. The first few days had gone by without any serious problems, he'd slept well and Spencer had behaved himself.

The sound of his roommates playing cards was welcome background noise and a good sense of camaraderie had sprung up between them all. Even the staff's mood lightened considerably and they looked to be enjoying themselves, despite the onerous task of being in charge of forty teenage children! Some hilarious episodes would make the school magazine upon their return Jamie was sure:

One group of sailors had sailed off into the distance,

unable to turn their laser as the wind picked up. They were rescued by motorboat, whilst another group at the same time actually sank their vessel when some bright spark decided to take out one of the bungs. The instructors were not best pleased, but at least the craft had been in shallow enough water at the time!

Another group actually broke the Jacob's Ladder, which wasn't the biblical ladder to heaven, but a fiendish team-building contraption. A classic team event that uses a giant-sized ladder suspended from two enormous poles, Jacob's Ladder is a true test of co-operation, balance, co-ordination and a degree of strength. The rungs of this giant ladder are spaced approximately five feet apart.

The challenge is to work effectively with a partner using good communication and team work and help each other reach the top. Marsh Green successfully managed to get a group of ten people up in one go in a terrific display of togetherness, only to break one of the rungs with their sheer weight. The repercussions of that particular episode were quite substantial and the Outward Bound centre apologised for the rest of the day. They were all fed extremely well that night!

One incident involved Jamie's group and he giggled as he remembered it. His group were on the trapeze. This activity involves being strapped to a harness that is then attached to a belay. You can't fall off! Jamie thought the idea of climbing a very tall telegraph pole and standing on a ridiculously small platform perched on the top was not especially challenging, until he actually climbed up there.

Jamie made the fatal mistake of looking down and for a moment his vision blurred as vertigo momentarily set in. He quickly looked back to the sky and clambered arms and legs everywhere onto the platform as the telegraph pole began to sway alarmingly. Once at the top, you have the impression, despite the fact that you are harnessed, that you could fall off and really hurt yourself.

Jamie tried to put that horrific thought out of his mind as he shuffled forward on the platform. His toes were right at the edge. He was aware of the rest of the group chanting his name, but he zoned out completely and prepared himself for the second part of the challenge. Suspended two metres away was the trapeze bar itself. The aim was to throw yourself from the platform through the air and grab the bar. This goes way and beyond what your mind and body want to do.

Jamie gulped. He could feel the adrenaline pumping through his body as the telegraph pole continued to sway. The trapeze bar swung tantalisingly close, but the thought of throwing himself off filled him with dismay. He could feel the palms of his hands become clammy and his breath quickened. He could hear everyone chanting the countdown.

"Three."

"Two."

"One!"

On 'one' Jamie threw himself into the unknown. His fingers reached for the trapeze bar and remarkably his hands grasped the bar. He breathed a huge sigh of relief as he swung gratefully. He could hear everyone cheering and a surge of achievement flowed through his body.

"Yes! Yes! Yes!" he shouted. He let go of the rope and hung in the air in his harness. The instructor lowered the rope until his feet touched the ground.

After that it was the turn of the rest of the group, to varying degrees of success. Some did it in no time at all, a few got to the top but wouldn't jump and a couple of show boaters upon reaching the bar swung their legs up and hung upside down twenty feet up in the air!

Mr Andreck was with them and his students coerced him into having a go. He didn't look keen on the idea, but not wanting to lose face, he quietly got himself ready.

JC leaned over to Jamie and whispered, "Sir doesn't look very happy. Look how white he's gone."

Jamie looked at sir and couldn't help but agree as their teacher hesitantly began to climb up to the top. "Yeah, he does look a little pale."

The group stayed quiet sensing that something interesting was about to happen as the instructor who oblivious to the feelings of the group and looking slightly bored made the same tried and tested encouraging noises. It wasn't having much of an effect on a very wobbly Mr Andreck. He finally made it to the top and wrapped his arms around the platform.

The group craned their necks to watch and their teacher was looking incredibly uncomfortable. His eyes were screwed shut, his lower lip was trembling and he looked about to burst into tears. Their teachers and instructors all talked about 'stepping out of your comfort zone'. Their buzz phrase for the week. Well, it certainly looked like their teacher had leapt out of his and was struggling to find a way back in again!

Finally, the instructor twigged and realised his charge was struggling. He shouted to Mr Andreck to get his attention and encouraged him on.

"You've got two options sir. Either climb back down, or get onto the platform and walk off. You're attached and perfectly safe." Mr Andreck didn't look entirely convinced, but taking a deep breath slowly began to haul himself onto the platform. "Well done sir, well done," cried the instructor.

The group cheered as he finally got his feet onto the platform. The telegraph pole wobbled as he tried to get his balance. Suddenly he stopped still and his face went green.

"I think he's going to be sick!" shouted one of the group.

Jamie looked up. Their teacher was swaying with the roll of the telegraph poll and looked strange. He had turned grey, his face covered in a sheen of sweat. He gave a lurch as his stomach gurgled and then without warning released a jet of vomit.

"Take cover!" The group scarpered screaming with mock disgust as Mr Andreck emptied the contents of his lunch onto the instructor below, who couldn't move as he was attached to the convulsing teacher above.

The children watched, some in amusement, others feeling sick themselves, as another wave of Mr Andreck's lunch splattered down from above onto the head of the instructor. Mr Andreck looked down at the mess he'd made and offered a weak apology to the instructor, who looked thoroughly miserable. The instructor to his credit gave the teacher a thumbs up, shook off some of the sick and started the countdown in revenge. The children joined in and Mr Andreck gave them all the thumbs up and jumped. He soared across the gap and made it to the cheers of the waiting group below who were still waiting at a safe distance, just in case!

It had been hysterical and Jamie was still chuckling to himself when a claxon sounded outside his room bringing him out of his reverie and back to the present. He swung his legs off the bunk and jumped down onto the dormitory floor. The others packed up their cards and made their way outside chattering noisily to find out which expedition they'd been assigned to go on.

Setting off

Jamie and the other thirty-nine excited teenagers congregated on the lawn of the Outward Bound centre. Throughout the week, the instructors and their teachers had assessed them. They were ranked in suitability for various overnight expeditions into the mountains.

There were four camping excursions, but the one that everyone wanted was Helvellyn. It was viewed as the most exciting. With the added bonus of walking Striding Edge, a dramatic knife-edge path with sheer drops either side, its element of danger and adventure had the most allure. The attraction of this particular adventure had taken on even more mystique at lunch, as one bright spark had said that there are more accidents on Helvellyn than on any other mountain in the Lake District!

There was an eager buzz as they waited nervously. Jamie didn't mind which expedition he went on, as long as he was with a couple of his mates. Spending more time with JC would be especially good. There were some who didn't want to go at all and of course the competitive crew who desperately did! The teachers had that smug we know but you don't expression that adults seem to adopt before announcements are made. They were being pestered by the obvious few but their only response was to 'wait and see'.

Woody strolled out grinning broadly. "Thanks for your patience everyone," he began. "As you know there are four expeditions awaiting you all. This is the finale to your trip here in the Lake District. Have you all enjoyed yourselves so far this week?"

A boisterous cheer went up.

"I'll take that for a yes then," he beamed. "I'd like you all to know that your headmistress, your teachers

261

and all of us have been hugely impressed with you this week. These expeditions we've designed are all perfectly safe, but vary in terms of difficulty in terrain and in gradient. A couple of the expeditions will be across the rolling fens, yet others of you will climb to quite a height to get to the top of some our higher hills. Whichever trip you go on, it will be one you will enjoy. We guarantee it! A bold statement I know, but you will really love the experience of camping out in the Lake District.

"You have all practised using the cooking equipment and how to put up your tents. These you will have to carry as well as spare clothes, an evening meal and your breakfast." Woody produced some silver packets from his pocket and held them up.

"This is supper!" A ripple of disbelief spread through them. Jamie smiled. He'd seen these on the Discovery channel. "These are vacuum packed ready meals. We try and keep things as simple as possible. What I'm holding in my hand is a curry. You simply boil up some water, add the contents and simmer for five minutes or so. It may not look like much, but this is the sort of stuff that the army uses and they are delicious."

"Have you got any steak Woody?" piped up Tommy with a grin.

"Sorry chap, no such luck! They haven't come up with a way of doing that just yet." He paused for effect, then looked at the assembled throng. "So, to the groups themselves. Let's start with Helvellyn."

An immediate hush descended. "Drum roll please." Immediately all the children started drumming on their legs, until Woody made a 'cut' sign with his arms. "The boys and girls on the Helvellyn adventure are: Francis, Charlie, Jamie, Tommy, Spencer, Calum, JC, Zac, Suzie, Tobias and Eddie. Well done you guys.

You have impressed everyone this week with your determination and teamwork. Your headmistress will be coming with you and what you need to do now is to go to the stores, pack your bags and receive your instructions. I will be taking your group, so let's go."

Envious faces watched Jamie and his group as they jauntily walked to the stores. Jamie wasn't sure whether to act pleased or not. The twins didn't care. They were giving each other piggybacks and pulling JC's pigtails as they went past, so there was no guilt there; it was the way they usually behaved! He decided to remain chilled so as not to rub other people's faces in it. Spencer on the other hand antagonised everybody, as he turned and gave them all a 'losers' sign on his forehead.

The stores were old stables, now used as space to store every piece of equipment that could be needed in the ever changing climate of the Lakes. Earlier in the day they'd packed their rucksacks with waterproofs, spare clothes, a sleeping bag, and most importantly their Primus stove. This was a windproof stove that needed special skills to ignite and keep going, but Jamie was assured would boil water in a force nine gale! They'd spent an hour perfecting the art of this earlier on and were confident that supper would be a feast whatever the weather.

Jamie was sharing a tent with Tommy, much to his relief. He and Tommy argued good naturedly as to which part of the tent they'd each take. The poles were the heaviest and most awkward. A quick game of rock, paper, scissors, sorted that one out and an obviously pleased Tommy gleefully handed the poles over to his tent mate. Once this small matter had been decided, the rucksacks were packed with the heavier pieces of equipment near the bottom of the pack. This was to help balance the walker and ensure that the lower back took the brunt of weight. They were ready.

Woody checked everyone's rucksacks and they put on their walking boots that had been waterproofed earlier with dubbin. One more final kit-check and they were ready to load up the mini-bus for the short journey to their starting point, the little village of Glenridding.

The chatter on the bus was at deafening levels and twice Miss Bareham had to ask them all to be quiet. Woody just turned up the radio, which added to the commotion and Jamie's head was ringing when the bus came to a halt. Everyone jumped out and popped on their rucksacks. Tommy groaned immediately as he slipped the straps over his shoulders. "How am I going to carry this heavy rucksack up there?" he grumbled pointing up at the summit of Helvellyn in the distance. The girls skipped up and danced around him.

"We're fine," they teased. "What are you? A wimp?"

"Aren't yours heavy then?"

"Light as a feather," they crowed, dancing around like cheerleaders. "Give us an E. Give us an A. Give us an S. Give us a Y. What does it spell? EASY!"

Jamie didn't believe them. His was heavy too. It was going to take a monumental effort to walk up there. The girls were showing confidence, but he knew they'd soon quieten down as it got steeper. Jamie looked over at Spencer who was patently ignoring everyone. He was staring intently, even meditatively up at the mountain and looked in a trance.

Jamie found himself reaching for the orb in his pocket, unnerved by Spencer's mood. It vibrated comfortingly, then fizzed and crackled with energy making his fingers tingle. He forced himself to think about something else when Woody sidled up next to him.

"Ready to go?"

Jamie smiled, "Think so Woody."

"No thinking about it. Let's do it!" He whistled quickly three times and the small group gathered. "Okay team, gather round and we'll get going in a moment. The plan of action is to walk out of Glenridding and up to Red Tarn, where we will camp this evening. The path we will be taking crosses fields and then as we climb, there will be steps in the hillside path. Take your time, there is no rush, but it is important to get yourself into a good rhythm as you walk. Singing helps.

"I'll lead the way, but along with Miss Bareham will be chivvying you along. The walk isn't especially far, about five miles, but it is the gradient and the added burden of your rucksacks that will make the going quite a challenge. We will be stopping frequently for drinks, but if you run out of water, don't worry, there are plenty of fresh water creeks to replenish supplies as we climb higher.

"The weather looks good up to about seven thirty tonight. It's midday now, we'll stop for a sandwich at one-ish and should make camp by five at the latest. We will need to be quite quick from there, as the weather will close in on us overnight, with high winds and some rain, so cooking quickly will be essential. It'll be an early bed I'm afraid, but you'll be able to chat and play cards if you brought any along." Francis thumped Charlie in the background in irritation. He'd obviously forgotten!

"Now, now boys. You'll be too tired to do much else and besides you'll need your sleep for the final push to the summit in the morning. Depending on the weather, we will be going up one of two routes to the peak. We should be lucky as it is forecast to be fine tomorrow and with little or no wind, we can traverse along Striding Edge to the top without any trouble at all. On the other hand, if the weather isn't kind, we can still reach the summit, but we'll have to take a different route. Everyone okay, then let's go."

Woody's group cheerfully followed him out of the town, through a gate and into a field. He quickly turned left and started to follow the valley alongside a small river. The valley was perfect – simply magnificent. A typical English scene; cattle grazed peacefully as the last of the swallows swooped around them, preparing their young for the long journey south.

Jamie had never really listened to his parents when they said that there was no country in the world that could compare to England when it was at its best. He always thought they were just being melodramatic. But looking at this valley it was unlike anything he had ever witnessed before. Miss Bareham slid alongside him.

"Simply breathtaking isn't it? I keep humming a little Elgar. *Pomp and Circumstance* I believe." Jamie just nodded, agreeing, but not sure what he was agreeing to. He watched open-mouthed as his headmistress started humming loudly and waving an imaginary baton! "Perhaps it's just me, but isn't it just, well, green!" she exclaimed once she'd finished.

Jamie looked again at the view and he nodded again. "Yes Miss, I'd quite like to paint for a while, but I might run out of green!" She laughed at this and bounded off to chat with someone else.

Jamie was amazed by the change in their usual undemonstrative and severe headmistress. He was still a bit wary of her after the incident in the assembly hall and had tried to avoid her as much as he could. He shook his head. She was definitely different today. Maybe she was like this at home and during the holidays? She was like a schoolgirl. She had a twinkle in her eye and kept bouncing from person to person pointing out something of interest or just generally socialising.

The group of walkers fed off her enthusiasm and were soon chatting happily amongst themselves. Jamie fell in step with JC and his initial fears about Spencer's strange mood dissipated quietly into nothing as they chatted happily.

Base camp

The scenery became more dramatic as they climbed higher. Appreciating the view was largely ignored, as the going was hard work. The well-worn path increased in gradient and, as Woody had intimated earlier, steps began to appear. The party trudged ever upwards in silence concentrating wholly on putting one foot in front of the other.

Jamie gratefully dumped his rucksack onto the floor during a break and took a welcome swig from his water bottle. The temperature was warmer than normal this high up and the air was still. The muggy atmosphere appeared to worry Woody. Jamie watched as he looked about him, concern etched on his face.

"Two minutes everyone. We need to keep going. We've got another hour and the weather is beginning to look ominous. We need to be sheltered if it closes in." He talked animatedly for a minute or so with Miss Bareham before they nodded in agreement. A quick clap from Woody and groaning they set off again.

The next hour was long. The lack of a breeze and the energy sapping temperature drained the life out of everyone's legs. The adults did their best to keep everyone going, promising that the imposing ridge coming up would be the last. There were cries of protest from everyone as they traipsed to the top, but true to Woody's word they rounded a small bend and discovered a small stone building nestled snugly into the hillside.

Woody stopped to explain. "This, girls and boys is our Outward Bound shelter, a type of bothy. People trekking up the mountains use bothies for free and they are often used instead of tents. The idea is that you leave them as you find them. They are very basic, but can come in useful if the weather gets really bad. This one is exclusively for us should we need it."

"What if it gets really cold camping Woody?" someone asked.

"Well, a fire will be set up inside ready to light if we need it. Oh and another thing up here. There are no toilets, just a spade, which we'll get later to make our own makeshift toilet."

Someone squealed. "No loo Woody? Grim?"

Woody explained. "I'm afraid so, but it'll be far enough away from the camp-site and we'll cover it over when we're done. If you don't want to use the hole you can disappear into the bushes!" The others laughed at that.

"Best to let everyone know where you're going, so there are no surprises!" agreed their headmistress with a snort of laughter.

Spencer leaned in to Jamie and whispered, "I wouldn't want to see her bum. It would give me nightmares for weeks!"

Jamie laughed and agreed. For once, Spencer had said something friendly, conspiratorial admittedly and not nice about someone else, but friendly nonetheless. They started to follow Woody away from the shelter to the campsite and Jamie fell into step next to Spencer.

"Spencer?" Jamie began. Spencer said nothing, but nodded his head allowing Jamie to continue. "Are we okay? I mean, this week you've been less," Jamie struggled to find the word, "less confrontational. Have you decided to let things be?"

Spencer smirked and shook his head almost sadly. "Jamie, you and I have never seen eye to eye, and if I was honest I'd say I've never liked you. Not sure why." He shrugged and continued. "Can't like everyone I suppose. The football thing was cool for a while but I bear a grudge." Jamie's heart sank. He knew it was too good to be true.

Spencer continued, "I know that you had something to do with that weird incident at school when everyone turned against me. It's got something to do with that weird thing that you carry around with you. How you got it from the river and survived the weir I'll never know. That really aggravated me and when you came out of that car crash without a scratch I just knew something wasn't right!"

Jamie began to protest, but Spencer cut him off.

"You need to listen! I don't believe in magic, but I can't be the only one to notice that peculiar things have been going on. Perhaps the others don't see it, or perhaps they choose not to, but things between you and me? Well, they aren't over."

The jovial atmosphere of a second or two was gone. Jamie wished he hadn't said anything. He tried to walk away, but Spencer tried to bar his way. The twins, sensing trouble, stepped in.

"You all right Jamie?" asked Charlie.

"This squirt giving you any grief?" added Francis.

"No, it's okay fellas." They looked doubtfully at Jamie. "Seriously. It's fine. Spencer and I were just talking."

Spencer grinned as the twins walked on ahead, each looking back every so often. "Still need your minions then Jamie?"

"No more than you used to Spencer. They do it out of friendship."

Spencer laughed nastily. "They'll drop you, like they did me."

"Spencer, I've done nothing other than try and be nice. I'd like to try that with you if you'll let me?"

"No chance. You and I will have our moment. Just waiting for the opportunity." And with that he picked up his pace, brushed his way past the twins and struck

270

up a conversation with Woody at the front. Tommy caught up and saw the look on Jamie's face.

"You all right pal?"

"Not really. Spencer does my head in. Do me a favour? Just keep an eye out for me. Okay?"

Tommy worriedly agreed. "Of course, but you really ought to talk to an adult about this."

"Probably, but I can't help feeling that they'd do their usual. You know, nod in understanding and say that they'll keep an eye on it. But you and I know that adults are adults. They quickly forget and besides, teachers have more than one kid to keep an eye on."

"Still, I might just chat quietly to Miss Bareham when I get a chance."

Jamie didn't argue with his friend and nodded as the party reached what appeared to be the camping area. Woody popped his pack on the floor and addressed everyone.

"This is our camping site. Welcome to Red Tarn."

Jamie looked about him and despite the troubled conversation with Spencer, was completely blown away by the view. Although bleak, the water of Red Tarn sparkled in the late evening sun. Insects danced across its still waters, leaving outward reaching circles on its clear surface breaking its mirror like quality. It looked curiously inviting and he felt like diving in.

Directly behind lay the summit of Helvellyn, a thousand feet up, and on either side of the lake two knife edged ridges surround them forming a bowl shape. There was the forbidding Striding Edge on one side and Swirral Edge on the other. It was spectacular. Jamie could hardly believe they were going to be spending the night here before attempting to reach the summit in the morning. Looking back down the valley was just as spectacular and he could see that everyone in the party felt a real sense of achievement.

"The tarn is one of the highest in the Lake District, lying at an altitude of over two thousand feet. It has a depth of twenty-five metres and if you are feeling brave you can swim in it."

"Will it be cold?" asked JC.

"Oh yes, very cold indeed, but very refreshing. The tarn is popular as a rough camping site with mountaineers and contains a very rare fish called the Schelley."

"Are they like piranhas?"

"Do they bite?"

"No not at all, but keep your cameras ready as they are very shy!" He frowned, looked up at the sky, checked his mobile phone and turned serious. "Everyone listen up. There is bad weather coming and things may get a little wild this evening. We should keep our party of tents close together just in case."

"Just in case of what?" someone asked.

"Just in case we need to evacuate to the shelter, but we shouldn't need to." Perhaps it was Jamie's state of mind, but Woody didn't look all that convinced.

"I've never had to before, but there is always a first time! Please don't worry, if you listen carefully to my instructions all will be well.

"Now if you look down the valley you can see some natural hillocks. What you need to do is find as flat a spot as you can and try and hide behind it. What I mean by that is you should have the crest of the hillock if front of you and you should pitch your tent so that it is facing into the wind. The opening of your tent should be facing the tarn. The wind when it comes will whistle up the valley, over the hillocks that will protect you and then fly past either side of the tent. If you pitch your tent sideways on it'll get flattened.

"Once you've found a spot, I'll come and check. Don't worry. Pitch your tent, spark up the Primus stoves and boil some water for your supper. I think we've got just over an hour before the rain starts. One last piece of advice. Keep your wet weather gear close. You may well need it." He clapped his hands together. "Get to it campers. Go! Go! Go!!"

For the next hour, no one really spoke. Whether Woody's frame of mind had affected them all, or possibly it was the oppressive atmosphere, it was hard to tell. The air was still. It was the calm before the storm and they could all sense that the weather was about to break anytime soon. Each group found a spot and erected their tent as Woody had instructed. It was hard going though, as there was no breeze and Jamie could feel the sweat trickling down his face. The humid atmosphere had rendered them silent and they were driven by a need for shelter and a good supper.

Before long Jamie and Tommy had their tent in a good position. They were happy and hammered in the tent pegs gustily in case of high winds. Woody approved with a thumbs up. Sleeping bags were unpacked and all their equipment was moved away from the sides of the tent so no rain could seep through. Their wet weather gear was ready at the entrance. They felt safe and secure and Tommy offered to get the water from the tarn. Jamie readied the stove for supper.

He was about to light it, when he decided he ought to go and test out the hole in the ground. He paused for a moment, unsure whether to leave the tent unguarded, but nature's call was stronger than tent preservation. He felt sure everyone was far too busy to engage in tent shenanigans. He had a quick scoot around to see if Spencer was about, but couldn't see him. He zipped up the tent just in case.

Jamie returned as quickly as he could, but as he approached he immediately saw something was wrong. The tent had collapsed and Tommy was standing next to it looking confused.

"What happened Tommy?" asked Jamie.

"Dunno mate!" They both looked at one another and simultaneously came to the same conclusion.

"Spencer!"

"That no good, rotten scumbag," said Tommy angrily. "Where is he?"

They looked around and then there he was, not more than fifty metres away, sitting nonchalantly on a small mound, staring at them. They caught his eye and gesticulated angrily. Spencer gave them a cheery wave, then got up and disappeared. Tommy was about to give chase when Jamie held him back.

"Not worth it Tommy. Not worth it. Come on, let's get this tent back up, he's only let down the guy ropes and collapsed a couple of poles. We'll have it back up in no time."

Tommy hesitated, but looked up at the sky and decided that Jamie was right. Grumbling obscenities under his breath, he and Jamie had the tent back up quickly without too much trouble. A quick inspection inside revealed nothing was missing and within minutes the water was on the boil ready for supper.

The storm

The curry they had for supper wasn't bad at all. Jamie and Tommy feeling full and rather pleased with themselves reluctantly went down to the edge of the tarn to wash up when the first rumble of thunder rolled across the valley.

"Come on Jamie. Quick!" said Tommy. "I love storms. Let's get back to the tent. It's about to get quite feisty. We'll have a fantastic view." Jamie wasn't quite so sure, but he wasn't going to hang around in the open to find out.

The boys lay in their tent side by side, with the entrance open. They were resting on their rucksacks and had their waterproofs on, just in case. They had a terrific view of the tarn and the imposing mountain of Helvellyn behind. The sun was setting. On one side the sky was an angry red, and on the other black clouds were building fast. Suddenly, lightning flashed at the edge of the storm front.

"Did you see that?" laughed Tommy excitement in his voice. He turned serious for a moment. "Did you know that lightning is over forty thousand degrees Fahrenheit? A bolt of lightning heats the air along its path causing it to expand rapidly. Thunder is the sound caused by the rapidly expanding atmosphere."

Jamie wasn't quite so excited, but laughed at Tommy's enthusiasm and thumped him playfully on the arm. Tommy just talked about Manchester United most of the time, so this was an unexpected surprise!

He too was fascinated by how the storm was building and forming before their very eyes. With a start he recalled the words of the warrior and worried for a moment that this was his doing. He shook his head trying to dismiss the idea as ridiculous. As they watched, clouds billowed up joining the black mass that was already formed. It was going to be a big storm! Another crack of lightning flashed across the sky, piercing the gloom that was descending. A roll of thunder could be heard reverberating across the mountain range and up the valley.

"You nerd! Since when were you so interested and knowledgeable about storms?"

"One July, we had a holiday in Colorado. It was awesome, really hot, but every evening at that time of year storms would roll in through the valleys between the mountains. Dad used to get over excited and jump around like a kid. He was hilarious. Mum would just roll her eyes as he bounced about. He loves storms and spent hours outside trying to get a picture of forked lightning."

"Did he ever get one?"

"Eventually. At first I couldn't see what all the fuss was about, but he took me out during one massive storm and tried to explain what was going on."

"Was it dangerous?"

"I guess so, if you were out on top of one of the mountains, but we were safe under cover."

"Is this one going to be as big?"

Tommy thought for a moment. "I wouldn't have thought so. The Rockies are so massive, you could watch the storms develop from a hundred miles away. I still think it's going to be a good one though." He laughed again as lightning lit up the night sky and he thumped Jamie back before he had a chance to hit him again. "Did you know you can count how far away the storm is?"

"I had heard, but how do you do it?" Jamie asked rubbing his arm.

"Well, after you see the lightning, you count in seconds until you hear the thunder. For every five seconds you count they reckon it equates to a mile."

"Equate?" Jamie laughed. "You really are a storm nerd aren't you?"

Tommy pretended to look studious. "I'm afraid so young man. With me around you'll learn something new every day!" They both jumped and giggled nervously as thunder boomed loudly in the distance. "Okay Jamie, keep a look out for the next bit of lightning then let's count."

They watched for a while as the dark of early evening descended on them and the dusky storm clouds rolled in. The wind began to pick up and started gusting with ever increasing speed up the mountain valley towards them. The storm built up in intensity as they watched. It literally bowled in, enveloping and essentially surrounding them. Lightning flashed and the boys began to count.

"One...two...three..." At fifteen the thunder boomed, louder than before and he felt sure he could hear a shriek from one of the nearby tents.

"Three miles away then Tommy?"

"Correct," asserted Tommy, as a gust of wind made the tent rattle and strain against its guide ropes. "Quite glad we're in the tent, otherwise it might fly away!"

Jamie looked worried. "Serious?"

"Not really, but it is going to get quite wild. I wouldn't be surprised if Woody decides to evacuate us all to the shelter before too long. The rain is going to hit us soon."

Almost as soon as Tommy said this, the first splatter hit the fabric of the tent. "Should we close up the front?" asked Jamie.

"Let's keep it open for a while, otherwise we can't keep watching the storm," Tommy replied, as another flash of lightning pierced the gloom.

"Wow!" both boys exclaimed, as the forked

lightning came down nearby. They began their count again and only reached ten this time before the thunder boomed mightily. Almost instantaneously, the wind picked up rattling the sides of the tent and the rain increased in intensity as it fell from the sky in sheets.

"Quick, shut the entrance!" urged Jamie. Tommy zipped them up and then both boys struggled into their sleeping bags in the enclosed space, laughing as they bashed one another in their clumsy attempts.

"They say that these tents are storm-proof, but I don't rate its chances!" shouted Jamie over the din the falling rain was making. They lay on their backs listening to the storm batter the tent and the wind howl around the makeshift camp. It really felt as though it had taken on a personality of its own and was desperately attempting to rip them from the valley floor in a fit of pique. Lightning flashed again, illuminating the gloom of the tent. The boys laughed at each other's faces.

"You looked like a ghost mate," chuckled Tommy.

"Not surprised Tommy, this is pretty intense!"

They quickly counted again and only got to six this time, when the thunder boomed, deafening them.

"That's close! Really close. Hold on tight!" It was raining incessantly now and with the wind bursts that tried to uproot their tent, it was getting pretty scary. Lightning flashed again, illuminating Tommy's face. He didn't look quite so excited by the storm now they were slap bang in the middle of it. Thunder boomed menacingly a second after. The storm was upon them.

Jamie had never experienced a storm like this before and definitely not at such close quarters. Again, he half wondered if the warrior hadn't caused it, but he dismissed the thought as storms happened all the time didn't they? The tent buckled first one way and the other in the wind. The rain lashed the tent and the thunder and lightning seemed insistent in staying overhead. They lay huddled together, hoping it would end soon, as another boom of thunder seemed to make the very ground shake and Jamie clutching the orb tightly in his hand, wondered how everyone else was getting on.

"I thought you said it wasn't going to be a big storm!" shouted Jamie.

"I think I was wrong."

"You okay?"

"Bit scared actually."

"Me too!"

Suddenly, a voice pierced the gloom and the boys shouted in surprise, clutching one another. "Kids. Are you all right?" It was Woody. "A couple of the tents have collapsed and I've got to get everyone to the safety of the shelter. You guys are next. Have you got your waterproofs on?"

They unzipped the tent, grateful to see an adult. Woody shone in a torch, rain dripping off his coat. "You have, good! Grab your torches, but leave everything else."

The boys scrambled out of the tent and into the ferocity of the storm. It was wild! It was pitch black and despite the fact they had torches, the artificial light did little in the way of piercing through the bedlam. The rain hammered straight down onto their heads and the wind whistled around them, almost lifting them off their feet. Woody was shouting at them, but they couldn't hear. He came up close once he realised and gave them a thumbs up. They answered in the same way and did their best to follow him. They had to bend double to avoid being thrown to the ground. Within a couple of agonising minutes, they had forced their way through the tempest to the door of the shelter.

Woody struggled to open the door for a moment, the

storm seemingly reluctant to let them go. He fought with it furiously until it gave way and all three of them fell into the comfort of the shelter. The wind followed them in, scattering dust and small bits of paper. Woody jumped up and grabbed the door which flapped back and forth, seemingly with a mind of its own, and then putting all his weight behind it finally shut it. Instantly the noise in the room ceased and the storm was firmly shut out.

Jamie looked around. Of the party of ten, they were numbers seven and eight. The rest were huddled around a bright and inviting fire, warming themselves after their torrid experience. The others turned and waved sheepishly and the twins as ever, seemed positively excited by the whole experience. JC smiled warmly and he was relieved that she was safe.

Miss Bareham had volunteered to fetch Spencer and Harry from the final tent, whilst Woody busied himself by a small gas stove boiling some water for some hot chocolate. Another burst of wind threw itself at the small windows and made the door rattle, as Jamie and Tommy took off their wet gear and hung it up to dry. Suddenly the door burst open again as two figures entered and Woody rushed over to help shut the door.

Miss Bareham was there with Harry, but Spencer wasn't there. She looked worried.

"Spencer's disappeared!" she exclaimed.

"What happened?" asked Woody.

"I got both boys from the tent, but there was a crack of lightning nearby which was frightening. We dived for cover and when Harry and I got up again, Spencer was gone."

"Did you look for him?"

"Of course I did! What sort of person do you take me for?" shouted Miss Bareham, making everyone jump.

Woody reached across and put one of his huge hands on her shoulder. "It's okay, I'm not accusing you. I just need to know where to look first."

Miss Bareham looked embarrassed. "Sorry Woody, take no notice of me. It's just a stressful situation to be in and I take the welfare of these kids very seriously."

"I know that, don't worry and no offence taken. Let's both go and look for him. Kids, stay warm and one of you keep an eye on the water. We'll be back as soon as we can."

The two adults left the relative safety of the hut, opening the door with some difficulty. The wind whipped in as if trying to find the occupants inside and then petered out suddenly as the door was firmly closed. The group breathed a sigh of relief. The violence of the storm had frightened them all and now that Spencer had disappeared no one quite knew what to say. The girls huddled up next to each other and the boys stayed close, the twins back to back.

"Did you hear that?" JC whispered.

"Hear what?" someone answered, "All I can hear is the wind."

"That." She listened again, encouraging the others to do so. Loud scratching could be heard at the door.

Jamie got up and beckoned the twins over. He nodded at them, grasped the door and flung it open. Everyone jumped as Spencer bounded into the room dripping wet with a broad grin on his face.

"Shut the door!" someone cried. Jamie grabbed the door and using all his strength managed to force the wind out again and closed the door.

"Where have you been?" demanded Tommy. "Woody and Miss Bareham are out there looking for you."

"Yeah, I saw them a minute ago," he replied shaking himself like a wet dog.

JC got up. It was obvious she was angry. Jamie felt a pang of something but let it go, stepping closer in case Spencer lashed out. "Why didn't you say anything? They are out there risking their necks trying to find you."

"Yeah, I know. Great isn't it? About time someone took an interest in me."

"Me?" JC was incredulous. "This isn't a bloody game Spencer. People do care about you, if you'd only just stop being so selfish and self-centred."

Spencer shrugged and grinned. Charlie moved forward, fist clenched, but Jamie stepped in the way.

"Leave it Charlie, he's not worth it."

Spencer shrugged again and then suddenly thumped Jamie in the stomach, kicked Charlie in the shins and upended the pan of water. He gave everyone a wave, bowed theatrically, opened the door to the maelstrom and ran back out into it, whooping like a banshee. Tommy raced to shut the door as Charlie hopped about and JC dropped to her knees to check on the stricken Jamie who was gasping for breath.

"What was that for?" she said. Jamie couldn't speak and rolled around in agony. The rest of the group were stunned.

"Why did he do that?"

"Is he mad?"

Jamie managed to get his breath back, but was feeling sore and Charlie was prowling around looking really angry, when the door burst open again. All the children jumped as Miss Bareham came in declaring that they had found him and to move away out of the fire so he could get some warmth.

"But Miss…," began Calum.

"Not now Calum!" retorted his head teacher.

"But Miss, he was here only a moment ago. He thumped Jamie and kicked Charlie, then went back out into the storm."

"Nonsense." Calum was about to argue some more, when Woody appeared carrying a prone Spencer. To the adults it looked as though they had rescued a wet, bedraggled and frightened fifteen-year-old boy, suffering from exhaustion. The children knew better and eyed the situation in complete disbelief. Spencer's acting was worthy of an Oscar. As if on cue, he groaned pathetically in Woody's arms.

JC spoke up, echoing how they were all feeling. "Miss, he is faking. We can all testify that Spencer was here only five minutes ago causing trouble as Calum told you. He's putting on a fine performance for you." Their headmistress looked troubled and Woody began to eye the boy in his arms with less concern, as he laid him gently next to the fire. He encouraged him to sit up and poured some hot tea from a flask.

Spencer groaned impressively and took a weak sip, whilst the others looked on in amazement at the sheer audacity of his performance. Miss Bareham found one of the spare blankets and after taking off his wet jacket wrapped it around the now shivering boy. There was a degree of tutting and gasps of astonishment from some of the others. This seemed to make up the mind of their teacher.

"Now, I can't believe that you truly think this has happened. Perhaps he popped in then went out to find us." JC tried to interrupt. "No, young lady. No. This evening has been difficult for us all and I think a lot of what has happened has been exaggerated by the storm. This boy needs warming up and it's obvious to me that he is cold and scared and, for those very reasons, I will be ensuring that he gets warm and recovers. I think he is genuinely cold and I will not, not, be argued with. I have taken on board what you've said and I'll think it over."

And with that she sat away from them all, but close enough to Spencer to show that she expected no one to question or give him any grief! Woody said nothing but sat in the corner of the room. The rest of the group huddled close enough to the fire to keep warm, but far enough away to show their disgust and their solidarity.

All eyes watched Spencer as he continued to put on a fine performance and then when he thought Miss Bareham wasn't looking, turned his head slightly so the others could see him. He opened his eyes, grinned and winked at them all, wiggling his fingers in a mock wave. Francis growled quietly and using his two fingers, crossed them across his neck. Spencer grinned once more, before groaning theatrically again and coughing, prompting some concerned attention from Miss Bareham.

Jamie looked over to the corner of the room and saw Woody frowning. Had he witnessed the silent exchange between them? He sighed and hoped so. The storm continued to rage outside and at least they were all safe for now. He closed his eyes and tried to get to sleep.

Mist

Jamie woke suddenly and sat bolt upright. Something had startled him. Groggily he sat up and looked around. For a moment he didn't know where he was. He rubbed his eyes. His body was sore and he wearing all his clothes for some reason. Where was his pillow? Where was Duster, or the poster of the bright orange McLaren MP40 on his bedroom wall? He wasn't at home that was for sure.

He rubbed his eyes again and a nearby groan began to bring his thoughts back to reality. His breathing slowed as he began to relax. A gentle snore emanated from next to him and he knew for certain where he was. He was half way up a mountain. In a hut. Sheltering from a storm.

Jamie listened and thankfully all was still now. The storm must have blown itself out. He looked at his watch, which read five thirty, and yawned, contemplating sleep again. He decided against it and stood up stretching the aches away. He looked at the floor, which was scattered with the sleeping and peaceful bodies of his friends. How they'd all slept he'd never know. The floor was uncomfortable and despite the rage of the storm, it appeared that they'd all fallen asleep eventually. He wished he had a camera. It was quite a sight. He shivered slightly despite the warmth in the room. The fire was still burning and the heat of ten bodies had kept the temperature comfortable. It was pretty smelly though and he wrinkled his nose in disgust.

Tiptoeing around the sleeping mass of teenagers Jamie made his way to the window. Looking out, he could see nothing. He wiped the window with his hand, clearing away some condensation and looked out again.

Still nothing, which was strange. It was not night-time that much was obvious, as the light was bright, but his confused early morning brain just couldn't work it out. He looked out and knew he should be seeing a mountain scene, but instead it was an all-encompassing sea of white. It was as if they had suddenly been transported into a dream. Jamie rubbed his eyes again. Perhaps it was a dream? Some pretty weird things had happened to him recently! It was eerie.

"Mountain mist," whispered Woody who'd sidled silently up next to him. Jamie jumped and nearly shouted out loud. Woody chuckled. "Sorry. Couldn't resist it."

Jamie's heart slowed down and he had a chance to recover. "It's really strange isn't it?"

"It certainly is."

"Will it clear away, Woody?"

"I'm not sure Jamie. It should do. I won't know until we go outside and check for any wind. I think it's time to wake everyone up and go and have some breakfast."

"In this?"

"Sure, it'll be fun."

Jamie shrugged and stepped toward a sleeping body when Woody stopped him. He pointed at Spencer. "What's the story with you two?"

Jamie paused, unsure whether to confide in Woody. "He doesn't like me. Pure and simple. He never has done and has made it clear he never will. Not that I'm bothered about that, but I just wish he'd leave me alone."

"Have you done anything to deserve it?"

"Probably. Certainly in his eyes I have. I think I've just helped other people to see him for what he really is."

Woody looked thoughtful. "And that is?"

"A bully Woody, a mean bully. Sad to say, but I don't think he's a very nice person. Some people just aren't I guess."

"Well, stick by me today and I'll say the same to Miss Bareham. She seems to have a bit of a blind spot where that boy is concerned."

Jamie smiled knowingly. "So did everyone else, not so long ago." He shrugged. "Come on, let's wake everyone up."

Woody wandered over to Miss Bareham and Jamie gently began waking up the rest of the crew. It didn't take long for everyone to be yawning, stretching and talking excitedly about the events of the previous evening. Spencer had woken up as well and was keeping quiet, watching the reaction of the others like a snake. Francis and Charlie eyed him with open hostility, whilst the others looked at him with no less disbelief than the night before. They still couldn't believe the sheer audacity of his actions, but seemed to decide as a group that ignoring the problem was the best course of action.

Jamie glanced over at Woody, who was in conversation with his headmistress. She in turn was listening, head slightly to one side. She nodded in agreement, slicked her hair back and popped it into a pony tail, before making her way over to the children. She beckoned Spencer over and coughed to get everyone's attention.

"Morning everyone. I hope you all slept well. What a storm last night and I'm glad you're all safe and sound this morning. It's a great relief to me I can tell you." She paused for a moment as if unsure of what she should say, then made up her mind. "Something went on last night apart from the storm. It doesn't take a genius to sense a bit of an atmosphere in here this morning. I think it's time we sorted this out. Spencer, come over here please." Spencer sauntered quite casually over to their headmistress, but didn't catch the eye of anyone. Jamie knew what was coming.

"Spencer. I want you to answer me honestly. Did you make up last night's events and come here before we found you outside?"

Spencer looked up and now brazenly stared at everybody daring them any of them to say anything different. Without a pause or any show of remorse he spoke clearly. "No Miss." Jamie knew what he had to do. This was his mess and he had to sort it out. He knew, he couldn't say why, perhaps it was his heightened sense of understanding since the orb had been in his possession, but he knew this wasn't going to be solved by adults. The others gasped and looked at Jamie. Jamie would talk to them later if he could, but Spencer would have passed a lie detector test today. It was almost as if he believed the lies he was telling. Miss Bareham was immediately irritated.

"Be quiet!" she warned.

"Jamie. Did Spencer come back into this shelter whilst we were out looking for him? And, more importantly did he strike both you and Charlie?"

Jamie closed his eyes and could feel the orb supporting the decision he was making. He could feel his fingertips fizzing. He looked at Woody and nodded slightly, enough for the leader to understand his decision, then looked at his teacher square in the eye.

"No miss." There was a stunned silence. The others couldn't believe what they hearing or seeing. "No miss," he reiterated, "he didn't."

"Thank you for your honesty Jamie." Charlie was about to step forward, when he caught Jamie's eye. Jamie felt his power rise within him as he looked intently at Charlie.

"Step back Charlie," he projected from his mind.

"Step back and let me deal with this. Okay?"

He could see Charlie wavering.

"Step back now!" he ordered.

The orb sparkled in his pocket as Charlie nodded and stepped back obediently into line. Miss Bareham caught the move and asked him if he had anything further to add.

"No miss," came the solid reply. There was a gasp again. Spencer remained emotionless. "Right then. We are all agreed then. I'd like everyone to come up one by one and shake Spencer's hand to show there are no bad feelings." She looked straight at JC. "As one of my ambassadors for the year group, perhaps you'd like to lead the way and go first?"

She stared intently at JC, almost daring her to resist or protest, but JC kept her head low and stepped forward. She avoided her teacher's glare and held out her right hand to Spencer. "Look up please, young lady." JC looked up at Spencer and surprised them all by giving him her brightest, warmest smile.

Spencer, slightly perturbed by this, slowly proffered his own hand and they shook. She held his gaze and his hand until he looked away. The others watched this, wondering how they should follow and as they did, noticed her left hand hidden behind her back.

She had her fingers crossed!

Jamie watched as a flicker of understanding spread throughout the group. Of course she hadn't meant it. One by one, each of the others took turns to shake Spencer's hand, offering similar ingratiating smiles, but all the while keeping their fingers crossed. Miss Bareham looked pleased at how things were turning out, unaware of the deception, but Woody had noticed. He nodded in grim understanding and silently began to clear away all the stove and the other bits of equipment they'd taken in with them, stacking it all by the door.

Only Francis, Charlie and Jamie were left.

Francis stepped forward, the same false smile upon his face and for a moment Spencer looked worried. Miss Bareham noticed and gave him a reassuring pat on the shoulder, encouraging him to take the extended hand. He did so and Francis gripped Spencer's with a look of determination on his face. Jamie felt a warm glow sweep through him as Spencer grimaced ever so slightly. Spencer wiggled his fingers, not wanting to let on how much that had hurt and braced himself for the next handshake. Charlie's.

Charlie stepped forward and repeated the process. Unbeknown to Miss Bareham, but in view of the others, he intentionally stepped in close and trod firmly on one of Spencer's stocking clad foot with his. The major difference being was that his were clad in a size nine hiking boot! Sweat began to break out on Spencer's brow. Miss Bareham frowned slightly and the others watched Charlie let go, twisting his foot ever so slightly as he moved away, grinding Spencer's toes beneath. Spencer's eyes widened, but he didn't cry out. Charlie took his place by his brother, who gently nudged him with his shoulder to say well done. It was Jamie's turn.

Both boys held out their hands. Electricity seemed to fizzle between their fingertips. Neither was surprised and no one else in the room seemed to notice. They paused and Jamie cocked his head slightly unsure of what would happen next. They tried again and the moment their hands clasped, something incredible happened.

A kaleidoscope of images hit Jamie's mind as they connected and the orb vibrated urgently in the pocket of his jacket. It was a warning.

Memories.

Not his.

Then whose?

Spencer's!

The images flew at him at great speed almost overwhelming him. Spencer's life flashed before him. Spencer as a baby, happy times as a toddler, confused feelings about his mother, triumph at walking, riding his bicycle, a male figure appeared sporadically, close, but not close enough to reach, his face clear for a moment then indistinct.

Marsh Green College began to appear in the thoughts. A wave of power, controlling the emotions as Spencer's reign of supremacy at school and in the village came through – happy times it seemed. And then things began to slow and become more vivid.

The incident at school and then a picture of himself – instantly he was hit by a hammer blow of hatred and staggered in his mind.

The football final, the winning goal and another image of Jamie – another lightning strike of loathing.

The weir incident, Jamie again. More vitriol.

Then Jamie began to appear again and again, more quickly. Feelings of malice, revenge and hatred flowed into him until the vision turned red. The colour of blood, then everything went blank. Jamie staggered back from Spencer releasing his grip. Everyone was staring at him and Spencer was looking at him curiously.

Did he know what Jamie had just seen? Jamie hoped not. He was genuinely spooked by the experience and looking at the others, wondered if he'd given anything away.

"Are you okay Jamie?" asked Miss Bareham.

"I'm fine," Jamie lied. "Just feeling a bit tired and emotional."

The others laughed and this seemed to break the tense atmosphere, much to Jamie's relief. Despite everything that had happened to him, he still hated to be the centre of attention. Miss Bareham seemed satisfied with her attempt to smooth things over and as quickly as she initiated the whole thing, she moved on.

"Woody. Over to you." Jamie walked as steadily as he could over to his friends and tried to be normal. All he wanted to do at this moment was to fall over and curl up in a ball. The whole vision thing had really scared him and he couldn't get the colour red out of his mind. He wasn't sure what it all mean, but one thing was clear! He would stay well clear of Spencer and not for the first time wondered if he'd made the correct decision. Should he have come clean about last night's episode? What would Miss Bareham have done? Nothing, he surmised, but make things worse.

He harked back to the warrior's continuous warnings about Spencer and idly wondered if he should have done something about him in the past. He shook his head, trying to get the implications of such action out of his mind. It wouldn't have been nice. At least he knew what Spencer really thought of him!

"Grab your belongings kids," Woody said cheerfully, breaking his confused thoughts. "We're going back for breakfast at base camp."

They peered out of the window and someone called out. "But we can't see anything!"

"We'll get lost!" declared someone else.

Woody opened the door and beckoned them to follow him outside into the early morning mist. Anxiously they followed, unsure of what would happen to them if they walked into this sea of white. They gathered around Woody who didn't speak, but instead gestured that they should follow him in silence. Puzzled, they did as they were asked and followed Woody blindly like the children in the Pied Piper story, the incident with Spencer for now forgotten, but Jamie wondered how long it would take for someone to challenge him about it.

As they ate breakfast, a discussion began about the mist much to Jamie's relief. He wasn't sure he had an answer to why he'd behaved in such away in the hut. He listened as most of them described the mist as walking in or on a cloud. Others pronounced it as like having cotton wool in their ears, the sound was deadened. Some bright spark suggested they were in a bad dream with millions of sheep, which raised a few laughs.

Charlie described it as like walking through a doorway and into a dream. He looked into space and hummed, closing his eyes. Without opening them, he continued to explain that it felt like indistinct shapes and silence, an acute awareness of life around him, but unable to describe who, or what, it was. He felt touched by the quiet, as if someone greater was sending them a message.

A burned sausage flew at him. He ducked grinning.

"Only joking. It is a bit a weird though. I do like it, but the mist seems to deaden all sound. Try banging that pot Francis." Francis turned to pick up the pan and as he did so Charlie threw the sausage back at him. It hit him on the back of the head.

"Oi! Who threw that?" He reached down to throw the sausage back when Woody coughed to get everyone's attention. Despite his unease Jamie couldn't help but smile.

"Good work everyone on clearing up the site and managing to cook breakfast."

When they'd arrived back at the campsite earlier, they had all feared the worst. Each tent had been flattened by the ferocity of the wind, but thankfully none had been completely blown away. The weight of their belongings and their enthusiastic peg hammering the night before meant that everything had been saved.

"Now, believe it or not, this mist will clear soon." There were murmurs of disbelief, but Woody just smiled. "Believe me it will. There's a light breeze and the sun is coming out. There will be perfect conditions in about half an hour. This will give us time to wash up and pack your tents before we attempt to scale the summit."

"Will we be able to walk Striding Edge Woody?" someone asked.

"Yes indeed. Conditions will be perfect." A cheer of excitement went up. "Now get to it campers." He grinned. "And don't forget to wash those pans carefully."

Striding Edge

A buzz of anticipation swept through the group, all fears from the night before a distant memory. Jamie felt relieved that no one seemed bothered about last night and he decamped without saying much. Without warning the mist suddenly vanished. One minute it was there and the next it had gone. It was if someone, somewhere, had switched on an enormous extractor fan and sucked it all away!

It was a beautiful day just as Woody had predicted. The sky was a clear blue, with the odd cirrus cloud high in the sky. The only evidence of the storm were patches of flattened grass and the odd puddle between the rocks. The summit of Helvellyn stood proudly, enticing them up and for most, they really believed that they would make it to the top.

Woody put a waterproof sheet on the grass and instructed everyone to put their rucksacks on it. He explained that they would return for these as they descended back to the valley later on that afternoon down the less intimidating Swirral Edge. As the group gathered he turned serious.

"Now everyone must listen very carefully. What I am about to say is important. What we are attempting today is perfectly safe, but you must take care. I wouldn't be allowed to take you otherwise. We will be walking up a path over there." He motioned over his shoulder and they could make out a distinct path up to a ridge in the distance. "Once we reach the crest of the ridge which is called Hole in the Wall, we will turn right and within a hundred yards we will be on Striding Edge. There are two or three clearly defined paths. We will be taking the widest one, but you still need to keep your wits about you.

"At some points there are some sheer drops, at others the drop is gentler, but it is still a long way to the bottom. Try not to peer over the top or look down if you are afraid of heights. None of you should be after watching you on your high rope activities this week. After about three-quarters of a mile it's a simple scramble to the summit. Easy really." He grinned. "Everyone ready?"

Another cheer went up.

"Then let's go."

Woody led the group and as ever the girls were close behind him chattering away. Spencer and a couple of the others followed on behind them, with Tommy, Calum and Jamie bringing up the rear with Miss Bareham. Within ten minutes they'd reached the Hole in the Wall. Everyone was relieved not to be trudging along like snails with their temporary homes on their backs for this, the final part of the expedition. A quick water break was had and then they began to follow Woody in single file along to where the infamous Striding Edge began.

Woody was in front, then came JC, Suzie, Calum, Charlie, Francis, Toby, Spencer, Jamie, Tommy, Zac and Miss Bareham. Soon enough, Woody turned and gave everyone a double thumbs up. They had reached Striding Edge. They fell into silence, in awe of what they were about to do. The views were spectacular.

Following with care they had to concentrate. It was manageable, but the path narrowed at some points meaning it was single file only. Loose stones clattered down the ravine on either side and they had to place their feet with care. Confidence grew as they continued on and the summit of Helvellyn drew ever closer. No one was really talking, there was no need. The scrunch of feet on the trail was the only indication that they were there at all. They could see for miles and felt on top of the world. Jamie smiled as up ahead, Calum tried to touch the vapour trails of the jets above with his fingers.

In front of Jamie, it looked as though Spencer was beginning to tire. Woody had made it clear that they should keep at least a couple of metres between each other lest anything should happen. Jamie slowed down so that he maintained the gap, but in doing so increased the distance between himself and Toby in front of Spencer. No one else had seemed to have noticed, but Jamie began to worry.

Spencer didn't look back, but Jamie could sense that something was awry. He readied himself for some sort of confrontation and he knew he should exercise extreme caution. He appealed to the orb for help and it buzzed in his pocket, affirming that it was there. Its support strengthened his resolve and he approached the now limping Spencer.

"Are you okay Spencer?" Jamie asked. Spencer sat heavily against a rock and groaned.

"It's my ankle, I think I've twisted it." Jamie was unsure of what to do. He looked around for help. In front the group were trudging on and Miss Bareham was about twenty metres behind. He decided to help.

"Let's have a look then." Jamie crouched down to take a better look, but as he did so Spencer suddenly stood up, kneeing Jamie full in the face, splitting his lower lip instantly. Blood poured into his mouth and his vision blurred. He barely had time to put his hand to his damaged mouth, when a cry of 'look out' came from behind. The orb was vibrating wildly in his pocket and instinctively he threw himself to the floor as close to the middle of the path as he dared.

Jamie breathed heavily, shocked at what had just happened. He touched the orb in his pocket. It was scorching hot, but rather than burn his skin it seemed to rouse his spirits and he made an attempt to sit up. He could feel its power rejuvenating him and he concentrated the energy to his mouth. The bleeding stopped and he could feel the split healing over. The orb crackled with energy in his pocket. Boy and orb connected and he knew his time was now.

Shaking his head carefully to clear his vision, Jamie struggled into an upright position. He looked up at the sky, which was strangely dark. Had the knee to the face damaged his sight in some way? He rubbed his eyes and looked again. There was nothing wrong with his vision; it was Spencer's leering and hateful face blocking the sun.

"Get up," he growled. Jamie didn't think about it. He just did as he was asked. He wasn't frightened. The orb had given the confidence to do what needed to be done and he crackled with energy, ready to strike if need be. He didn't feel any anger, which he wasn't sure was a good thing or not. If he allowed his rage to take control he would have just swept Spencer clean off the edge, but in front of everyone else that would be tantamount to murder. His senses were alive and he felt a calmness of both mind and spirit.

The two boys faced one another, a steep, sheer drop on either side of them. Spencer grinned nastily and tilted his head to one side as if listening to voices. He nodded, as if some conclusion had been reached. Jamie was aware of other people shouting their names and the distinct shape of Woody looming closer over Spencer's shoulder. He knew they'd never make it in time and Spencer lunged at him. Jamie stepped back at the same moment, which took Spencer by surprise and his right foot slipped on some loose scree.

Arms flailing, Jamie watched as Spencer lost his balance and fell heavily to the ground with a thump, close to the edge of the precipice. He scrabbled to try and get up again, but his feet couldn't get any grip. Realising his predicament as the edge of the path began to disintegrate he screamed in terror. His body began to slip inexorably into the abyss and his fingers searched frantically for some sort of purchase on the disintegrating surface. His body began to slip away from the path, until only the crown of his head was visible. His hands desperately gripping the path were the only things stopping him from falling to his death.

Jamie watched all of this happening with macabre fascination. It was happening quickly, but his mind was working faster. Two possibilities seared into his mind. The first, rather worryingly seemed quite appealing as he heard the warrior's voice speak to him.

"Let him fall," the warrior declared. "It'll be a tragic accident and you my friend will enjoy a quiet life. Think what you could do with the orb, if you put your mind to it. Forget the wish, be strong, join with me!"

It took a second or so for Jamie's true character to shine through. The possibility of ending this all was tempting, but he'd never be able to live with himself. Besides, he'd been set a task to help people. Think of the wish, his inner dialogue continued. Never mind the wish, his mind screamed at him, save Spencer!!!

Jamie shook himself from his reverie and sprang into action. He threw himself to the floor and spread his weight across the path. Toby and Tommy appeared white faced. The boys were scared. He barked at them, the power in his voice made them obey instantly.

"Don't stand there staring. Lie across my legs." They didn't argue and did as they were told as Jamie, now weighted down, reached over the precipice and looked down. Spencer was hanging precariously, a sheer drop of a hundred feet below him fell to a narrow path where inexplicably sheep were traversing. He shouted at Spencer. "Spencer, grab my arm."

"I can't," cried Spencer desperately. "I don't know where you are."

Jamie touched his arm and felt a bolt of hatred pierce him between the eyes. He let go again quickly, then tried a second time. "I'm right here. I'm going to grab hold of your forearm. When I do, grab hold of mine. Okay?" There was no answer and Spencer slipped again. "Okay?" he shouted.

"Okay," came the exhausted reply. Jamie touched Spencer's arm once more and again the painful rush of Spencer's emotions threatened to wash over him. "On the count of three. One…two…three." Jamie gripped Spencer's arm just as both his hands slipped off the edge.

Jamie's mind was hit like a battering ram. As well as the now familiar feelings of hatred a rush of sheer terror flowed into his brain making him cry out in pain. The adrenaline in his own body was now pumping through his veins. He breathed deeply and took the weight of Spencer as he clung onto his right arm and tried to block out the emotions of the other boy. Spencer's other arm flailed about helplessly as he swung above the chasm. His weight was incredible and it felt as though Jamie's arm would pop out of its socket. Sweat instantly poured from his brow.

"Spencer," he gasped. "Grab my other arm. I can't hold on for much longer."

Spencer understood and desperately reached for Jamie's outstretched arm, but missed. Someone screamed as Jamie, with Tommy and Toby sitting on top of him, slipped an inch closer to the edge himself. Spencer tried again, but missed once more. He tried a third time. Jamie managed to get a grip of Spencer's jacket and hauled him in. Both boys were now locked together in a seemingly deadly embrace. The adults appeared, ashen faced and Woody had grabbed hold of

Jamie's ankles, whilst Miss Bareham stared grimly over the edge.

Jamie closed his eyes and reached out to the orb. He felt the mysterious object, which had so long been his constant companion, explode into life in his pocket. A bolt of power flowed into him making his arms tingle. He no longer felt scared. He was determined. Spencer would be saved. He gripped Spencer's arms hard making the other boy cry out loud. He breathed in and heaved. An almost superhuman strength took over his arms and slowly he began to haul Spencer up towards him. The bodies holding him kept him stable and, now understanding, Miss Bareham and Woody both followed his lead and lay next to Jamie.

Jamie heaved again and this time Spencer's head appeared level with Jamie's. Miss Bareham reached out and grabbed the stricken boy by the scruff of the neck, as did Woody. It was crude, but effective and with one final heave from them all, they hauled the stricken boy safely back onto the path.

There was a stunned silence, as Spencer lay sprawled on his back, eyes closed. The only hint that he was alive was the gentle rise and fall of his chest. The pressure on Jamie's ankles relinquished as Woody got up and knelt down next to the prone figure of Spencer. Toby and Tommy got off Jamie and Miss Bareham who was also up, helped him onto his feet and then enveloped him in a bear hug. The others cheered in relief as a grinning Jamie was released from the appreciative clutches of his headmistress. He reached into his pocket to touch the orb in thanks and the world stood still…

He had helped the final person.

The final piece of the orb's existence clicked into place and in his mind, images of those he'd helped froze for an instant and were gone: Tommy, Calum,

Duster, Grandma and now Spencer. The feelings he had had when he'd helped the others were now intensified and for a fleeting moment he felt almost godlike. He was imperious, righteous, all encompassing.

The power within him was awesome and though it was incredible he was momentarily petrified by it. It surged to a crescendo and then disappeared and he knew that the prophecy had been fulfilled. He had his wish. The orb ceased to vibrate in his pocket and for a fleeting moment, Jamie felt a terrible sense of loss. A warm glow emanated again as if to placate him and the world started up once more…

Tommy clapped him on the shoulder, "You're a hero mate."

Jamie had to shake himself to realise where he was. On Striding Edge, in the Lake District. He came to. "Wow, oh wow." He sank to his knees in shock at what he'd just done.

"How did you do it?" asked a worried JC who'd carefully joined them.

Jamie shook his head. "I don't know, I just don't know."

Tommy passed him some water. "Here, have a swig of this." Jamie gratefully took the water and took a greedy glug. He wiped his mouth and got up again. He looked at JC. "Spencer?" he asked.

"He's okay Jamie," she answered. "Here, come and have a look." Spencer was indeed standing up and leaning on Woody who had his arm around him. He caught Jamie's eyes and smiled warmly, for perhaps the first time ever. Jamie sighed in relief. It was all over. He'd helped five people. He'd defeated the warrior. It was all over. All he needed now was to make his wish.

"Jamie," called Spencer. "Come over. I want to thank you for saving my life." The others cheered him on as he walked over. Spencer held out his hand and

Jamie took it nervously, unsure what would happen when they touched. Nothing, but his grip was surprisingly strong. Spencer smiled gratefully, but Jamie watched him with care. Was there still something lurking behind those eyes? The others were cheering and hugging each other but the atmosphere between the two boys was still cold despite the smiles. The two adults were looking on, delighted by this apparent reconciliation.

Spencer's grip tightened as he pulled Jamie in for a reluctant hug. Jamie was decidedly uncomfortable now, as Spencer's embrace tightened. It was beginning to hurt and unbeknown to everyone else, every muscle in Spencer's body was taut. He was ready to strike. This wasn't over after all and Jamie didn't have the orb to help him. He was on his own.

Make the wish! Make the bloody wish! his mind screamed at him. He couldn't escape from Spencer's clutches and he could see that he was being intentionally turned so his back was to the sheer drop. Make the wish, make the wish.

Spencer released Jamie from his embrace, but still held onto his hand and with the other hand gripped his shoulder, hard. Everyone clapped and cheered. Jamie felt helpless and couldn't speak. No one could see what was happening and he was too scared to shout out. He was utterly and totally on his own. He shut his eyes and concentrated.

He made the wish and hoped that it had worked.

When he opened them again, Spencer was looking at him with a tear in his eye. He nodded and Jamie nodded back. He smiled at Jamie, embraced him once more before he shuffled them both to the edge. There was a stunned silence and a cry of 'no' before the realisation of what was happening sank in. It was too late.

Without a word, Spencer threw them both over and out into the void.

Epilogue

Flowers and cards adorned every available space and a helium filled balloon bobbed gently on the currents of the air-conditioning in the hospital room. A prone figure lay in the bed, chest moving faintly up and down beneath the crisp, white sheets. Pale hands lay over a light blanket and a peaceful, almost serene face betrayed no pain, nor emotion. The prone boy slept in a vegetative state, IV drips in his arm and a heart monitor bipped next to him quietly.

Since the attempt on his life, Jamie had been in hospital in a coma for nearly five months. His broken bones had mended and despite the height of the fall, the doctors were frankly amazed that he had survived at all. When the helicopter had finally managed to locate him, they had found a twisted body, clutching, for reasons unknown to them, some sort of crystal ball. The orb, now completely inert, lay in the drawer next to his bed, all life in it gone.

Spencer's body was never found despite a major search in bad weather. Spencer's parents, distraught at their son's cruel actions, pleaded that his body be allowed to rest wherever it lay. Jamie's parents magnanimously agreed.

Jamie's family had moved him from the hospital in Manchester to one nearer home, so they could remain by his bedside. Each of them took it in turns to keep a constant vigil in case he regained consciousness. The doctors were hopeful at first, but the longer he remained in this state, the less likely they thought he would ever wake up.

Grandma was with him. She talked to him quietly, telling him news of home and of Duster who pined for his master, subdued and mostly asleep on Jamie's bed, reluctant for walks or his food. She stroked his hair and for some reason opened the drawer next to his bed, retrieving the orb, which the paramedics had been unable to prise from his hand until he had reached the hospital.

She turned it over quietly in her hands and closed her eyes concentrating hard. She remained in this state for some while. Sweat began to form gently on her forehead. A single drop of perspiration ran down onto her nose and fell onto the orb, which fizzled faintly for a moment and went out again just as quickly. She smiled weakly, kissed her grandson on the forehead and hobbled back to her chair using a walking stick for support, a memento from her car accident.

When Jamie's parents appeared, they found Grandma fast asleep. They quietly pulled up chairs and each held one of his hands. They looked at one another sadly and issued their own silent prayers for their son's recovery. Exhausted with worry and affected by the peace in the room, they soon fell into a sleepy trance like state, Mum with her head next to Jamie, Dad resting his chin on his chest, asleep.

In the quiet of the room, a finger twitched and an eyelid flickered. A second finger trembled ever so slightly and eyes began to move behind their eyelids, as something incredible began to happen.

Mum woke up and looked down at Jamie's hand as it moved again. She reached across to her husband and gently woke him up, not wanting to believe what she was seeing. She put her fingers to her lips as her husband looked at her questioningly and motioned for him to look at their son. As if aware of the situation, Grandma too had awoken and was watching the scene with wide eyes.

The heart monitor next to the bed began to beat more strongly and Jamie's parents had to sit up straight as his hands began to twitch. A nurse appeared at the doorway and nodded at them all smiling gently. She gave them the thumbs up and shut the door quietly behind her allowing the family to enjoy this moment, whilst she fetched a doctor.

Both of his parents held his hands gently. Suddenly, they felt pressure back and Jamie's eyes opened, blinked rapidly and then opened experimentally again. He looked around, unsure of his surroundings and then recognising his parents tried to speak. Dad shushed him and kissed him gently on the forehead. He turned to face his mother.

Her shoulders were shaking with emotion and she was crying silently. Tears dropped onto the bedclothes, as she laid her head on her son's shoulder. Jamie reached up and stroked her hair gently. She recovered her composure slightly and sat up and closer to her son, now returned to her. She picked up his hand and stood up, placing it on her enlarged stomach. His eyes widened, as he felt his unborn sister move and he laughed gently, as a single tear fell from his mother's eye onto his cheek.

Jamie was still feeling confused, but the realisation of what he had wished for made him smile. It had worked! He began to sit up and Dad rushed about, propping him on a couple of pillows. He groaned as he tried to sit up. He was sore. His eyes began to focus and he saw his grandma sitting in the corner, smiling at him. Mum was next to the bed, hands resting protectively on her belly. Dad looked at him and said simply, "Welcome back son."

A faint hint of movement in the room caught Jamie's eye and despite his befuddled brain, he sensed something was wrong. A tendril of vapour had trickled from his mouth as Dad had said that last word. Mum shivered and asked if someone had turned up the air conditioning. Jamie looked over at his grandma who was reaching frantically for her stick, terror evident on her face. She, like Jamie, knew what this meant. He didn't know what to do. He had no idea where the orb was, or whether it would activate after he'd made the wish. Perhaps that was what Grandma was trying to reach for.

Jamie watched helplessly as Dad wrapped a cardigan around Mum's shoulders and pressed the assistance button next to his bed. His lips were cracked and his mouth dry. He tried to speak but couldn't. Grandma struggled to her feet and began to hobble across the room. She was obviously going for the orb. Her eyes were wide. She tried to tell him where it was, when the room shimmered and mist flowed in.

Ice crystals formed on the eyelashes of his parents and in a second they were frozen to the spot. Grandma had reached the bedside cabinet and was reaching for something when she too was routed, frozen in mid motion. Jamie shivered, not from the cold, but from fear. He was here! The warrior was here!

The mist billowed slightly as the figure he recognised, walked through it and stood by the bed.

"Greeting and salutations!" said the warrior, dressed from head to toe in his obsidian armour. "I must congratulate you. The first of us in generations to have beaten me. A rather fitting way to have ended it all, wouldn't you say?"

Jamie couldn't move. Terror flooded his veins.

"You may well be wondering why I'm here?" The warrior laughed out loud and Jamie cringed. "I can see by the look on your face that you think I've come for your soul." He shook his head. "A deal is a deal. You won the challenge. You can keep your soul. Besides, I have one belonging to someone else."

Jamie's heart sank, he thought he knew who but

didn't dare say his name out loud. He tried to sit up again and a sharp pain between his eyes made him grimace. He knew what was coming and tried not to show any fear. The mist billowed again as a second figure began to materialise. "Oh no!" He managed to splutter.

The figure approached, the gait and swagger of his nemesis was unmistakable as he split the fog. Grinning inanely, Spencer stood next to the warrior and stared triumphantly at Jamie, who shivered uncontrollably.

"This boy needs no introduction I take it?" chuckled the Warrior. "I watched his attempt on your life and moments before he left his, I made him an offer he couldn't refuse. He serves me now."

Spencer made to step forward, murderous intent in his eyes which he no longer had to try and hide. He reached for Jamie who cried out painfully. "Keep him away from me!"

The warrior held out an armoured arm and Spencer took a step back snarling. "He will keep, my new protégé. We have other matters more pressing."

Jamie felt marginally better at hearing this, but he still didn't trust the warrior. He licked his cracked lips and managed to croak, "Why are you here?"

"You will still join me. I cannot just take you as I could have done before. You must willingly join me."

"I will never..." The effort of talking was exhausting Jamie.

"Yes, yes, I know that," the warrior replied. "Hence my visit. You just need a little, well, persuading shall we say."

Jamie had no idea what he meant.

"Any thoughts?" asked the warrior as he began to stalk around the room. He placed one huge hand around the throat of Jamie's grandma and began to squeeze. Spencer laughed nastily.

"No!"

The warrior growled menacingly. "I should have killed the old woman whilst I had the chance. No matter. No, it's not her I'm here for." He released Grandma and turned to Jamie's dad. Jamie pleaded silently for him to leave his parents alone, when realisation hit him like a hammer blow. He tried to move his legs out of bed, but he wasn't strong enough and tears began to flow down his face with the effort. The warrior laughed as he watched. He snorted in derision at Jamie's dad and had reached the prone figure of his mum. He walked around her and his head towered over hers. Jamie now knew what was at stake.

"Please no," he managed. The warrior's eyes widened as he wrapped his arms around Jamie's pregnant mother and gazed at Jamie, triumph gleaming in his piercing blue eyes.

"She will be mine! Your sister belongs to me!"

Jamie clutched his chest as a terrible pain racked his body. He reached out a hand in desperation, trying to clutch at the warrior. Laughing loudly, the warrior slapped him away, before turning on his heels and leading Spencer from the room.

Another spasm of pain shot through Jamie's body and his vision swam momentarily as the two figures receded. He desperately tried to follow them, but the pain in his chest was too intense. His mind went black and he fell, unconscious, in a tangle of sheets onto the freezing cold tiles of the hospital floor.

Lightning Source UK Ltd.
Milton Keynes UK
UKOW03f0625110414

229803UK00002B/11/P